SUCH A STRANGE LITTLE GIRL

J. A. BAKER

Boldwood

First published in Great Britain in 2026 by Boldwood Books Ltd.

Cover Design by Dawn Adams

Cover Images: Shutterstock and Adobe Stock

A CIP catalogue record for this book is available from the British Library.

Paperback ISBN 978-1-83561-209-5

Large Print ISBN 978-1-83561-207-1

Hardback ISBN 978-1-83561-206-4

Trade Paperback ISBN 978-1-80656-999-1

Ebook ISBN 978-1-83561-208-8

Kindle ISBN 978-1-83561-210-1

Audio CD ISBN 978-1-83561-201-9

MP3 CD ISBN 978-1-83561-202-6

Digital audio download ISBN 978-1-83561-204-0

This book is printed on certified sustainable paper. Boldwood Books is dedicated to putting sustainability at the heart of our business. For more information please visit https://www.boldwoodbooks.com/about-us/sustainability/

Boldwood Books Ltd, 23 Bowerdean Street, London, SW6 3TN

www.boldwoodbooks.com

To friends everywhere. May you never be like any of the characters in this book.

Men kick friendship around like a football, but it doesn't seem to crack.

Women treat it like glass and it goes to pieces.

— ANNE MORROW LINDBERGH

The truth is rarely pure and never simple.

— OSCAR WILDE

PROLOGUE

Glossy and viscid, the sight of it roils her guts. Pooling around her, the crimson liquid grows ever closer as if attempting to follow her, trap her even. She swallows and stares at it in horror, repulsed by its gleaming quality, its putrid metallic stench. Cloying and inescapable. No matter how hard she tries, she can't seem to tear her eyes away from the growing expanse of blood. She is mesmerised by its eerie glow, fascinated and disgusted in equal measure at the fact the human body is able to hold such copious amounts of fluid; fluid that seeps and spreads seemingly without end. She stares at it, wondering when it will stop. *If* it will stop. At some point this will all be over. It *has* to be. She cannot stand here for much longer, watching. Waiting. Surrounded by the stench of death.

Feet twisting in panic, she snaps out of her stupor and steps back, thinking what a miracle it is to have it surging through our veins. For our hearts to keep pumping day after day, the spilled blood on the floor the very thing that fuels us, the thing that keeps us alive. And then she is propelled back into the moment by a sound from nearby, reality hitting her like a speeding truck.

Horror clings to her skin, crawls up her throat, an angular jagged rock that sticks in her gullet, making it difficult to breathe. She swipes a hand across her forehead, its clamminess repelling her. She is shivery yet her face burns, her flesh fiery like a furnace. A fusion of hot and cold clashes within her. She has done this to herself. She has made this awful thing happen. She is the one to blame and must accept that fact. It is what she does next that counts, how she acts in the next few minutes that will determine the future. *Their* future. She is here for a reason and mustn't forget that. She has been caught off guard by this unfortunate incident and now has to focus on what comes next.

Time judges her, every second that passes putting her closer to getting caught. On the wall, the hands of the clock curve their way around the plastic face, the noise of each staccato movement ricocheting in her head. She needs to leave, to get as far away from this place as possible. And yet still she watches, unable to look away. Unable to move. Her gaze fixed on the blood that continues to leak out of the body that lies sprawled at her feet.

The figure is still; no convulsing, no gasps for breath. Nothing at all. The thick dark liquid continues to worm its way ever closer; its appearance, how it glistens in the dying light, catching in the back of her throat, causing her to retch. It's everywhere now, the stink of near death; it leaches into her clothes, her hair. Soiling every inch of her. Climbing through her pores and leaving an imprint deep within her soul.

She won't ever forget this moment. She can't erase it from her mind. How could she ever blank out such a monstrous event? And yet, it wasn't meant to be this way. It was an unplanned error. Things escalated. Became unmanageable. She made a terrible choice, her temper unspooling in spectacular fashion. This whole episode is an awful mistake. But it *has* happened and now there is no going back. She has to deal with it, do what she can to escape from this situation unscathed. Blameless. Anybody who knows her would realise this wasn't planned, that this isn't like her. It just materialised. Like an out-of-body experience. She watched from another place, hovering above as violence occurred. Screaming, shouting. Cries for mercy. And blood.

Oh God. So much blood.

Her breathing is a rasp. She stops, listens out. Silence all around. Only the deep thrumming of her own heartbeat as it pulses and whooshes in her ears. The rhythmic pounding of her conscience. Of sorrow and sadness. Of what could have been. Should have been.

Then a guttural moan. A sudden spasm as the body tries to drag itself across the floor, like a snake slithering to safety, sliding away from its predator. Away from her.

She steps back and falls, fear and dread at the sight before her making her dizzy and unsteady. Consuming her. It's what comes next that fills her with horror. The unknown.

Scrambling to her feet, she backs away. She needs to move, to escape this madness, but is all out of ideas. Her DNA is everywhere, the stamp of her presence so deeply embedded into the house she may as well stride into the nearest police station and offer herself up for imprisonment. Tell them to lock her up and throw away the key.

But not yet. There has to be a route out of this situation. A way to remain free. A way to get what she came here for.

She wills her brain to snap into action, to fucking well *do* something. Give her some answers to save her skin. But her thoughts are too jumbled, a snarl of terror and anger and confusion. And then something else catches her attention, causing her scalp to prickle, the hairs on the back of her neck to stand on end. A noise from upstairs. The thing that brought her here in the first place. The thing that belongs to her.

The lingering brain fog that has clouded her thinking suddenly clears, the sound from above splintering her thoughts, spurring her into action. She steps over the bloodied figure on the floor, ready to do what needs to be done. To take what is rightfully hers. It's clear to her now, everything slotting into place. The bloodied figure is simply collateral. It's not how she wanted things to pan out and she isn't a monster, but if she doesn't move quickly, it will all have been for nothing.

The floor is spongy beneath her feet, the room swaying when she finally breaks out of her torpor and darts up to the bedroom. This scenario seems so out of kilter, so far removed from how she hoped it would be when she visualised this moment all those weeks ago, but everything is too far down the line to back out now. Who will care for Elise if she doesn't finish what she has started? A pain shoots through her abdomen at the thought of the child, *her child,* a phantom painful griping sensation tugging at her in the space where her uterus should be. Where it was before it was cruelly ripped from her body by an army of ruthless strangers.

The landing area is a dim murky place, blinds pulled shut, shadows enveloping dark corners and pushing them into obscurity. She stops, her breath hot and sour, fear rooting her to the spot. She tells herself to move. There isn't enough time for inertia. This is what she wanted. This is her moment, the glittering prize lying so close to where she stands she can almost feel the warmth of the child, see her sleeping body nestled safely in the next room. She stops, closes her eyes and inhales. She can almost smell her, the soft scent of baby skin an alluring intoxicating fragrance that makes her light-headed with desire and a sense of yearning so strong it is all-consuming. Impossible to ignore.

A creak as she pushes open the door, but then something else stops her. A noise from below. The rattle of metal. A key being inserted into a lock, then the click of a handle being turned and the sharp bristling sound of a door brushing against a doormat. She hears feet stepping on wood followed by the unmistakable slap of a briefcase as it is dropped on the floor, its sound echoing and clanging in her brain. She removes her fingers from the door handle, her palm hot, limbs cold as ice.

He's home early. He isn't meant to be here. He is on a business trip. Why is he here and not on a flight to New York as planned? Is this a trap? Has she been duped and stumbled into this scenario like an unseeing idiot? Her mind angled towards one thing and one thing only. Blinded by her need, her grasping desperation to take what is hers.

And then the unmistakable gravelly timbre of his voice as he calls out his wife's name, the sound of it pushing needles of ice up and down her spine. She realises then that there is no way out of this situation. This is the final instalment of her life as she knows it. After all the pain and the arguments; after all her thwarted attempts and the terrible unbearable heartache, at long last it is finally coming to an end. And all she feels is relief.

PART I

1

BLAKE

'Perhaps it will help you come to terms with what took place all those years ago?'

I can feel Arthur's penetrative gaze boring into me, trying to delve inside my head. See how I function and determine what drives me. I'm sure he already knows more about me than I know about myself. I'm not an idiot. He is attempting to get me to offload, to tell him what happened. My silence speaks more than a thousand words ever could. He picks up on my reticence and changes tack, drumming his long slender fingers on the wooden surface while he thinks of another way. The noise of the constant drumming rattles in my head like the rumble of distant thunder. A portent of an incoming storm.

'Or if talking proves too traumatic, why don't you try writing it down in the form of a letter? Some things are easier to put on paper than voiced out loud. The spoken word is often lost amidst the surrounding noise, or frequently misheard and misinterpreted by the listener. The written word, however, is a solid thing, something we can return to time and time again. We can re-read and absorb it long after words uttered have vanished into the ether.'

Suddenly, I'm interested. Writing is something I *can* do. It's my forte. The thing I enjoy more than anything else. The thing that has helped keep me sane these past few years. I have hobbies and activities that I carry out on a daily basis to help pass the time but putting my thoughts down on paper is the backbone of my existence. And a letter. To her. Already my stomach is knotted; fear and exhilaration a heady combination that is making me dizzy.

'That sounds appealing,' I say, my voice no more than a whisper. I daren't show too much enthusiasm, my guard constantly up for fear of being caught out and wounded.

If the past has taught me anything, it's that dread and disappointment are never far away, unwanted bedfellows always lurking, waiting to strike when we least expect them.

'So you think that perhaps you can write a letter? Tell her how you feel.'

Excitement continues to pulse through me. I'm already formulating my first correspondence, Arthur's words of advice no more than white noise in my ears as he continues speaking. He is correct on that score. We all have the ability to block out things we don't want to hear. The roar of excitement in my head is far louder than Arthur's sage advice.

'I think I can do that. It sounds challenging but I enjoy being tested, being made to think.'

Arthur's small nod and half-smile tells me that he is happy with my response. I have agreed to his terms, made him feel as if I am endorsing his idea. Which of course I am. Arthur's superior status is something that will always divide us, keeping us on different sides of a whole. Our symbiotic relationship serves us both well. The healer and the healed.

I leave the room feeling lighter than I have for some time, my mood buoyant, my mind firing off in all directions as I think about how I am going to start my letter. The letter that has gone round and round my head for the past few decades. The letter I should have written before now. The letter that is key to me turning a corner and being who I have always wanted to be.

Dusk settles, a ridge of resplendent ochre settling across the rugged ridge of the hills by the time I have worked out how to write my opening clause. It needs to be just right, to set the tone for the rest of the conversation. Friendly, not too formal. Inviting, not intimidating, but more than anything, it has to capture the essence of who I am, as if all the planets have aligned and the universe is waiting for us to be reconciled once more. Always together, never apart.

I settle in my chair and let the words flow, each one leaving me in a heady rush. Each one laced with love and integrity and honesty.

1 January

Dear Lucy,

Where to begin. I guess it will be easier to go back to the start of us, but our beginning feels like such a long time ago, our memories so deeply entwined, that I'm not sure what to write first, how to unpick all those early events and recollections and encapsulate them in an opening sentence. So instead I will begin this missive with an apology. An apology for leaving it so long. I should have written to you before now but life has been busy and difficult and time has run away with me as I'm sure it has with you. We are both older now. Older but not old. Wiser too, I hope. Then again, you always were an emotionally intelligent individual, smart beyond your years; the brightest and cleverest person I knew. I trailed behind you, basking in your warmth and radiance, hoping some of your glitter would be passed onto me. It never happened. I remained your dull friend, always hidden in the shadows, a skulking bystander pulled along in your slipstream of goodness and happiness, but in truth I didn't mind. Just being your friend was all I ever wanted. You were always enough for me. Until you weren't. We won't go there just yet. Another time perhaps, when we become reacquainted; comfortable enough to dig that bit deeper without hitting bone and causing a lasting injury. Without the jarring nerve-jangling sensation that comes with closeness when all civilities and good manners have been exhausted.

Anyway, I digress, something I do a lot these days. Being cooped up in this small apartment has me chattering endlessly when I do finally meet somebody who is prepared to listen or someone who is simply too polite to stop me. I will try to not bore you with the minutiae of my life. The last thing I want to is for you to stop reading this letter before you have barely begun. As always, I long for you to use your precious time and spend it with me. Some things never change, do they? Always needy, I am still desperate to dedicate my time to doing things with you. To have you pore over my words and allow me to climb inside your thoughts, nestling up like a slumbering child who takes up every inch of space in your head.

Anyway, back to my reasons for writing to you. I have never been a huge believer in the whole New Year, New Me thing; all those promises and resolutions waiting to be broken, the cracking of each one loud enough to shatter glass; each shard sharp enough to pierce flesh. But now that I am older and full of reflection and consideration for this thing called life, I have decided it is time to take stock. To slow down and think, be the person I have always wanted to be. And the person I have always wanted to be begins with you, dear friend.

Do you recall our first day at school? That traumatic brain-melting day when our lives collided, fusing us together. Forging a friendship that otherwise would not have worked. We were an unequal match, you and I – children from very different backgrounds. Same neighbourhood but starkly different families. I guess we rubbed along together prior to attending school, playing together in the street, but our memories of that time are too dim for us to remember. It's that first day in class that has stuck with me. In theory, it shouldn't have happened, us remaining close for all those years. Soul mates forevermore. But it did, didn't it? I believed it then, my slowly developing brain telling me that our lives would follow the same trajectory, that we would walk the same path side by side, and I still believe it now. Which is why I am writing this letter, to keep that connection going, to ensure it doesn't sever. I feel anchored to you, Lucy. You are as much a part of me as one of my limbs, as deeply rooted in me as one of my major organs. You are the beating heart of me, keeping me alive, the thought of you infusing me with happiness and a wash of light when life seems dark and dreary. I see your smiling face in my head and suddenly the clouds part to reveal the sun behind; a blaze of shimmering gold in an otherwise normal day. Am I romanticising? Viewing everything through rose-tinted spectacles and using flowery poetic language to paint a very different picture to how things actually were? Probably, but if I can't speak frankly about my feelings at this point in my life then I may as well remain mute for the remainder of my days. And I don't want to do that. I want to tell you how I feel in the hope you will see how much I have missed you. In the hope you will read this letter and possibly even take the time to write back. I expect little but wish and hope for plenty. Just a word or two would suffice, Lucy. Just enough to keep me company and warm me through on these long wintry evenings.

Here I go again, veering wildly off track. Seeing my traits and habits written down in black and white is mildly disconcerting. It's like viewing myself under a microscope, warts and all. Not a pleasant experience. I hope that my writing to you will serve as a reminder of how flighty and whimsical I am. How unlike you I am. You, who was always so steady and reliable and smart and thoughtful while I dipped and swerved my way through life. I will try to do better. To be better. I have a long way to go before I can consider myself as considerate and kind as you, dear Lucy, but I'll never stop trying.

Anyway, back to that first day at school. I recall the feelings of dread, the sensation of that warm trickle of liquid as it trailed down my legs and pooled on the linoleum flooring at my feet. Fear misted my vision, horror at the situation in which I found myself swirling in my gut like boiling tar. I was rooted to the spot, too hot and humiliated to put up my hand and ask for help, sweat pasting my brow, making me sticky and uncomfortable. So you did it for me. Even at such a tender age, you were able to see my predicament, to detect how embarrassed and frightened I was, and you took charge, speaking to the teacher, gently taking my arm and leading me out of the classroom. I will never forget that moment. The quiet sense of camaraderie. The relief of being noticed and cared for. At only five years of age, in a strange place, tongue-tied and crippled with shyness, I knew you would be my ally.

My closest friend. I was timid and reserved but I wasn't stupid. I knew level-headedness and leadership when I saw it, and I saw it in you. I wanted it for myself, that poise and confidence, the ease with which you carried yourself, as if the world and everything in it would always be yours, but knowing that it wasn't who I was or would ever be, I opted for the next best thing. You.

Staying by your side, doing what I could to keep you in my sights was in the forefront of my mind. You were my safe person. My sanctuary. The one who never ever let me down. Until that fateful day, that is. That awful gut-wrenching day when our worlds spun out of control, sending us whirling in opposite directions. But we have a lot of ground to cover before we speak of that. I promised to start at the beginning and there is a lot to get through, far too much content for one simple letter, so I will save it all for further correspondence. I promise to tread with care. We owe each other that much. And a whole lot more.

I pray that you reply to this letter. I don't think I could bear it if you didn't. The thought of you tearing up my heartfelt words and throwing them in the bin would break me, but it's a chance I'm prepared to take to get our friendship back on track.

We had a lot of good times, didn't we, Lucy? More than most. The good outweighed the bad, that much I do know. If you can find it in your heart to reply, it would mean the world to me. I don't go out much these days. It is always the wrong type of weather, or the wrong sort of person walking past my window when I glance out, so whenever possible, I stay indoors. Safer. Easier. People are unpredictable creatures. Unreliable and selfish. I am sure that you of all folk will back me up on that score. What I do know is this – my life would be a whole lot easier with you in it. Please consider writing back. I have missed you more than you will ever know and now wait patiently for your reply.

Love, Blake.

2

BLAKE

I clutch at the letter, my palms sweaty, a tremor running through my body. It's unbecoming, a woman of my years behaving like an excited teenager in Arthur's presence. I try to act nonchalantly, as if none of this bothers me in the slightest. Even though it does. My nerve endings are alight, my stomach knotted.

'Would you like to read the reply to me?'

His question catches me unawares. Stupid really. Careless of me to be so unprepared. I should have expected this. I should have been ready for his stark gaze and shrewd manner. And yet I'm not. I feel out of sorts, like a child caught stealing sweeties, my hand still firmly lodged in the jar, a fistful of sugary treats grasped tightly in my hot bony fingers.

'Not really. Not yet.'

He nods as if he understands. He doesn't understand. He thinks he does, but I have always been good at hiding things. Even from myself. But he will know more soon enough. Given more time, he will know the ins and outs of my story as well as I do. Except that with the passing of time, I'm not entirely sure of all the details any more; things have become blurred in my mind, creases appearing where there used to be firm straight lines. Some of the images are grainy and lacking in colour. I'm hoping these letters will help restore that period of my life to its former glory, injecting vibrancy and clarity and helping to banish the fog that lingers there. Lucy and I deserve that much, or at least Lucy does. It seems rather haughty to think that I actually deserve anything at all, as if the world owes me a chunk of positivity and happiness. It doesn't. None of us are owed anything. We get out of life exactly what we put in.

'So how are things?' he asks, his gaze fixated on the piece of paper in my hand. 'Everything going well?'

'As well as can be expected,' I say in return, because that is what he wants to hear.

There are days when I get the feeling Arthur is ready for me to pour my feelings out so he can mop them up and help dry my tears. That has happened in the past. But today isn't one of those days. Today he appears busy and keen to be elsewhere, which suits me because I would rather be elsewhere as well; in fact, I would rather be anywhere but here. I want to be alone in order to digest Lucy's reply, to pore over every word and allow myself some thinking time as to how I will formulate my next letter to her. Because there will be another. And another and another and another. I will write until I have no words left, until my thoughts are dry and desiccated.

'Have the nightmares stopped?'

I sigh. The nightmares.

'Yes,' I say, because I want this to be over with. 'The nightmares have all stopped.'

'You seem edgy today. Is it because of the letter?' He nods at my lap where Lucy's reply sits.

'Not edgy. Excited actually.'

'And you have brought the reply with you. Are you absolutely certain you don't want to read it to me?'

The staccato hammering in my chest increases. I swallow and close my hand around the letter, my fingers clutching it as if it is about to grow wings and take flight.

'Yes, I'm certain. I want to be alone while I read it.' I cock my head to one side and summon up a smile. 'If that's okay?'

Arthur's hands block out the light behind him as he raises them in mock surrender and shakes his head. 'Absolutely. This is your private correspondence. I would never want to pry or intrude.'

We both know his statement isn't exactly true but I let it slide. Now isn't the time for excruciating nit-picking or raking over old conversations that would cause us both a great deal of embarrassment.

'Well, I guess since you're free of nightmares and are eager to read your letter, we can perhaps call it a day for now?'

I rise out of my seat a little too quickly, the room swimming around me when I stand. The heat is suddenly stifling, forcing beads of perspiration onto my forehead and causing my scalp to prickle. The need to be alone is suddenly overwhelming. I walk on unsteady legs and make my way out of the room to a place where everything feels cooler and less threatening.

The ambient temperature is perfect as I sit in my usual spot next to my window. I unfold the letter and stare at the words written there.

10 January

Dear Blake,

Well, this is most unexpected. What a surprise to hear from you. I admit, when I first opened the envelope and saw your handwriting (which hasn't changed) I almost threw it away. I was gripped by fear, the terror of what the letter might contain turning my insides to liquid. It was basic curiosity that kept me reading until the end. And it is basic manners that has made me reply. That and the fact I have missed you, but I won't bore you with that just yet. More of the emotional stuff later.

I'm not sure what to say, how to formulate a reply without it sounding overly nostalgic and maudlin. I was a tad frightened as I read your words. Anxiety had me in its grip, the fear that you had written to finally cut me out of your life after my previous transgression and lack of compassion regarding your circumstances all those years ago. It was enough to have me put this letter away before I read it through. I imagined you were writing to tell me that these would be the last words you will ever say to me. I was relieved to see that that wasn't the case. Thank you for that. Thank you, thank you, thank you.

Of course I remember that first day at school. How could I not? I recall your shyness and my horror that nobody had noticed your distressing situation. Not the child sitting next to you nor the teacher who sat and watched. Not even the adult who breezed past us, her gaze firmly fixed on other things. You had nobody. I had to do something to help. Leaving you alone to suffer wasn't an option. You would have done the same for me despite your quiet nature, I am sure of that.

You have said so many kind things about me that I'm certain aren't true, but reading them has helped to bolster my flagging self-esteem. Things haven't been easy since that day. That awful day when everything went wrong. I too live in a small place now, seeing few people, if any. I live a low-profile life. It's easier that way. I like the quiet; the safety and comfort it brings. The tranquillity too. There is a solace of sorts to be had when the nights draw in and I can be alone with my thoughts. Winter isn't my favourite season but it's pointless feeling low and despondent when the darkness comes. There is nothing I can do about it. I simply have to bide my time and wait for spring to arrive, the light nights bringing the promise of summer and warmth.

Funnily enough, I was thinking only last week about how fortunate we were to live where we did as children. To attend the same school and become firm friends. Otherwise we wouldn't have met, would we? I wonder if I too am also looking at things through a different lens. Time often warps our memories, bending them until they are so misshapen we hardly recognise ourselves or our own lives any more. Especially when we suffer trauma. And you did suffer, didn't you, Blake? And that was because of me. I let you down and everything that happened afterwards was all my fault. So before I go any further, I would like to apologise a thousand times over. I am so, so sorry for what I did to you, and I hope you can find it in your heart to forgive me. I'm guessing that you writing to me is proof that we've moved on from that disastrous period of our lives and can become close once again? I hope so, I really do. I've missed you more than you will ever know. I realise you might not think that, but it's true. I did a bad unfeeling thing that led you to the darkest of places. You weren't responsible for what took place. I am. It was and still is, all my fault.

Let me tell you a little about myself and my current life. I've changed a lot over the years. Sometimes I go to church. I realise you might find that strange given my upbringing but there we are. People often change and maybe I'm one of those people. I'm not a deeply religious person, but I do believe in spirituality. I honestly believe that if we look hard enough and listen to what is around us, we can learn from our mistakes and the mistakes of others. I've learned plenty from my mistakes, Blake. Have you?

Anyway, St George's is a small chapel close to where I live. I'm anonymous there, a lone figure sitting on a pew asking for help and forgiveness. Father McGuigan often speaks to me, gives me guidance, helping me to make it through the darkest of days. And my God, the dark days are many, which is why I'm grateful you have taken the time to write to me. I needed to hear from you at this point in my life. More than you could possibly ever know. The past suddenly seems so close, as if the years we spent together are edging ever nearer. The gap between what we were and who we've become is wafer thin. It's as if I went to bed one night as a youngster and woke up the next morning an adult. Our existence is distilled into a bundle of disjointed memories.

I'd like to write about those memories, the good and the bad. The things we did and didn't do. Perhaps together we can both piece it all together and create a full picture. A rich tapestry that has led us to this point in our lives. We're at an important juncture, you and I. It's time to slow down and reflect on our shared history. These letters are a way of doing that, so well done to you for starting up this joint venture. Me and you together again. And not before time. As always, you are the one who has kept the connection going. I've never been so good at it, have I? Always busy doing other things. Always leaving you behind.

Anyway, back to our formative years before I bore you half to death with my inane ramblings. Do you remember Miss Kielty, our first teacher? My God, she was hideous. Cruelty personified. I recall how frightened I was when she asked me to stand up and recite my three times tables. We were both just five years old, barely able to write our own names. I can still hear her caustic laughter, the way she curled her lip, shrieking at me to sit down, telling the other pupils that I was an idiot. We survived a whole year in her class. What doesn't kill you makes you stronger. And it did make me stronger, more resilient. Able to fight back. I think perhaps that was the turning point for me. The moment when I realised that the only person who would ever look out for me, was me. That was when it all began. Some might say it came before that point, but the image of that teacher's face screaming at me, her features crinkled with disgust at my obvious ineptitude, is something that will stay with me forever. Her dark eyes and sarcasm taught me that life can be cruel and we all need to be on our mettle to keep the demons at bay. The key to warding off life's cruel blows is to mete them out before they reach us. But not to you, dear friend. That was a mistake and I regret it every single day. Sometimes when the shadows fall, when that crushing strangulating stretch of melancholy hits hard, it becomes too difficult to discern an enemy from an ally. Maybe I was more like my mother than I care to admit. Like Miss Kielty, her obvious dislike of me shaped who I was. Who I became.

And what I did.

But I'm a different person now, I'm happy and settled and living a half decent life. Nobody's existence is perfect, is it? Mine is as good as it can be given what took place. I will tell you all about it next time I write. I don't want to flood you with too much information. Just enough to keep you informed and maybe even entertained, but not so much that I bore you to death. We lost each other once. Let's try to not do it again.

I'm now going to wait for your reply. I'm desperate to hear back from you. I hope you will keep me updated with what is going on in your life. Maybe we can forge a path together, make a joint effort to help us both become better people and do what's right from this moment on.

Please write back soon.

Love, Lucy.

3

BEFORE

Martha was convinced it was the cold that was doing it, the unpredictable British weather sending everyone a little bit crazy. Darkening their moods. Or maybe she was simply looking for reasons when there weren't any to be found. Maybe people enjoyed being miserable while she always tried to find a sliver of light on the greyest of days. On the roads and on the streets, ugly grimaced faces stared at her, bodies rushing past, cars spraying everyone with rainwater from the gutters. Drains bubbled and overflowed, people ankle-deep in filthy freezing water as they trudged past one another on their way to work. She felt sure it would never end. Every day she checked the weather forecast, glancing outside and praying for warmth, for the grey clouds to part and the sun to reveal itself.

'This is why British people move to Spain.' Isla spat out the words, her hair slicked down with rain, a heap of wet clothes slung over her shoulder as she yanked them off the washing line and added them to the pile that sat atop her collarbone. 'Ten minutes they've been out for. Ten bloody minutes of dry weather and then the heavens opened and they're wetter than when I lifted them out of the machine.'

The low fence that separated their gardens allowed Martha a clear view of her neighbour and friend. Even through the sheet of water, she could see Isla's sunken cheeks and haunted expression. Her dispirited stance, body bent and braced against the howling wind that buffeted her. She was a wisp of a thing, her skin grey, hair lank and uncombed. When it came to Isla, unlike the rest of the world, the weather didn't alter her demeanour. It was just how she was. How she had always been. All the howling storm did was exacerbate her low mood. Make her even more edgy and restless. Isla didn't look for slivers of light on grey days. It was as if she embraced the dirge and the shadows, refusing to seek out the warmth and the sunlight.

'I can give you a hand?' Martha's voice carried over the saturated lawn, bouncing off silken rose petals that wilted beneath the weight of the pounding rain. She had been in her greenhouse when the downpour came, fat wet splodges bursting out of a stray cloud that sailed across an already leaden sky.

'Ah, I'm fine, Martha. Ignore me. I've had a bad day. Bad week, truth be told.'

Isla's bad days and weeks stretched out like elastic. There was a time when she'd smiled, when the sun had shone in her world, but as the months and years passed, the rip in Isla's demeanour grew and deepened, her posture became more crooked, her expression set like stone. A scowl was her default stance, snarling at passers-by. Grunting at their attempts to initiate conversation. Isla's good days were becoming rarer. It was hard to remember when she last smiled, when she spoke without that growl in her timbre that Martha had learned to ignore. And yet Isla herself couldn't see it – how low she was, how it was part of her character, instead continually putting it down to finances or work or the weather. There was always something dragging her mood deep into the loam.

But even those grey days seemed halcyon compared to what Martha was seeing right now. This time it was different. Her stricken expression, her grey pallor. Then there was the weight loss. This time spelled a deep depression that would affect everyone in her orbit, friends and family doing what they could to help her back into the light. It loomed large like a hangman's noose. And it would be Martha who would have to accompany her back from the brink, reassuring her friend that life really was worth living. That there were things in her day-to-day existence worth getting out of bed for each morning.

'Anything I can help with?'

A sharp intake of breath and brief shake of her head and Isla was gone, scurrying back inside, the door slamming behind her. Then a protracted silence followed by a clap of thunder so loud, Martha could feel the vibrations pounding in her chest. Perhaps later, when Isla had had time to think, to mull over their conversation, Martha would go round there, invite her friend over for coffee. They could have it at home or perhaps go to the café on the corner of Belmont Road. A change of scenery, getting the poor woman out of that house, might prove beneficial. Finn was a good, kind man but blind to his wife's needs, smiling inanely and seemingly unperturbed when his wife refused to engage in conversation, her mind too crowded by all the commotion to think clearly. Or when she pushed his hand away as he tried to place it over hers while she battled another mental decline. He would smile and offer tea and biscuits to a woman whose world was crumbling around her. Isla needed more than a placid, caring husband. She needed professional help. Martha was no psychologist but she could listen, try to reassure the poor woman that things would improve. Whatever it was that was dragging her down, as a friend and neighbour, Martha saw it as her duty to help. Whether Isla wanted it or not.

* * *

'You can't make it better, Martha. Nobody can. I'm in a rut. Stuck in a dead end with no way out.'

Steamy tendrils curled up over her fingers as Isla clutched at the spoon, stirring at her coffee, her movements sharp and noisy. Each clank rattled Martha's nerves, her flesh stippled with goosebumps while she waited for Isla to elaborate. It had been a long time since they had sat and chatted like this, just the two of them offloading over a cup of coffee and a slice of Victoria sponge. How long had it been? Two months, maybe three. Martha stared down at a bare table. No cake this time. Neither had the appetite for it, Isla's mood and permanent grimace stripping away any hunger pangs or sugar cravings. Her eyes had darkened when Martha suggested they share a slice and so Martha had ordered only coffee, hoping the caffeine would provide enough fortitude to listen to her friend's outpouring of grief.

'Try me. Sometimes just talking about things can make them seem better.'

'Not this time, love. Not this time.' Isla shook her head, her eyes lowered, long lashes blinking repeatedly. She reminded Martha of a newborn foal, all fear and fragility, as if the world was too big and terrifying a place for her. As if she might slip off the edge of the earth and spin away, disappearing into the ether like an inconsequential speck of dust.

Martha wasn't about to pry. She wasn't a gossip, despising those who did. She loathed the type who gathered in covens, forensically pulling apart conversations, dragging down absent friends and shredding them until all that was left was the ruins of a once-respected individual. It wasn't her way at all. But she did want to help. Isla had to know she wasn't alone. Martha remembered all too well the days when the darkness had crept into the mind of her own mother, forcing her to take to her bed where she would slump for days on end while Martha got herself up and off to school on her own. Her mother would lie in the darkness of her bedroom while Martha cleaned the house and cooked meals in readiness for her springing up days later as if nothing untoward had occurred. As if Martha hadn't kept the house running while her mother battled her demons under the weight of a winter duvet and a bottle of whiskey. Although ordinarily not given to heavy drinking, once the fog had cleared and she was able to elaborate, she claimed that it helped her to sleep. Helped her to blank out the anxiety and the thick swirling mists; to turn her back on the greedy depression that gobbled up all the light in her world, casting shadows across her mind and obliterating everything. Even her own daughter.

'You look thin, Isla. I hope you're eating properly.'

A shrug followed by a protracted silence, the air around them angry and jagged as if any noise would result in it splintering and falling apart. Then tears bubbling out of large glassy eyes, running in rivulets down Isla's pallid cheeks. The sight of it softened Martha's tense frame, made her want to scoop up her friend and protect her from whatever was eating at her soul. She had seen before how demons could ravage somebody beyond all recognition. How they could strip and gnaw until there wasn't anything left to feast on.

'Oh, Isla, please let me help you. I can't just sit here and do nothing.'

The heat of Martha's own flesh was in sharp contrast to her friend's ice-cold hand as Martha reached across the table and clasped Isla's fingers, holding them tightly as if she were a precious object that might shatter at any moment. She plucked a crumpled tissue from her pocket and passed it across to Isla, who grabbed at it and held it to her face in an attempt to stem the steady flow of tears that bubbled like a swollen river about to burst its banks.

'Nobody can help me, Martha. There isn't anyone who can get me out of this situation. I don't want to keep it, he knows I don't, but Finn is already planning everything, buying books about milestones and teething, and searching in magazines and newspapers for names. I don't want this baby, Martha. I can't have it. I just can't.' Her words were a splutter between gulping sobs.

Martha's hot palm heated up her entire chest as she placed her fingers over her sternum, pressing down the flutter of anxiety that beat hard beneath her clothing. A baby. Dear God, she wasn't prepared for that. It was usually money or work or Finn being his too-affable self that stuck in Isla's craw and drove her to distraction, but this? This was the last thing Martha expected to hear. A baby changed everything. A baby in their household would tear apart the flimsy strands of their already threadbare life.

Martha held her thoughts, keeping them in check. One stray word could send everything hurtling off in the wrong direction. For many, this would be welcome news, but not for Isla. She had always stipulated that children were out of the question. Like Martha, her own childhood had been questionable. Dark and lonely. The difference between Martha and her friend was that Martha had wanted her own children, planning them and waiting patiently while they grew and blossomed inside her. She longed for children if only to prove to both herself and others that she could break the pattern of negativity and melancholy. She had an urge to demonstrate to a watching world that she could love and care for them unconditionally despite never having a decent role model in her own upbringing. And she did love them. Declan and Archie were happy and healthy. They were allowed to be children, free of the constraints of forced adulthood before they were ready. The early lives of her children would not emulate her own upbringing. She had made sure of it, promising herself as she sat across from the doctor all those years ago, listening as he spoke about the importance of looking after herself whilst pregnant, that she would be the best she could be for her children. And not just for her children but also for herself. Because self-care was a necessary function when battling a broken past, a history that continually reminded her of her background and inherited traits. A past that whispered in her ear, telling her how close she was to becoming her mother. A broken woman who barely functioned.

'Isla,' Martha whispered, her voice so low she feared each word would drift away, unheard, swallowed up by the pulsing thrum of the silence, 'you can make this work. You are a kind and loving person. You have a lot of compassion and forgiveness in you. You may not be able to see it now, but you will make a wonderful, caring mother.'

A cold breeze carried over her fingers, the air thin and sharp against her flesh as Isla snatched her hand away and stood up, her chair scraping across the floor with such ferocity, Martha felt herself recoil.

'I have to go. I can't talk about this now. I'm too tired for it. Too tired for any of this. Just too bloody tired for everything, Martha. I'm fucking exhausted with nowhere to turn.'

She was gone before Martha could say anything more, Isla's hunched figure passing by the window, chin tucked deep into her chest in a bid to escape the driving rain that pelted at her face. Even allowing for that, Martha could still see her friend's slightly crazed expression, her cold, frozen features. Her combative stance and gait, as if the world was set against her. As if she was determined to rail against whatever fate decided to throw her way. Even the positives; the days when the sun shone endlessly and the news was filled with hopeful stories that didn't tarnish or depress weren't enough to help Isla through. Depression came from within, Martha knew that but had nothing else at hand, nothing to offer her friend except the promise of sunny days and a hopeful smile.

Despite living two doors down, it was another month before Martha saw Isla again, her phone calls going unanswered, her gentle raps at the door duly ignored.

She tried to keep her gaze averted from the bump that was already starting to show when Martha did finally spot her.

'Hi, Martha,' Finn shouted from the other side of the driveway, his hand raised. 'Just off to church. We have plenty to celebrate.' His smile, rather than being infectious, felt forced, a rictus expression, his flesh stretched across the angular bony features of his face. She could understand Isla's mild annoyance, Finn's imperviousness to the obvious exacerbating the problem. Rather than trying to find a solution or attempting to work through issues, Finn's answer was to act as if they didn't exist. Paste on a smile and plough through the debris with breath-taking bravery that would fell a lesser person. In many ways, his demeanour was child-like; frivolous and excitable in the face of adversity.

Isla slunk into the car before Martha had a chance to meet her gaze. But she could see the scowl on Isla's face, her features lined and folded like a scrunched-up slip of paper. Church was Finn's love, his sanctuary, not Isla's. She did it to keep him happy. Isla had nothing; no protection, no place she could shelter when the world became too busy and violent for her. A lonely, fractured childhood had cemented the idea in her head that God didn't exist, leaving a young Isla to rot in the arms of a woman who didn't love her. Martha had tried to explain to Isla time and time again that love took many forms, that her mother had indeed loved her, but like Martha's own mum, she'd simply been too ill to show it. She wanted to say it again, to shout it across the driveway as Finn backed the car out onto the road and set off to the place he appreciated more than his home, taking his wife with him. She wanted to shout that God might not be able to help Isla but she certainly could. Even Martha's small efforts brought more joy into Isla's life than attending mass and taking Holy Communion with a man who was blinkered to his wife's illness.

Finn's Ford disappeared around the corner, leaving Martha standing alone, wondering what the future held for her friend, and how she would cope once the baby came along, turning an already fractured woman into a completely shattered one.

4

BLAKE

19 January

Dear Lucy,

I'm happy to hear that you are content. I'm excited about the two of us focusing on the good times, the places we visited together, the fun we had. Because it hasn't all been bad, has it? I recall times when we laughed till we cried. Times when we lay on the grass with the sun beating down on our necks, birds wheeling above us in a clear azure sky. Those are the times I want to remember. The soft white clouds. The buzz of insects. The best of times. Not the grey days. The miserable days. The days when life didn't seem worth living. Those blissfully joyous moments when the sun seemed to shine that little bit brighter and the grass was the most beautiful shade of green, its silken sheen swaying in the soft summer breeze like waves on the ocean are the days I liked the most. Those times are the ones worth remembering. Sometimes even now, the shadows inch their way in but at least now I recognise them for what they are. I guess we all have our bad days. Me more than most. Do you have bad days, Lucy? Or do you still breeze through life like you always have, as if nothing is amiss? Even in the bleakest of moments when the world felt as if it were about to shatter into a million tiny pieces, you still managed to rise and greet the day with a smile. Sometimes I longed to see the dark side of you, for your skin to split open and observe as those demons came slithering out, fangs bared, claws primed for the kill. But they never did. Maybe you were better at hiding them than I was. Although I do recall a few darker incidents, but I guess it's still too early in our renewed friendship to speak of them. So for now, I'll pretend that everything was perfect.

Do you think I'm a good and decent person, Lucy? I'd like to think that the answer to that particular question is yes, but I do know that you possibly harbour some less than savoury feelings about me. That's because I did some less than savoury things when I was younger. But I'm different now – a changed woman. At least that's what I have been told by those around me. I try to be kind and reflect on my behaviour and hope that those traits come across in my letters, but you will have to forgive me if now and again I sound abrasive. I still have days when I am slightly off kilter. When that happens I take some time out to recalibrate, to retune my brain and emerge a better person.

Do you remember when we were about eight or nine years old and decided we would take ourselves off up to the hills for the day, telling nobody where we were going and arriving home late in the evening as the sun was setting? It was just too tempting, living as we did at the foot of the Cleveland Hills, staring up at them in awe and considered as too young or not careful enough to climb them. So we did what any adventurous child would do and disappeared without telling anybody, time running away with us as we lost ourselves in the splendour and beauty of nature. The adventure took a sour turn later that evening as we spilled into the street in an excited exhausted jumble to a gathering of worried people who were minutes away from calling the police. They were standing waiting for us at the end of the road, faces lined with anxiety. Except for one. I recall your mother, how she appeared unperturbed by your absence, rolling her eyes and shaking her head as you approached. Her face remained impassive as you ran to her full of apologies. I recall then how she pushed you away and stalked off into the house, slamming the door behind her, leaving you standing alone in the half-light beneath the lamppost. I called over to you and you went home with me where we ate a sandwich and drank a cup of steaming hot chocolate. I remember that so clearly, how you wanted to stay the night at mine; the look of dread on your face, the fear in your eyes at the thought of going back to face your mother alone. Your father was away working. He did a lot of that as I recall. Tongues wagged, people making wild unsubstantiated accusations about the state of your parents' marriage. About her treatment of you. But we ignored them. We never truly understood the gossip and what it meant. We were too young to comprehend any of it. Adults occupied one world and we lived in another, ours free of hatred and judgement. We were too young and naïve to understand and contextualise their comments. Besides, we had our own little friendship. A solid unit. We didn't need anybody else. We had each other and that was all that mattered. But now those accusations make sense. The gossip mongers were correct. And yet they did nothing, everyone going about their business while you suffered. I guess that's how it was back in the day. People didn't interfere in domestic incidents. Children got physically and emotionally punished in the harshest of ways and everyone turned a blind eye, leaving youngsters to suffer at the hands of the people who should have protected them. The danger rarely came from outside. Instead the monsters resided at home, the place where children should have been safe. The place where you should have been safe.

I also wanted you to sleep over that night. Somehow I knew that you needed to be protected from your mother. From her wrath and indifference towards you. My mum rang and asked if you could stay at ours after I pleaded with her. It was the weekend, there was no school the following morning, but your mother insisted you go home. I watched you trudge to your front gate, spine arched as if the weight of the world was perched on your shoulders.

I knew the next morning when I awoke that something was wrong. It was as if our invisible bond had been broken, the cord that stretched between us to keep us from harm, severed. I could sense it. The way my heart hammered deep in my chest. The way my body ached and my gut gurgled and pulsed. Something was horribly awry.

The heat of the rising sun forced me out of my bed, dappled spots of warmth speckling my skin, making me hot and uncomfortable. I knelt on the mattress, pulled the curtains aside, leaned to one side and stared down the road. If I craned my neck and pressed my face against the glass I could see your house two doors down. Everything appeared normal. Peaceful. Your mother's car was on the driveway. The blinds were closed. And yet something crept beneath my skin; a slithering creature I couldn't ignore. I had to know. I had to see you to settle the crippling sense of foreboding that puckered my flesh and made my head ache.

It was early, the streets empty, everyone sleeping. Except for me. My own parents were still in bed when I let myself out and set off to yours, curiosity burning a hole in my chest. I knew your house and its many idiosyncrasies – the creaking gate, the wobbly paving stone beneath the front window. The small pile of gravel we kept hidden round the back of the shed.

For emergencies, *you had said.* Like they do in the movies. Throw a handful at my window and I'll sneak down and talk to you.

Do you remember those small pebbles, Lucy? We had practised throwing them so often and failed, handfuls of them hitting the wall and spraying across the lawn like spent bullets. And then both of us scrambling about on our hands and knees in the darkness, trying to retrieve them before your mother noticed. Everything we did had to be beneath her radar.

It will be just another reason for her to hate me, *you had said.* Just another reason for her to send me to my room without any supper.

We treated those stones like precious minerals, and that morning I knew that I had to use them to check you were okay. Tiptoeing around your back garden and dropping onto my belly, I slid forwards, reaching through the narrow opening between the rickety old fence and the shed, fingers grasping for those pebbles that would let me know you were safe. I was met with a brush of soil and the odd blade of grass but no pebbles. I tried again, sweeping my palm across the ground but came up with nothing. They were gone. My first thought was that you had moved them, but before I could think anything else, a hand grasped at my ankle, yanking at me with force. I felt myself being dragged backwards, my sweater riding up over my stomach, dewy grass dampening my skin. I didn't have time to scream or call out. Another hand grabbed a chunk of my hair and my head was pulled backwards with such ferocity that my eyes watered and a whimper escaped out of my throat.

'She's not here. Whatever it is you're after, forget it and get the hell out of my garden.'

I stared up into the face of your mother, her frenzied expression turning my insides to liquid. I wished your father had been home. I wished I hadn't gone there, but most of all, I wished that morning that your mother would die so you and I could be left in peace. I trudged home after she let me go, teary-eyed, not knowing where you were and thinking how simpler and less fraught it would be if your mother was involved in a car crash or fell out of a window or took a tumble down the stairs. I thought of a hundred different ways in which she could die so we could be together without any fear or interference. I visualised your father meeting somebody pretty and delicate and happy. Somebody who smiled a lot and allowed us to play in your garden without the usual hollering that you had to go inside and do your chores, and that I had to go home and not bother coming back.

I have a vivid memory of telling you about that incident afterwards. The aftermath of that day was something else, wasn't it? The commotion outside your house, the look on your face as you were hauled out of the police vehicle and led back into the house by a stern-looking officer whose eyes were sharp enough to cut glass. Why do adults believe other adults, dismissing the word of a child as mere fantasy? Why are younger members of society ignored, their claims written off as fabricated nonsense? I think we know better now, don't we? Time has moved on and as a society we are more inclined to listen to what youngsters have to say, but back then your protestations were brushed aside, your mother claiming you had let yourself out of the house in the early hours of the morning to go searching for your father who was working in London. As young as you were, even you knew that walking from North Yorkshire to the capital city was impossible. An early morning jogger had found you huddled behind a clump of shrubbery in Great Ayton, shivering and frightened. Cold and alone. You had been there all night. Ever since your own mother had woken you and bundled you into the car in the early hours as punishment for coming home late the evening before. Our blissful adventure in the hills had resulted in you being ripped from your bed in the middle of the night and left stranded in the darkness miles and miles away from home. You were eight years old. Was it events like that that made you so brave and resilient, Lucy? I am guessing you operated on a fight-or-flight basis, always ready and prepared for the next episode. Always ready for the turmoil you endured in your own home at the hands of the woman who should have loved you more than life itself.

We were young, you and I. Just children. But we both knew what took place that day was beyond the pale. Of course beyond the pale was how you lived, your mother cutting and slicing you in thousands of tiny irreparable ways until in the end, the pain became too much to bear. But I'm getting ahead of myself. I don't want to drag you down or darken the mood. I just wanted you to know that I knew. I have always known, despite what the adults continually told me about you being badly behaved and running away. Your resilience and strength were the things that kept me by your side. Every time you overcame another adversity, my admiration for you grew a hundredfold. I so wanted to be like you, but we both know that we were polar opposites – me the quiet, awkward one and you the star that shone brightly, your effervescence drawing people to you so effortlessly it was mesmerising to watch.

I am finding it incredibly cathartic, this letter-writing process. I wish I had done it before now, taken the brave step to contact you after all these years apart. I have been foolish and stubborn and know now that the grudge I had against you has actually held me back. Bitterness is a barrier to happiness. I realise that now. There are lots of things I wish I had known when I was younger. With age comes wisdom. And bravery. No longer the cowering, shy child, I now have the courage to speak my mind. And speak it I will. So be prepared for me writing about some things you would sooner forget.

Next time I write, I will tell you about my garden. It's my precious space. A sprinkling of paradise in an otherwise dismal area. I have developed green fingers in my latter years. Who would have ever guessed that meek, mild Blake would suddenly become the type of person who can turn nothing into something? I have also taken up painting. I'm no Rembrandt or Picasso but I like to think I'm getting better with each consecutive attempt. There is usually more paint on me than on the canvas once I have finished but it passes the time and I enjoy it. It's the simple pleasures that I now appreciate. Small things can bring such a lot to our lives in so many immeasurable ways.

I hope you have found worthwhile ways of passing the time, Lucy. It's important to keep our brains active. We were both blessed with intelligence, but as was always the case, you often managed to get higher marks than me in every exam and test we took in school. I wasn't jealous, it made me admire you even more.

I am biting hard at my lip as I re-read what I have just written. I think it is now time to stop with the countless lies. I admit I was more than a little envious, but I never showed it and it certainly didn't impinge on the longing I had to be your closest friend. Maybe now is the time for me to apologise for any barbed comments I may have inadvertently made as we read through our exam results. I like to think I kept it under wraps, but emotions have a way of sneaking out and finding a target, like a heat-seeking missile programmed to destroy whatever is in its sights. I never meant for you to be my target, Lucy. You were and will always be my shining light. I always found you no matter where you were, your brightness and intensity always easy to locate. And I have found you once again.

I look forward to reading your reply.

Love, Blake

I fold up the letter and slip it into an envelope, pressing down the flap with such care and precision, anybody watching would think it contained a precious object, which in a way, it does.

I step outside and hear a voice behind me. 'Would you like me to take that for you?' Sandra moves in front of me, hand outstretched, her eyes lowered as she stares at my letter to Lucy.

'No!' My voice rips through the silence. I take a deep breath and make a concerted effort to keep my tone low and friendly. 'Thank you, but I'll manage.' My smile is wide and a little too forced. My neighbour always has that effect on me, her presence making me jittery and out of sorts.

If Sandra notices my demeanour, she hides it well. We have lived next to each other for the past few years and although we have very different personalities, we manage to rub along together without any drama or conflict.

'Okay,' she says softly. 'No problem. I'll let you get on.'

Guilt pricks me as she starts to walk away. Sandra means

well, always offering to help, always with a kind word. I just find her overbearing at times, often prying into my affairs with her relentless questions about my family and my life. Sandra is an open book, speaking regularly about her chequered past. I prefer privacy which seems to make her even more inclined to try and dig deeper into my background.

'Sorry,' I offer by means of an apology for my brusqueness. 'It's just that it's for a close friend of mine. We haven't spoken for years.'

My fingers are cold as I cling onto the envelope, pressing it against my chest for safekeeping.

'I understand,' she murmurs. 'Good friends are hard to come by. We should keep them close.'

Flames lick at my face as I recall a conversation with Sandra a few months ago. A conversation where she detailed how one of her friends died in a car crash in a vehicle that Sandra was driving. She was breathalysed and was three times over the limit. The case went to court and Sandra paid a hefty price for her recklessness. She now has no qualms about speaking about the incident to anybody who will listen. That is where we differ. I prefer to keep my personal matters private, but the more I internalise, the harder she tries to get inside my head and unpick my thoughts.

The sound of my door closing seems to reverberate as I push it to and head into my garden where everything always feels brighter and more peaceful, the raucous noise of the world hushed by the beauty of nature. I tilt my face up to the radiance of the low winter sun and let out a deep sigh.

5

BLAKE

30 January

Dear Blake,

Please forgive my shaky script, but my hands are trembling as I write this letter. I have always thought of you as somebody special even after what we went through. And we endured more than most. I am horrified to think you are still disturbed by something that happened many years ago. I have no memory of any veiled insults or barbed comments you made to me. If they were indeed uttered, then they clearly weren't done with any malice behind them. Or maybe by that point I had grown a second skin, become inured to invectives after living with my mother and putting up with her rages and indifference towards me.

Those hours after my mother left me in the darkness far from home as punishment for simply being a child and playing outside were the longest of my life. I had never been so frightened. Of course at that point I had no idea what lay ahead. What horrors my mother had in store for me. Being unceremoniously dumped in the middle of the night, miles away from home was just the beginning. But as you say, it helped me become a stronger person. For every insult she fired my way and every damaging act she heaped upon me, I grew hardier. More courageous. Her insults allowed me to grow. I had no choice. It was that or wither and die. I didn't do it to be brash or appear brave in front of others. I did it because there was no other way.

I have another memory. It has just popped into my head so please indulge me while I ramble. You and me walking to school one foggy morning, the iciness biting at our flesh. Winter was approaching but we were brave and foolhardy and decided that coats were for losers, the two of us striding along as if we owned the world. How innocent and naïve we were. Had we known what was about to take place, we would have tried to camouflage ourselves amidst the tentacles of thick fog that curled around us; smoky fingers that could have pulled us to safety. Pulled you to safety.

She appeared out of nowhere, springing out of the shrubbery, cartoon style, eyes bulging, fingers curled into claws. We almost laughed. Almost but not quite. We could see that something was not right, her expression slightly crazed, her posture primed for violence. Do you recall that moment, Blake? I'm sure you must. I had endured abuse at that point, but for you, it must have come as a shock. A rude awakening to the fact that people can be cruel and thoughtless and selfish, carrying out nefarious acts on whomever they please. I have been told many times that I come across as confident which is a thinly disguised slur for arrogant, but I've often wondered in the intervening years if they targeted you because you looked meek and mild. In truth, I was as frightened as you and would have reacted in exactly the same way. Abuse from my mother was one thing, but to have an angry, unhinged individual try to drag me into the bushes and beat me senseless is another level of fear. It would have terrified me as much as it terrified you. You fought and scratched them off while I stood, frozen, my limbs refusing to move, my throat clogged up with shock and dread. By the time I found my voice and screamed, she had managed to rip your sweater and left grazes on your skin from the ensuing struggle. You put up a good fight while I did nothing. So when you say such lovely things about me, please remember that day. The day when I stood by and did nothing to help you. I am anything but confident and definitely not the shining star you think I am. My failings are plenty. What I am is human, and humans are flawed, damaged creatures in so many ways. We make mistakes and do terrible hideous things. Since that time I have raked over it in my head, what I could and should have done. But we were children and what's done is done and cannot be undone, so I hope you can forgive me for my ineptitude that morning. I never got to apologise back then and suddenly feel the need to do it now. When I say I am sorry, I really do mean it.

We moved on from that day as watchful children, never quite settling back into childhood the way other youngsters did. You were understandably jumpy and wide-eyed at every unexpected noise while I carried on trying to protect you. I'm sure at some point, we put it behind us, or maybe I did, but I'm certain it stayed with you, the trauma of that assault, the violation haunting you for a long time afterwards. I once recall, many years later, you stating that the attack was recompense for you having a blissfully happy childhood compared to my car crash of an upbringing, so maybe we became equals afterwards. I don't want to dwell on it too much. Continually raking over a distressing incident isn't healthy. And I should know.

On to better times. Maybe now is the moment to let you know about my recent achievements. They don't amount to much but I'm proud of them all the same. Although I don't travel too far these days, I gain a lot of pleasure from pottering around my garden and tending to the flowers and shrubs. There is a magnolia tree next to where I spend my days and when it's in full bloom, there's nothing in the world quite like it. The pale pink and white remind me of the halcyon summers we spent wandering through the woods and up into the hills where we would stand like rulers of the world. Below us, we could see the urban sprawl of industry that brought the place to life. Plumes of steam billowed out of cooling towers and we would watch, enthralled, as the world flourished beneath us. I don't recall the exact day when we stopped climbing those hills, but at some point we became teenagers, too busy and too cool to continue with our childhood adventures. Other pastimes beckoned as we developed into fledgling adults. That was when the real changes took place, but I'm getting ahead of myself. One step at a time.

You say you've taken up painting. We both used to enjoy drawing and sketching back in the day, didn't we? I once got a piece of my artwork framed which gave my confidence a much-needed boost. I realise you think I'm blessed with self-assurance but that's just a mask for my insecurities. I have as many fears and moments of uncertainty as the next person. As I said earlier, we are each and every one of us only human after all. Gardening is a tranquil hobby, and I adore the colours and scents of the flowers, especially after the rain. A down-pour seems to bring out the perfume of each blossom, latent aromas bursting and rising into the air from damp petals. My safe space is a riot of colour. I did say that my achievements don't amount to much, didn't I? But as we get older, small things can mean such a lot.

I hope I haven't upset you too much with the mention of that assault. I feel that if I don't speak of it now, then I never will, and it has burned a hole in the core of me for so many years, it's now time to let go of it.

You are right about these letters being like a form of therapy. Strange, because it's as if we still have so much left unsaid, which is hard to believe when you consider we've known one another since we were toddlers. You would think we would have run out of words by now, everything there is to say already voiced, yet here we are, still so much to speak about, and so much still unsaid. Perhaps ours was a friendship made in heaven.

Until hell nudged its way in, that is.

And it was hell. I try not to think about it too much. Maybe later when we've said everything there is to say, then perhaps the time will be right to tackle that sordid, disturbing era of our lives. It's the elephant in the room, the hulking great immovable object that haunts us every day. We can speak about the nice twee times all we like but it won't make the awfulness of what happened go away.

I will sign off with a piece of news that will hopefully bring a smile to your face – I've become a grandparent! My daughter gave birth to a baby boy and they have named him Lewis. I have yet to meet him as the distance between us is too great, but am assured both mother and baby are doing well. He weighed a whopping 9lb 2oz and has dark hair and blue eyes, just like his father. My dreams are now filled with images of his tiny cherub-like features and I hope that one day soon, I'll get to meet him and hold him in my arms. I debated whether I should mention this piece of news to you given your circumstances but felt sure you'd be happy for me. I hope that is the case. You and I go too far back to hold grudges or keep secrets from one another, don't we? I know you as well as I know myself, your features and thoughts as familiar as my own. We each have our passions and devils to deal with. The person closest to us is often the one we push away, and for a while that happened, but we're back together now, Blake, and I'd like honesty to be the thing that seals our friendship; the glue that keeps us bonded. No more lies or hurt. Just truth and tenderness. I think we owe it to one another, don't you?

Your letters have given me hope for the future. Just goes to show that happiness can rise out of the shadows. Smouldering embers of a fire that once ravaged us have slowly rotted into the soil and now green shoots are springing up, ready to blossom and flourish into something beautiful.

Listen to me, waxing lyrical and getting mawkish and sentimental. It was you who was always the wordsmith. Your flair for putting together a well-crafted sentence and weaving it into a compelling story was something I always admired. And it brought in a handsome income for you as well. Even though some of your stories were derived from real experiences, I never complained. Writers are told time and time again to draw from their own encounters and write about what they know. So you used your wealth of knowledge about the lives of others to write your novel. You told my story too, didn't you, Blake? You told the world about my childhood and the battles I fought every day; battles and trials that gouged a huge hole in my formative years, leaving me bruised and bloodied. Not that I minded. Or perhaps I did a little. I've made a promise to be honest so to start lying to protect you at this juncture would amount to hypocrisy. So yes, maybe deep down, I felt slighted at your portrayal of me in your book. But I'm sure you already know that. I've forgiven you and we've moved on. The future is what matters now. Let's make it a good one and not spend time brooding over a difficult and painful past that we cannot change.

Anyway, I've bored you enough with my inane ramblings. I'll sign off now and wait excitedly for your reply.

Love, Lucy

'You look decidedly happy. Anything new to tell me?' Arthur's smile is a rare thing to see, his slightly crooked teeth gleaming like diamonds.

I want to reply that he too looks like the cat who got the cream but instead nod and explain that I am happy and everything feels on a level. Stable and easy.

'How's the painting going?'

My art classes. I feel myself slump a little. Writing has taken up most of my time, my other pastimes now relegated to the back of my mind.

'I'll get back to it.' From somewhere in the room, a draft skids over the back of my neck. 'At some point.'

'You've been busy with other things, I take it?'

He's fishing for information. Arthur already knows I've been busy with my letter writing. His less than subtle technique won't get me to open up and bare my blackened soul. My letters to Lucy are private, as are her replies. Lucy and I have a shared history, things that nobody else knows or should ever get to know. There is nothing to be gained from me telling the world about what we endured. Not yet anyway. The grim inevitability of it all coming out at some point fills me with dread, but I refuse to let that notion depress me or detract from my current spell of happiness. Today is what counts. Tomorrow's problems can wait.

'I'm content. That's what counts, isn't it?'

The squeak of his leather chair fills the room when he leans back, his stereotypical stance making me smile. We both have our roles and we each play them well.

'Of course. But at some point, perhaps we need to speak of your friend. And what took place. Yes?'

Fire heats up my face, flames licking beneath my skin, charring my bones. This is Arthur at his best, slowly unpicking the fabric of my life while I desperately clutch at stray fibres, trying to keep everything intact. Trying to stop my life from coming apart and falling in a heap at my feet.

I could speak of it right now. Or I could just tell Arthur to fuck off and leave me alone, to stop trying to ruin my happiness with his constant probing and relentless questions.

'At some point,' I say quietly, barbed wire cutting at my throat. 'But not yet. Not today.'

The scrape of my chair against linoleum signifies that this conversation is over. I stand on unsteady legs and head to the door, knowing that soon my private letters to Lucy will be read by him. It's just how it is. But for now I'm enjoying keeping her to myself.

I slam the door behind me, the echo of my sudden departure a sad reminder of how little power I have over my own life.

6

BEFORE

'I wouldn't ordinarily dream of asking, Martha, you know that, but I've tried everything and I simply cannot get through to her.' Finn stood on the doorstep, his eyes dark, his thinning hair lank and unwashed.

Martha stared at his slightly equine features and ashen complexion, wondering what really happens behind the closed doors of their home. Wondering why the man who was practically glued to his wife's side was unable to see what was painfully obvious to outsiders.

'Give me two minutes to let Charlie know what I'm doing, and I'll be straight round.'

Finn's countenance and sloping gait as he walked back home tugged at Martha's emotions, cutting deep into her humanity with a savageness that scared her. Finn never asked for help with any of his wife's episodes. Ever. It must be bad. Dread was a clenched fist in the base of her stomach.

Charlie was dozing in the armchair when she peeked her head around the doorframe. It was the end of a fifty-hour week for her husband, day after day of fixing cranes and being on call-out. She wouldn't wake him, shouting upstairs to the boys instead that she was going to see Isla and wouldn't be long. In truth she had no idea how long it would take or what she was about to be faced with. A sullen Isla who refused to get up off the living-room floor? She had dealt with that in the past, managing to coax her up into the armchair before Finn arrived home from work. Or maybe it would be an angry Isla who'd once taken it upon herself to smash ornaments against the tiled fireplace, only stopping when she drew blood on her hand from a shard of broken pottery. There was so much that Finn didn't know, so much shielded from him. Was it any wonder that man strolled through life without a care in the world? Isla seemed to save the worst for Martha, her behaviour curbed and vaguely acceptable once her husband entered the house.

'I'll only be half an hour. No shenanigans, you two!'

Pulling the door closed with a muted click, Martha wove her way through parked cars and a snarl of shrubbery, and nudged Isla's front door open with her hip, stepping inside, her movements and footfall soft and ghost-like.

At the top of the stairs stood Finn. A tall figure of a man, his silhouette casting a shadow across the landing. Everything about him was eerie; from his long, smooth fingers to his deep unrelenting gaze, and yet having known him for over a decade, Martha was aware that Finn didn't have a malicious bone in his body. What he did have to deal with was Isla's mood swings, her unpredictable ways and steadfast refusal to bend to his will to procreate and have the many children he so desired. His church was his life and Isla came second in so many ways. He was a kind man but blind to her needs and often unable to deal with the aftermath of her moods and bouts of depression. And Finn only saw the half of it, work and religion taking up most of his time. Martha supposed he was better off praying at mass, although why was a mystery to her. Even God had no answers when it came to Isla.

Martha crept up the stairs and gently nudged Finn aside. She felt his body lean at an awkward angle, his posture bending like willow. For such a large man, his stance felt as soft and as pliable as butter. His large feet stumbled as he stepped away, defeated by his wife's stubbornness. Isla had won this one. For once, she was in control.

Martha sat on the floor and placed her ear next to the bathroom door, gently rapping at the wood, doing what she could to appear tender and sympathetic despite a flicker of exasperation slowly combusting in her chest. This was a delicate moment, one that required a woman's touch, not the lumbering gait of an overly devout man who relied on prayer to solve every issue and problem. Isla needed to hear the voice of a friend who had always been there for her and was now doing what she could to get Isla to acquiesce and let Martha inside.

'Isla. It's me. I know you're upset but if you unlock the door, we can go somewhere quiet to chat.'

Silence. Nothing except the sound of Martha's own breathing and the whoosh of her blood as it roared in her ears, the growl of it making her dizzy and disorientated.

'Come on, Isla. I'm not here to judge. All I want – all *we* want is for you to be happy.'

The heavy drumbeat of nothingness reverberated off every wall, knocking at Martha's skull like a hammer against stone. She turned to Finn, her voice gravelly. Brimming with authority. The very thing Finn lacked.

'We need to get her out of there. Did she take anything in with her?'

His response, the look of helplessness on his face, the shrug of his shoulders as he shook his head to convey his lack of understanding, brought forth a wave of anger that threatened to engulf her. This was what Isla railed against; her husband's inability to read the room, to read his wife and take decisive action to stop her from hurting herself.

'Razor blades, Finn? Any medication or alcohol?'

'I'm not sure. I don't think so. I've asked her to pray, to get God to help us, but she isn't answering me.'

Martha's skin sizzled. Frustration built in her gut. This was what Isla was up against day after day. It was like repeatedly slamming her head against a brick wall.

'Finn, why don't you go downstairs and make us all a cup of tea?'

The shuffle of feet as he sidled away lowered her blood pressure, the pain in her eyes dissipating the farther Finn moved away from her. A good man with plenty of love in him but so horribly blinkered it was a wonder he didn't walk headlong into traffic.

'Isla, Finn has gone. It's just me here now.' She pressed her body against the cool grain of the wooden door, her palms flat on the floor for balance. 'He'll be back in five minutes. If you unlock the door now, I can come inside with you and we can talk in private.'

A low click followed by a creak. Heart thudding, Martha slid through the tiny opening, swallowing down the gasp at the sight before her. Fingers trembling, she reached up and turned the lock, making sure nobody could get to them, then crouched next to Isla's crumpled, dazed body, fear pounding in her temples.

'How much have you had, Isla? Please tell me you haven't drunk the whole lot?'

Martha could see by the glassiness of her friend's eyes, by the pastiness of her skin, that Isla had consumed the full bottle of gin. She thought of the unborn child nestled in Isla's womb, the tiny infant purportedly protected from the outside world in the warm cocoon of her friend's uterus, and the damage that Isla may have done to it. Martha had read about such things. She had no medical training but common sense told her that alcohol could do terrible things to a foetus. Brain damage, learning difficulties, physical deformities. Any number of issues could arise from this level of consumption. And then there was the danger of alcohol poisoning. Isla wasn't a drinker. The odd glass of wine now and again but apart from that, very little. Her body wasn't accustomed to or prepared for such a large amount in one go.

'I wanted rid of it. I don't want this baby, Martha. I've heard about people who drink gin and lose their babies. I want to lose my baby, Martha. I can't have it. I just can't.'

A splutter followed by a coughing fit as tears ran down Isla's cheeks. Martha shuffled closer and placed an arm around her shoulders, Isla's skeletal frame a shock to her.

'If he could – or if I could...' Her slurred words tailed off, eyelids drooping as she leaned against Martha's chest and, in a matter of seconds, fell into a deep drunken slumber.

Hospital. Somehow, she had to get Isla to the hospital. Martha would have to ignore her friend's protestations and anger at the whiff of medical intervention and do the right thing. She had to make sure the baby was okay. This was no longer just about Isla. A helpless baby's life was at stake. Finn should have seen the signs. He should have got Isla the help she obviously needed instead of hauling her along to mass every Sunday as a way of cleansing their souls and asking for forgiveness for their collective sins. Isla's soul was currently in meltdown and the man was too dim to see it, his devotion to his church blinding him to everything else.

Isla's spread of dark hair fanned out like a halo as Martha laid her friend's head on a folded towel. She needed time to think. To plan. To get it just right without any of Finn's ecclesiastical guidance and counsel. And what if this wasn't the first time? What if Isla had been secretly drinking for the entire pregnancy? Martha closed her eyes, shook away that thought. She needed to focus on the here and now. Adding to the current issue with wild accusations and guesses would only make things worse.

After carefully peeling away her friend's cool thin fingers from her chest and sliding from beneath her clutches with stealth-like precision to save waking her, Martha stood and unlocked the door. She was greeted with a pair of staring eyes when she slipped out of the bathroom and onto the landing area, Finn's expression child-like. Such innocence in the face of trauma. The man had no idea what he was up against, his guileless ways completely ineffective when it came to knowing how to handle his wife and her complex needs. Martha knew what should be done but was aware that that particular option was out of the question. A termination of the pregnancy would go against Finn's beliefs. It would possibly end their marriage. For now, she had to deal with the immediate problem; call an ambulance, get Isla hospitalised. Make sure the baby was unharmed.

'We need to ring 999, Finn. Can you do that for me?'

A second passed, two then three, his blank stare an unnerving sight to behold, his dark pupils tiny pinpricks that bore into Martha as if he was searching for answers she couldn't give, until eventually he sprang into action, galloping down the stairs, hollering into the receiver that his pregnant wife was ill. Yes, she was definitely pregnant; no, she didn't have any additional medical needs; and yes, she needed to be seen as soon as possible.

Martha sucked at her teeth and fought back tears. If only psychiatrists and therapists were as easily accessed as doctors of medicine. Finn didn't know about the empty bottle of gin his wife had consumed in the hope it would end the pregnancy. He didn't know about how desperate she was, how her mind was in freefall. Finn didn't know much at all. But he would find out soon enough. Once they reached the hospital and the medical team assessed her, he would discover just how far Isla had fallen. How she was trying to dig a deeper hole rather than clamber out of the one she was in. But for now, Martha had to go back in the bathroom and comfort her friend. She had to try to rouse her and make her aware that the medics were on their way.

* * *

The arrival of the ambulance in a blaze of glory with its wailing siren was enough to force Isla upright into a sitting position. Even in her dazed state of mind, she was aware that things were about to implode. Glassy-eyed, she looked around, a sudden dawning in her expression. A flood of colour rushed into her pale cheeks, her neck peppered with humiliation. The empty bottle sat at her feet. Martha pushed it away out of reach, fearing Isla would attempt to hide it. The doctor had to know what and who he was dealing with. No cover-ups. No lies. No more deceit or fabrications that would allow Isla to slip even farther into the abyss.

'Martha, what's...?'

'Shhh. You're going to be fine, Isla. I'm going to unlock the door and let the medical team in.'

The growing bump hindered Isla's attempts to escape, her ballooning midriff making her clumsy and un-coordinated. One rapid sweeping motion and Martha had the bottle grasped in the palm of her hand, her fingers curled tightly around it while Isla sat slumped, a forlorn sight, her hair askew, eyes dark with shame.

'I haven't been keeping up with my appointments for this thing.' Her finger prodded at her stomach, a long nail resting on the arced solidity of her abdomen. 'Not even sure why they want me to go anyway.'

Martha had every answer at the ready about checking the baby's heartbeat and Isla's blood pressure, but remained silent. They both knew that Isla's question needed no reply. Lashing out with pointless rhetoric was Isla's default stance when the world crowded in on her, when people with their endless interrogations and Finn with his constant requests for her to attend church pushed her into a corner like an animal caught in a snare, teeth bared, a snarl erupting from the back of her throat.

Outside, a gust of wind stirred the trees, their branches creaking and groaning like the guttural rattles of a dying man, each scrape and moan laced with desperation. Martha bit at her lip, thinking that even the noises of nature in its many forms became threatening when she was close to her friend. It was as if Isla's presence, her low mood and despondency, had the power to drag everything and everyone around her down to ground level where it was cold and gravelly and far from the warmth of the sun.

A sudden sound from behind the door cut into Martha's thoughts. The crackle of fabric. Footsteps. Voices. Then a gentle knocking that had Isla backing away, legs propelling madly until her spine was pressed up against the cold tiled wall. Martha suppressed a sigh. Her friend was a sorry sight. Like a frightened lumpen child attempting to hide from a particularly wicked deed.

'Come on, let's get you up.' Arm in arm, she hauled Isla to her feet and opened the door.

Finn stood outside the bathroom, face stricken. It was almost impossible for Martha to conceal her exasperation. A married couple acting like a pair of helpless children, one of them pregnant, the other locked in a world of devotion to a deity who had turned his back, leaving the pair of them to thrash and flounder about like dying fish. This couple needed to up their game, was Martha's first thought. Be the steady reliable people this baby needed in order to survive.

'She's drunk all of this. Take care of her.' Martha stepped aside, watching as Isla fell into the chest of a startled medic. 'And take care of that poor unborn baby.'

* * *

It would be another two months before Martha saw Isla again, their eyes locking as they sat opposite one another in the place of respite that was Isla's temporary home after trying to terminate the pregnancy herself. The same place where she had learned to master the art of feigned acceptance of both her condition and her unborn child in a bid to get back home. None of the so-called professionals could see beyond Isla's gushing words when asked about the baby. They took it all at face value, assuring Finn that she was improving and would soon be fit to be discharged. Martha had a burning desire to scream at the purported professionals that she was lying, that Isla would say exactly what they wanted to hear in order to get them off her back. But Martha knew that she was a lone voice howling into the void when it came to Isla and her crafty ways. Which was why she stopped her efforts, figuring if Finn didn't care enough to see beyond Isla's brittle veneer, then why should she waste her energy? Martha had her own family to look after. A job to go to. A house to run.

The baby was born unharmed three months later. And that's when the real problems all began.

7

BLAKE

18 February

Dear Lucy,

I'm happy you wrote back to me and would like to thank you for your honesty. Sometimes being truthful and upfront is painful, but always better, I think, than hiding behind a protective shield. By being honest, we leave ourselves open to slings and arrows and so although I feel shocked at your mention of me making a handsome living off the back of your misfortune with my writing, I do admire your bravery. I'm not the type of person to take umbrage at the slightest bit of provocation (which is why we're still friends and also still in communication after all these years) so I think it's best we don't speak any more of the stories I wrote about that period of your life. The only thing I would add is that I like to think I did it with sensitivity, but maybe you disagree? I think it's a valid argument and nothing will shift my viewpoint. Anyway, it's all in the past and as you so accurately said at the end of your letter, a hopeful future is more important than a fractured past.

I am delighted to hear you have become a grandparent.

Family is what matters. Not money or possessions or any of the things people spend their lives chasing; it's the ones closest to us, our blood relatives, that make life worth living. As you know, I will never become a grandmother so will live my life vicariously through you by reading about the small precious addition to your family. Maybe that's why I chose my writing as an outlet, something to fill the vacuum in my existence. I lost two of the only two things that ever mattered to me, and so I turned to writing to pass the time. Little did I know that one thing would lead to another, and a publisher would offer me a large advance for my words which set me up financially for the next few years. I didn't do it to spite you, Lucy. It just happened and I would have been a fool to turn down such a lucrative offer. It did, however, come at a price. But you already know that, don't you? Please don't disappoint me by pretending otherwise. I couldn't bear for you to insult my intelligence.

I'm not lonely. You need to know that. I am often alone but never lonely. I hope when you do finally meet your grandchild, you realise how lucky you are. I've managed to fill my days with the other pastimes that I mentioned in my last letter because my family is sadly lacking. Many are not as unfortunate as me and you are one of those people. When it comes to being surrounded by loved ones, you should consider yourself very blessed. I would if I were you, but I'm not you, am I? I am me, a barren childless woman who lives alone with only my thoughts for company. Such a bloody awful cliché. Such a bloody awful life.

The assault when I was a child – it never really left me. I managed to tuck it away, refusing to brood over something I couldn't change, but yes, it was a disturbing moment. I guess I should consider myself lucky you were there with me other-

wise things could have turned out very differently. Why didn't we report what happened that day? It remains yet another of our secrets. We have plenty of those, don't we? Things we kept between just the two of us. That's why we can't ever drift apart. Nobody knows me as you do and I know you like no other. We're as strong as forged steel, you and I. A solid unit. It's our many dark moments that hold us together.

I still write on occasion (not only these letters to you), although I don't submit my manuscripts for publication any more. I still like to dabble, penning short stories and articles that nobody will ever read. They're stashed in a manila folder beneath my bed. Maybe one day I will show you them, that is if you're interested. I wouldn't want to show you them if you choose to not read them. God forbid I ever do anything that would upset the delicate equilibrium of your perfect life.

Sorry.

Sometimes it just comes out; all my resentment and bitterness. It leaks out like acid, burning everyone around me. I seem to be terribly adept at hurting people. It's one of my defining features. I will try to do better, Lucy. Because you don't deserve my wrath.

Anyway, back to when we were small and just getting acquainted; when life was exciting, the future crammed with opportunities. I loved that time, seeing little or no danger. Even the attack didn't diminish our need for adventure. There was one thing, however, that began to eat away at my confidence – your beauty and buoyancy as you turned from a neglected little girl into a beautiful teenager. You had none of the awkwardness that I possessed. You did have the bruises though; those awful beatings your mother gave you. They were horrific. Only I saw those scars on your skin. You hid your distress as well as your mother hid her violence, hitting you where it wouldn't show. I knew though. I remained voiceless, watching from the sidelines as you endured the worst treatment possible from the woman who was supposed to love you unconditionally. I guess we have that much in common, don't we? Each of us watching soundlessly as the other was attacked, both of us doing little or nothing to assist.

Your blemish-free sculpted features and flawless deportment always gave you the edge over me. I was smaller, everything about me less noticeable. Less striking. People often commented on your piercing blue eyes and long dark lashes while I stood by, wishing somebody would for once, just once, say something complimentary about me. But what was there to say, really? I had small nondescript eyes, flyaway hair and the beginnings of acne-covered skin. When I did eventually develop some finer points, it was because I worked on them, using a small amount of make-up, and applying conditioner to my dry, frizzy hair. Doing whatever I could to remain in your league. To remain by your side. Because I never told you this, but I was always terrified you would find somebody better. Somebody confident and beautiful to replace me. Fortunately you didn't, and the frumpy friend gradually morphed into somebody who was able to walk beside you without appearing too dowdy. No longer plain Jane; with a little application and a lot of effort, I was able to transform myself into somebody who although didn't turn heads as you did, no longer shrank and wilted in your shadow like a desiccated flower deprived of rain and sunlight.

Are you still as beautiful, Lucy? Or has middle age finally caught up with you? It has dented me for sure, stripping away the layers I spent years carefully applying. They were superficial anyway, masking the real clumsy, ugly me beneath. I'm back to who and what I was before I learnt the art of disguise.

On another note, I'm sorry to hear about the death of your father. I realise it happened quite a few years ago, but of course, we drifted apart so I feel the need to convey my apologies for not attending his funeral. He was a decent, quiet man, always working hard. Always somewhere on the periphery of your existence. I recall you once mentioning that neither you nor your mother held the same love for the church that he did. Maybe if he had been around more, your mother would have treated you a little better. With him out of the house she was free to show her ire towards you in many varying forms, whether it was belittling you in front of friends and doing what she could to chip away at your self-esteem, or taking the belt to you because of some imagined slight. It's just as well we had each other back then, isn't it? This is going to sound terribly selfish, but whenever I saw your red eyes, sore and swollen after a bout of crying because of what she had done to you, it made me feel slightly better about myself. You see, seeing you distressed served as a timely reminder that my life was actually rather good. I had nothing to feel downhearted about. I have gone over it time and time again and think perhaps Schadenfreude played a part in my reactions. It's not something of which I am particularly proud but already I feel better for telling you. I was always a little jealous of you and although my heart broke when I saw your physical scars, there was a small part of me that delighted in your misfortune. Why? Your presence and mental strength was your undoing. It sparked something inside of me. No matter how painful those beatings were, no matter how rude and insulting your mother was towards you, you always stood tall, rising above it, refusing to let her break you. I was overcome with a range of emotions as I observed your stamina and fortitude, and that's because I was weak and insignificant. What did you have inside of you that I didn't? I asked myself that question over and over. Perhaps your natural beauty went deeper than anybody realised and you were as gilt edged on the inside as you were on the outside whereas I was ugly through and through. I think that is what started it. My envy. The green-eyed monster. I never showed it or spoke to you about it but it was always there, lurking. I knew one day that it would be the undoing of me. Of us. Did you ever suspect? I like to think I hid it well, but dark, festering emotions always have a way of sneaking out and making themselves known, oozing out of the tiniest of fissures and tainting everything in close proximity. I was a different person back then and I want to apologise for my behaviour. I'm now fairly comfortable in my own skin. A contented individual who rarely looks in the mirror. There's no need. I am who I am just as you are who you are.

Not gilt edged at all.

A memory has suddenly catapulted into my brain. A memory of you doing something you would sooner forget. Not so perfect after all, eh, Lucy? I don't mean to dampen our happy mood but I do wonder if you recall that day? The day when you showed me how even the most perfect of people can do imperfect things. Maybe deep down, you were as odd and as strange as me. A strange little girl with the darkest of intentions.

I look forward to reading your next letter.

Love, Blake

8

BLAKE

'You seem on edge. Everything okay?' Maya observes me closely. Maya, my friend and neighbour with her kind words and watchful eye.

She and I get on well. Better than my relationship with Sandra, who has a loose tongue and a dubious past. I have a feeling that her drink-driving conviction isn't her only crime.

'Ah, I'm fine, Maya. Been better but also been worse.'

She smiles and touches my arm and for a brief moment I think I'm going to cry. Tears burn at my eyes. I blink and turn away, hoping she hasn't noticed. I spent enough of my formative years being weak and feckless. Now is the time to start fighting back, to stop being the victim and getting dragged along in the slipstream of other people's lives. I am my own person and time is marching on. Soon it will run out and I'm going to be left asking what I've done with my life. With no partner, no family and no career, I am an empty husk. Even now after all these years, I hanker after having a family of my own. A child I can pour all my love into. And I would love them unconditionally. They would spend every second of every day surrounded by love and compassion and warmth. Not like many children who enter this world unwanted and unloved. Cast aside like pieces of dirt. I hoped that writing the letters to Lucy would fill the void in my life, but it doesn't feel that way at all. This morning I woke with an ache in the pit of my stomach at the thought of getting up and having nobody. Arthur, Maya and Sandra are the only people in my life. Maya is the closest thing I have to a friend; Arthur and Sandra are merely acquaintances, Sandra an irritating neighbour with no respect for personal space or boundaries. I am suddenly overcome with a rage so intense and fierce that it scares me. Like a furnace exploding inside my head.

'Got to go, Maya, not feeling too good.' Before she can protest, I slip back inside, Lucy's reply to my last letter tucked deep inside my pocket.

I lied to Arthur about the nightmares. I still have them and they're as vivid now as they have always been. Last night I woke drenched in sweat, my heart pounding, head thrumming. It took an hour before I was able to get back to sleep and even that was fitful. Every time I closed my eyes, images flooded my mind, forcing me awake. Today feels like a wasted day, as if I'm wading through treacle; every movement an effort, every thought tinged with despondency and self-reproach. Also pain at what the future holds. I have made the decision to write to Lucy, but what if it all goes horribly wrong? My future seems uncertain, everything unbalanced and out of kilter.

I perch on the edge my bed, the floor soft and spongy beneath me, everything around me feeling flimsy and brittle. This needs to stop, I know that. I have fewer years ahead of me than there are behind. Time is of the essence if I am to make amends with Lucy and forge ahead with the rest of my life. And I want to do that, I really do. There is a reason I struck up this correspondence and I need to see it through to the bitter end.

28 February

Dear Blake,

I'm not sure where to begin. So much offloading in your last letter that I've had to take some time to gather my thoughts before penning this reply. There is a lot that I want to go over in response to your comments and I think the best way to do that is in order.

Firstly, let me address the matter of your writing. I am over the fact you wrote about me and I am glad you still find the time to write, but relieved that your stories now remain private. Having every part of my life made public never sat well with me. I think you know that and I think you probably knew it before you did it, but went ahead regardless. What does that say about you and our friendship, Blake? What does it say about how you feel about me as a person and a purportedly close friend?

Secondly, thank you for congratulating me on my grandchild. As I said, I debated whether to mention it given your circumstances, and am aware of the fact you will never have grandchildren of your own, so hope you didn't think me insensitive but excitement got the better of me and I couldn't not tell you about my expanding brood. My daughter and her partner are already talking about another addition to their little family, so who knows? Maybe my small family will continue to expand.

Next, Blake, you were far from ugly or awkward. Always by my side no matter what, you were the most beautiful person I knew. In spite of our differences and the events of later years, I never thought any less of you. Beauty comes from within, and you possess such a wonderfully vibrant spirit that it would be impossible to look at you and not think of you as anything but handsome; a striking individual with an unshakeable loyalty to those closest to you. Throughout my life, you have always been there, Blake. Always at my side no matter what. Even when I craved solitude, there you were, waiting in the wings. Always present. Always hanging around.

As for the beatings meted out by my mother, I think the less said about them the better. I still have scars both internally and externally, and would rather forget about the whole thing. It's easier to leave it all behind. Sometimes the weight of emotional baggage becomes too much to bear. Dragging it along is exhausting and damaging. I have neither the strength nor the patience to continually think about what took place so I leave it well alone. With that decision comes peace and a sense of stillness.

Thank you for taking the time to speak about my father's death. He was a quiet presence in my life. Too quiet, doing little to stop my mother's actions, but I loved him regardless. As I grew older I realised that I couldn't change him or lessen his devotion to the church, so gave up trying, ploughing my energy instead into my schoolwork. I just wish he had given me as much attention as he gave to his faith. His continual prayers didn't improve my life or strengthen the relationship between me and my mother. It certainly didn't mend her damaged brain. And it definitely didn't heal my broken body. But as you said, I appeared confident and have a face that turned heads whenever I walked into a room so at least that's something, isn't it?

The final thing you mentioned is something of which I have no memory. After reading it, I'm beginning to wonder if you ever really knew me at all. I've gone from being practically perfect to possessing a dark soul; a person who carried out something dreadful. So dreadful you refuse to tell me what it was. What did I do that day, Blake? Did I hurt somebody?

Surely someone as purportedly perfect as me wouldn't do anything bad? I've wracked my brain and come up with nothing so you're going to have to remind me of that day in your next letter. We got into a few minor scrapes over the years as do all youngsters but I can think of nothing so serious that it is etched into my brain, although it appears it is deeply etched into yours. Does that make me forgetful or does it make me completely selfish? I like to think I'm neither but will wait for your reply to discover what I did that was so heinous it has left a lasting impression on you after all this time.

Now that we have got to know each other all over again and have clearly dispensed with the social niceties, I'd like to speak of the time we spent at Whitby. Do you remember that holiday? For once, my mother allowed me to accompany you and your parents on a short break to the seaside. I can't recall what year it was but think that maybe we were twelve or thirteen years old. A difficult age for two young girls, our lives fraught with changes both physically and mentally, our minds tied up with apprehension at what the future may hold. I was excited and hoped for a lovely break with my best friend but things didn't turn out as planned. I'm sure you know what I'm going to say next, don't you? Neither of us need a reminder about it and as you have clearly indicated, your memory is as sharp as ever, remembering things that have fallen out of my brain. The incident on Pier Road. As I write it down, that day is coming back to me with startling clarity, the terror of it searing my skin like a white-hot branding iron. Was it really an accident or was it deliberate? At the time I was convinced it was a mishap, both of us messing about near the edge of the water as teenage girls are wont to do, but now with hindsight I think that perhaps there was malice behind it. Is my assumption correct, Blake? Because if we are going to be open and honest about things, I would like to know, all these decades later, whether that knock against me was, as claimed, an accident or was it that you were you trying to end me? The day before, I had made the mistake of reading your diary. I was wrong to do it. I know that now. I knew it then, but I was young and immature. I realise that is no excuse and I'm not trying to justify what I did, but we all make mistakes and I made the grave error of reading your innermost thoughts, and worse than that, mocking them. The thing is, seeing those words written down in black and white was a shock to me. I needed time to digest what I'd seen, but you caught me in the act and ripped the journal from my hands, shouting that I was invading your privacy and had no right to see what you had written. You were right of course. But I was left reeling and before I could stop myself, the words came spewing out, a torrent of abuse and outrage, combined with hilarity that you could think such thoughts, let alone put them to paper. My father was a much older man – thirty years your senior. He was a tall, lumbering, characterless albeit harmless individual, and you had portrayed him in your diary as some sort of Hollywood superstar, fawning over him and spouting desires that no young female should ever entertain, especially if that man is the father of your best friend. I told you to rip out the pages and burn them, that you were an idiot and that I hated you. Even now I can still feel the flickering flames of horror that lit up my face as our argument escalated. It was your mother who calmed it down, using her soothing tones to sort out our troubles. I apologised to you later and you assured me that it had been written in a moment of madness and that you had already torn up the diary. But then the following day occurred and I felt sure the two incidents were connected. I still recall the horror of finding myself hurtling down into the water after you accidentally lost your footing and bumped into me. We had been looking down at the waves, a frisson of excitement taking hold at the fact there was no barrier between us and the water below. What tame lives we led back then to be so excited by such a small thing. Turned out it was no small thing at all. It was almost the undoing of me. Your father jumped into the freezing water after I fell, and dragged me to shore. I was a poor swimmer, thrashing about in a wild panic until he held me tight and pulled me to safety, laying me out on the cold, wet concrete where I shivered and cried for what felt like an eternity.

A crowd had gathered as I was hauled up the steps and onto dry land, row upon row of curious faces staring down at me. It took a while for me to get my breath back and for the fear to dissipate but when it did, I could see you kneeling beside me, your features contorted with horror. Were you really that frightened that day or was it all an act? Did you feign shock and dismay to cover your tracks? I hope I'm jumping to the wrong conclusion here but this thing has nagged at me for a few years now and I would rather speak about it than allow it to grow and fester and ultimately destroy our recently renewed friendship.

Before anybody could intervene and start asking questions, I was pulled to my feet, your insistence we go back to the cottage so fervent that your mother had to ask you to keep your voice down. I think you feared the police or somebody in authority questioning your movements before I fell. Back then, there wasn't any CCTV around to destroy your account of what took place, but you were obviously afraid of your story being picked apart with forensic precision and everyone finding you at fault. If I'm going to be perfectly honest, your inadvertent stumble that day definitely felt like a push. A hard shove when nobody was looking. Maybe I deserved it for being such a nosey, deprecating friend. I didn't deserve to die though, did I? And I could have lost my life had it not been for the quick thinking and strong arms of your father. The father you took for granted while mine seemed to care so little about me. You were lucky in so many ways and yet directed your ire at me.

We all trudged back to the cottage, heavy-hearted and soaking wet. Your mother ran me a hot bath and as I lay back in the soapy water and tried to gather my thoughts, I could hear you crying, stating how close you had come to losing your best friend. I realised it then, something that had niggled at me for some months if not years, sticking with me throughout adulthood – that despite our closeness and deep friendship, I would always have to watch my step whenever you were around. You had boundaries, Blake, and I crossed them at my peril.

I look forward to hearing from you and hope my account of that day hasn't unearthed any nasty raw memories for you. I just wanted to let you know that far from being the weak and awkward person you think you were, it simply isn't true. You were and undoubtedly still are a strong-minded individual with a will of iron. I pried into your innermost thoughts and mocked you. You did what many would have done in that situation. I just want you to know that I know and have always known that what took place that day wasn't an accident.

It was revenge.

Love, Lucy

9

BEFORE

'Have you fed and burped her, Isla?' Martha lifted the screaming child out of the bassinet and cradled the infant against her chest, the baby's hot body bringing a layer of perspiration to Martha's neck. Heat radiated from the newborn's tiny skull, her skin pink with desperation. 'Babies cry for a reason. They don't cry just because they are babies. That's not how it works, Isla.'

A shrug of the shoulders followed by a sigh. 'She was fed a few hours ago. I mean, how much milk does one baby actually need?'

A rock dropped to the pit of Martha's stomach. She swallowed down her misgivings and tried to soothe the poor child. 'They need as much as they need. If a baby cries then you try changing them and if that doesn't calm them, then you try feeding them and if that doesn't work, you try burping them or cuddling them. You do whatever it takes to comfort them and to stop the crying.' Keeping the exasperation out of her voice sapped Martha of every bit of strength she had. Energy seemed to be in short supply of late. She had very little in reserve for Isla's incompetence and lackadaisical parenting methods. And teaching somebody how to love their own child was a new thing to Martha. Even Martha's own inept mother had loved her, but Isla showed indifference towards her newborn and it was frightening to watch. If this was how Isla acted in the presence of another person, how bad was her behaviour when she was alone with her baby?

Dirty dishes and pots were stacked high in the sink when Martha marched in with the baby resting against her shoulder. It was impossible to find anything, the kitchen strewn with debris. She rummaged for formula, eventually finding a clean bottle and a tub of white powdery feed at the back of a kitchen cabinet. Nestling the baby in the crook of her arm, she made up the bottle, shaking it vigorously before placing the teat into the baby's tiny, puckered mouth. Tears bit at Martha's eyes, fear stinging her flesh as the child drained the bottle in less than a minute. How long had she been lying there screaming for food? And how often did this happen? The little one was barely a month old and a tiny scrap of a thing. Had anybody called to check on her progress or was she just being left to rot? Surely given Isla's medical history, somebody should be checking up on her, making sure all was well with mother and baby? Where were the community nurses and the health visitors? Where was the support network that was meant to be there for new mothers and babies?

'What about Finn? Where is he?' Martha stood and headed back into the kitchen where she prepared another bottle and then another before placing them in the fridge for later.

'At work. And then afterwards he's going to church. They've got an important meeting apparently.'

It was difficult to mask her inner rage, Martha biting at her lip with such savagery she could have sworn she tasted blood. She would speak to Finn when he got home. This was unfair. In fact, given Isla's state of mind and recent incarceration, it wasn't just unfair; it was downright dangerous.

Ten minutes was all it took to burp and change the little one after she had been fed. Her tiny body was swamped by the large bassinet as Martha placed her down and stood for a short while watching her sleep, her pale, thin lashes fluttering in a peaceful slumber as the goodness of the food flooded her tiny body. Such innocence in the face of utter helplessness and neglect. Martha knew then that she would have to do something. Despite having her own family and a full-time job, she knew that she was going to have to step in and guide Isla, make sure this baby didn't come to any harm. She and Isla were friends after all. It was what friends did for one another. Caring for babies was hard work. Lack of sleep and the constant crying could drive the most well-balanced of people to the edge of insanity. And Isla was anything but well balanced. She had come unstuck and was teetering on the brink before giving birth despite what the medical team believed. Sleep deprivation was adding to her despair. She needed as much assistance as she could get. She needed Martha now more than ever. Whether she wanted her or not.

Being constantly on her mettle, calling round as often as she could and attempting to get Isla conditioned to her new environment and routine took its toll. After only a month, Martha had lost so much weight, her clothes no longer fitted. Two months later saw her close to collapse. Rocking and feeding a baby as well as holding down a job as a supervisor in a large factory and caring for her own young children was more than she could manage. With jutting hip bones and a constant sense of unease that sat in the pit of her abdomen, Martha finally relented and saw a doctor, whose face told her everything she needed to know as he pressed at the lump in her distended stomach.

* * *

Three months after her gruelling routine of caring for Isla's infant saw Martha hospitalised, doctors passing on the grave news to Martha and her husband Charlie that her demise would be sooner rather than later. She hung on for eight days, slipping in and out of consciousness, asking after her boys, speaking of long since dead relatives and making Charlie promise to keep an eye on Isla's baby, telling him of her concerns, until at last, on the stroke of midnight one cold and breezy autumnal evening, Martha slipped away, leaving a void so large and deep that the whole family felt sure it would suck them in and they would never return from its dark, pitiless depths.

When Martha's family did eventually blink their way back into the light, Charlie decided he could no longer stay in the house without her. Martha had been the glue that held them together, the keeper of their fortress. Continuing to live in their home without her there was unthinkable and so within six months, he sold up and moved to a different part of town. A fresh start for him and the boys. A future without Martha.

The new family that moved in were a decent lot from what he could gather. They had a youngster almost the same age as Isla and Finn's little one. A little girl. Perhaps they would play together as they grew older, become firm friends. It was what Martha would have wanted had cancer not cruelly ripped her from their lives. Maybe once she found her way out of the fog, Isla would be the loving mother the baby needed. The loving mother that Martha had been to their boys. All kids deserved to feel wanted and needed and safe, didn't they? Maybe Isla had it in her to be that person, the one who showered her own child with care and attention. He liked to think that Martha's attentiveness and guidance had had some sort of impact on her friend.

God knows she had put enough effort in, neglecting her own needs, ignoring her health and the warning signs that something was not right with her own body in order to keep Isla on track with that damn baby. It was probably a good thing they had moved house. Charlie wasn't sure he could hold his tongue in that woman's presence, her lethargic yet strangely aggressive ways riling him to the point of wanting to scream in her face that she was lucky to be alive while his wife was buried six feet in the ground after slavishly tending to Isla's requirements without asking for anything in return.

The new owners moved in on a wet Friday afternoon, stepping foot into their new home with dreams of what lay ahead. They had heard of the family with the baby who was close in age to their own little girl. Possible future playmates. Possible firm friends. The opportunities for the two baby girls were endless.

* * *

Isla watched from her window, ignoring her daughter's yowling as the new neighbours lifted furniture out of the removal van with an absurd display of euphoria and vigour. They were giddy with happiness, smiling and laughing, their chatter echoing as it was carried by the wind and drifted towards her. Who were these people that displayed pointless elation while shifting sofas and tables in a torrent of rain? If there was one thing that irritated Isla it was unnecessary jubilation. It was jarring to see, sending a wave of anger through her. Isla continued to watch as the woman stood by, a baby perched on her hip while men carried and shifted dressers and chairs and boxes. Annoyance augmented in her gut as her own child wriggled and cried. Why was her life so difficult while others seemed to do things with such happiness and ease? None of it was fair, and with no Martha to help out, each day felt more difficult and longer than the last, Isla's list of tasks seemingly endless, her child more fractious with each passing day. She tried, God knows she tried, but it was as if her own offspring hated her, refusing hugs and turning away at each spoonful of food. The sleepless nights were another thing that sapped her of energy, making the simplest of daytime tasks seem mountainous. She wanted to be a decent person and wife and mother but every day brought a new trauma. Every day felt more difficult than the last. Information gleaned from magazines she had pored over in the hope of being a better parent didn't help. Remedies such as rocking and cuddling were impossible with a baby who appeared to hate her. Everywhere she looked, there were mothers and babies who were practically suctioned together, their smiles so wide it looked as if their faces were about to break in half. Isla couldn't stand it – the superficialness and sly glances at other broken mothers who couldn't or didn't have the energy to dance and coo and smile with their infants. It was all an act anyway. Deep inside, she suspected that most people were damaged. The only difference between her and other people was that she refused to hide it. Isla's flaws were always apparent to others. Not like this new neighbour who appeared to have it all – perfect husband, perfect figure and face, and most frustrating of all, a perfect baby.

'Come on,' she growled to her screaming infant, whose face had turned crimson while Isla watched the comings and goings of her new neighbours, 'let's get you fed, see if we can stop your incessant moaning and wriggling.'

The child's howls filled the kitchen as she strapped the young girl into the high chair while she prepared their lunch.

10

BLAKE

28 March

Dear Lucy,

I suppose you've noticed that it's taken me some time to write my reply to your last letter, and I'm pretty sure you understand why. I wanted to get it just right, you see. But as I've said, you probably already know that. And I'm also certain you already know what I am about to say. Words are weapons and once said cannot be unsaid, so I have written and rewritten this letter before settling on this version in the hope it gets my point across without sounding callous or offensive. Bitterness is never far from the surface of my skin so it has been difficult keeping it under wraps but I think, or at least I hope, I've managed to do it.

I'll speak of the memory I have of you doing something you would rather not shout about, later. First, I want to go back to that day at Whitby. It was stupid and childish of me to fawn over your father, but let's be honest here, what young girl hasn't developed a crush on an older man? Your dad was a quiet, gentle soul and with the benefit of hindsight what I possibly felt towards him was pity and admiration rather than love or lust. He had his church but he didn't have his wife. She was elsewhere mentally and his constant prayers to help save her soul went unanswered. So my heart went out to him, and I admit I became a little obsessed, spending all day, every day, thinking about him. My first mistake was writing it all down. The second was leaving it somewhere it could be found. What I did wasn't a crime. It was no more than a childish act of affection. But what you did was immature and hurtful. There, I've said it. You hurt me, but I got over it. I forgave you and got on with my life.

So onto the main question. Did I deliberately push you into the water? I'm not going to dignify that query with a response as the answer is patently obvious and I think you already know that. We seem to have stirred up a hornets' nest of memories here so I am left wondering if what you did all those years ago is worth mentioning, but will do it anyway, if only to satisfy your curiosity. I mentioned it, so it would be rude to lead you on with no sense of closure.

We were thirteen years old and had taken our usual route home from school, walking along the lane and reaching the bridge before anybody else could catch up with us. We always did prefer our own company, didn't we? Just the two of us against the rest of the world. Except that day, something dark crept into your soul, a rogue demon that slid beneath your skin and made you do something awful. Have you remembered yet, Lucy? Has the mention of the bridge brought the memory crashing back, a splintered recollection skidding sideways into your brain and knocking you off balance? I hope so. I will continue anyway because it's about time it was out in the open. You dipped your toe into the murky waters of delinquency that day and it shocked me to my core.

I never liked that bridge. A tall spindly thing that stretched across a busy road, it didn't feel safe. The handrails were low and the vehicles beneath us fast moving. I always ran across it, desperate to reach the other side, the creeping tingling sensation in my fingers and toes at the roar of fast-moving traffic making me nervy and uncomfortable. You always laughed, slowly striding across in your usual confident style while I waited at the other end for you. But that day you insisted we walk it together, your arm hooked through mine to hold me back. To make sure I was around to witness what came next. Did you do that so we would both be blamed if caught? Or did you hang on to me to allow me to see exactly what you were capable of? Confident, beautiful Lucy tarnishing her immaculate reputation with one act of madness.

It began with small pieces of plasticine you had taken from an art lesson in school. I can still see your face, your eyes glittering with excitement as you rolled them up into small bullet shapes, letting them drop onto the cars below.

'The odds of them hitting a vehicle are so low, we'll be lucky to see one of these little pellets stick,' was what you had said.

You made it sound like an experiment. A childish game. A dare. And stupidly, I believed you.

But that wasn't what it turned out to be. It was a silly moment of foolishness that rapidly morphed into a ghoulish nightmare.

I watched, stupefied, as you picked up a rock and wrapped the brightly coloured material around its sharp edges. An innocent-looking, plasticine-coloured weapon. I continued watching, gaze transfixed, my heart hammering as you tossed it over the side of the bridge. And then I observed in horror as it hit the windscreen of a passing car. The shat-

tering of glass and subsequent swerve of the vehicle trapped a pocket of air in my lungs that made it almost impossible to breathe. And then came the smash as the swerving vehicle hit another car, the collision of metal pounding in my ears and banging against my skull.

Before I could say or do anything, you grabbed my arm and yanked me away, our feet twisting beneath us as we exited the bridge, taking the steps two at a time and running into the woods. We continued to sprint through the foliage, dodging tree trunks and puddles, jumping over the beck and landing on a carpet of snapping twigs until we emerged out of the other side into dappled sunlight, our faces burning from our wild escape, our chests heaving and convulsing as we gasped for breath.

The rest of the walk home was conducted in silence. I didn't have the words to say what I wanted to say and I suppose you figured that silence was better than saying something incriminating. We took a vow that day – to keep schtum and carry on as if nothing untoward had taken place. That was our implicit promise. Never voiced out loud but always there.

That evening and for the rest of the week, I kept a close eye on the local news, absorbing every detail, scouring newspapers for stories of a driver being seriously injured by a rock falling from the bridge, but there was nothing. We had managed to get away with it. Or rather, you had. I wasn't a willing accomplice. I was hoodwinked into being present while you carried out the dangerous deed.

Now do you remember, Lucy? Is it all coming back to you?

I think you must recall that day. Something like that wouldn't slip anybody's mind. Not unless they were borderline psychopathic. Not unless what they did meant so little to them that they managed to push it out of their mind.

I think I've said enough about it now, don't you? Time to move on to other things. We seem to have descended into squabbling in such a short period of time and that isn't, and never has been, my intention. I got in touch with you because I want us to forgive and forget, to heal and remain firm friends. I hope you are of the same mindset. We are so similar, you and I, so I feel sure we can move on and speak of other things. Maybe those times we think of as happy and carefree weren't so happy and carefree after all.

Yesterday I took a stroll around my garden. The weather has been kind of late so I thought I would make the most of the weak sunshine. The views here are limited but being able to breathe clean fresh air is enough for me. It's a feeling of calm that washes over me as I trail my fingers over the silken petals and smell their soft perfume. Not lilies. They remind me of death. It's a sad association but one I cannot shake. Maybe it's their powerful, pungent aroma that puts me in mind of rotting corpses. Bodies with skin stretched like wax across bone-white features. Roses are my favourite. Any colour. I'm not particular, although I am rather partial to blood-red varieties.

I've probably either sent you to sleep or scared you with this letter. I hope it's neither but I do have an uncanny knack of upsetting people when what I really mean to do is bring things out into the open. Believe me when I say I would never intentionally hurt you. I hope you believe me. Do you believe me, Lucy? I really hope so otherwise what we are doing here is pointless.

Please don't be alarmed by this letter. We've got a connection going now and to cut it at this juncture would be heart-

breaking. We've come a fair old distance, you and I, but still have some miles left to walk. Let's do it together. We can talk and reminisce and try to mend the things that we broke along the way. Together we can hopefully scoop up the shattered pieces of our lives and make them whole again.

I beg you to write back and will wait excitedly to receive your next letter.

Your best friend

Blake

'I didn't get to speak to you yesterday. Is everything okay?' Arthur sits in his usual spot, his face puckered with unease.

I'm never sure if his concern is real or if his question about my welfare is something he feels compelled to say, lines he has spent years rehearsing. Maybe he practises in front of the mirror to get it just right.

'I'm okay,' I lie.

I guess we're both proficient at being what we're not, each of us hiding behind our perfectly painted masks. These letters are taking it out of me. I feel tired and irritable. Sitting across from Arthur is increasing my feelings of disquiet. The more I try to push those emotions away, the harder and faster they come back, like a drowning woman flailing and surfacing for air.

'Anything in particular you want to chat about?'

He's good, I'll give him that. He opens doors and leaves them ajar for all my issues to creep through. Not today though. Today exhaustion is winning and I'm too tired to speak coherently. Too tired for everything. Even my courtyard garden will have to wait.

'No, not really. I think I might just head back today if that's okay?'

'Feel free to do whatever you wish. You are your own person.'

I leave Arthur in his usual position in his chair by the window and head back, praying I don't fall apart along the way.

11

BEFORE

The days became longer, darker. Things had been bleak before Martha's passing, but without her friend and her daily assistance close by, everything was hopeless. She tried. God knows Isla tried, but nothing seemed to work. Finn was never home and the cries from the child went on and on and on. Some children were born difficult. Isla had read about it. A difficult birth led to a difficult child. And this little person was hard work from the get-go. Everything about her was trying. No matter how often Isla fed and held and hugged and rocked her, she was inconsolable, her screams loud and sharp enough to rouse the dead.

It was a dreary autumnal morning when the new neighbours intervened, the pair of them clearly disturbed by the sound of the child's howling.

'We're taking our little one out in the pram to get some fresh air. We can take yours as well if you like? Give you both a break.'

Isla was only too keen to hand over her hot, crying bundle, laying her in the buggy within seconds and placing an array of blankets over her tiny body to muffle the cries.

'You do what you need to do to catch up on housework or to

simply rest. We'll take her for a little stroll to the bottom of the avenue. Might even make it to the park if they both fall asleep.'

Isla closed the door before they had left the driveway, relief at the sudden silence, a hot soothing rush that clung to her skin and embraced her. She was free. For the next few minutes, she could be who she wanted to be. The person she had once been before her body became swollen and distorted, her brain foggy from lack of sleep.

Thoughts filtered into her mind as she staggered into the living room; unpalatable notions she tried to dispel. Pinpricks of realisation that she had just handed over her baby to two virtual strangers. People whose faces she had seen through windows, across garden fences. A spear of anxiety, like a flickering flame, shot through her. And yet it was tempered with something else: euphoria. And exhaustion. A lead weight pressed down on her, fatigue the likes of which she had never known before. It bit at her aching flesh and chiselled its way deep into her bones. Why had nobody informed her of how tiring having a child would be? The darkness was bad before the baby came along but at least there were occasional bursts of sunshine. Not any more. Shadows obliterated everything; no light ahead. Nothing at all.

* * *

It was the knocking that woke her an hour later; a series of insistent thumps that rang around the hallway and echoed in her dreams, hauling her upright and back to reality. Isla staggered up off the sofa and opened the door to two smiling people who were standing proudly on her doorstep, a happy sparkly-eyed little one held tightly in their arms. A cooing sound gurgled its way out of her daughter's tiny love-heart-shaped mouth. Was this really her child? The same one who wriggled against her and rejected the bottle and woke three or four times a night screaming in the pitch black, refusing to be consoled no matter what Isla did? The question of how they had pacified her baby – the child she had created and carried and pushed out of her body in a glutinous bloody mess – stuck in Isla's throat. The words she wanted to say wouldn't come. She couldn't bring herself to ask these strangers how they had managed to calm her fractious daughter when her own methods had failed so miserably; not just once but over and over and over; day after day, week after week. Each attempt at calming her troubled daughter, trying to connect with her, stretched out in her mind, reminding her of how useless she was. All this baby had ever done was upend her life and rob her of sleep, and now these fucking strangers had done in one hour what she couldn't manage in almost a year.

Guilt needled her. She would try to do better. To be better. She had made another human being, brought a small helpless child into the world, and seeing her daughter propped up in the arms of two unfamiliar people was like a slap to the face. Already, Martha's voice was ringing in her head.

'Just love her, Isla. Feed and hug her. Do what comes naturally.'

Except it hadn't come naturally, had it? Maybe some people weren't cut out to be parents. What if she was one of those people? She had never wanted children. Unlike Finn and Martha, she didn't have it in her to embrace parenthood. This child was an accident. A terrible mistake. The unwanted result of one night of passion. And even that wasn't so great. Sex with Finn was a perfunctory undertaking, something they did in the dark before drifting off to sleep. Isla had heard about post-coital slumbers and orgasms and all manner of other sex-related issues that seemed to be lacking in her own life. Finn was a reliable hard-working man, but he wasn't an enthusiastic lover who made the earth move for her. She'd had one boyfriend prior to meeting Finn which had resulted in a brief fumble in the dark that left her feeling less than impressed. And now she had a baby, and lovemaking and heady nights of lust and desire felt so out of reach she was certain she would never have sex with Finn again. One baby was enough for her. One baby was too much.

'She really is a delight, isn't she? If ever you need any help, please don't be afraid to ask.' Smiles stretched wide. Gleaming teeth. Perfect complexions. Who were these mannequin-like people standing on her doorstep? These glossy-faced individuals who stepped into each day as if anything was possible. It wasn't. Excitement and happiness and enjoyment of life was reserved for the few, and definitely not for the likes of Isla. The idea of respite from her baby daughter was tempting, giving her time to catch up on sleep and housework, but from now on, she would do what she could to keep these people at arm's length. She was better off alone, operating at her own pace away from the scrutiny of neighbours she barely knew. Her trust in people had been dented at an early age and she was too jaded, just too damn sceptical, to soften and allow anybody else into her life. She'd had Martha and now Martha was gone and that was that. Her life was closed off from others. And that was exactly how she liked it.

Her eyes flickered as she stared at their faces, watching as they chattered like excited schoolchildren. Even poor Martha had had her faults and failings, her bad days and times of joylessness and sadness. Isla had seen her exasperated and tired on more than one occasion. But not these two. These perfect robotic people whose connection to her daughter was stronger than her own. She hated them. And she hated herself for hating them but was unable to break out of the vicious cycle of malicious thoughts.

'Best be off. Got to get this little one ready for her playgroup.' Their eyes travelled down to their own baby, lying peacefully in the pram, staring up at them with large blue eyes from beneath a pristine coverlet. 'I'm Anna by the way, and this is my husband, Trevor.'

'Isla,' was all she could manage, and even saying that made her feel sickly and marginally dizzy.

'Well, lovely to finally make introductions, Isla. Anyway, hopefully we'll see a lot more of each other.'

Maybe it was her own bad genes that made the child the way she was. Hers or Finn's. Maybe somewhere way back in their family they had ancestors who were wild and untamed and brutal and miserable. Just like her. But not like her new neighbours with their glossy offspring and helpful ways and soothing voices.

Maybe Isla could learn from them. Be more like them instead of being who she was. Because she was sure that deep down who she currently was wasn't the real Isla. And who she currently was wasn't the way she wanted to be. Some days it was as if a monster had crawled beneath her skin and was injecting her veins with poison. She hated it. Loathed it. Concealed deep inside her was a happy, caring Isla who was aching to be free. She just didn't know how to entice her out of the shadows and back into the light.

'Thank you.' She reached across and pulled her baby daughter into her arms, the warmth and heft of the baby's small body triggering tears that bit at the back of Isla's eyelids.

Blinking, she closed the door and carried the infant into the living room, watching as the perfect people pushed their perfect pram down the path and closed the gate with a careful quiet click. A sudden wriggle, collective heat rising from their bodies, and before her new neighbours had opened their own front door, screams filled her living room, her child itching and stretching. Desperate to be free. Desperate to be away from Isla. It was all too much. The tears came thick and fast. Her own child was set against her. She could feel it, a powerful tugging sensation that ripped at her soul. This relationship was an ongoing battle between mother and daughter. And Isla knew at that moment that despite being tiny and relatively new into the world, despite not having control of her newly formed emotions, her baby daughter was winning.

12

BLAKE

14 April

Dear Blake,

How odd. I have no memory of the incident on the bridge. Are you sure you're not getting me confused with somebody else? It certainly doesn't sound like something I would have done. Being in trouble with anyone in a position of authority always frightened me. Still does, although these days I lead a fairly sedate life so chances of me ever being reprimanded for some paltry misdemeanour are slim to non-existent.

I read and re-read your last letter. I will admit that at one point I lowered my head and wept. Shall we start afresh? Only a few months into our letter-writing campaign and we appear to have descended into a form of madness, dredging up the muddy, soiled parts of our past that obliterated the good things we did. And it's the good things that count. I firmly believe that and hope you do too.

We should forget the diary and the bridge incident and begin again, talking only about the positive, happy times we had. Are you up for that? I guess it's been a kind of cleansing, speaking of the bad things, and now that we have done it, I think it's time to leave it all behind.

Each morning when I wake, I'm full of plans and ideas on what to do, but as the day progresses, I seem to run out of energy and end up doing very little. Perhaps it's my age, or maybe it's my condition. Have I told you about my condition? I don't believe I have mentioned it yet. It's my joints; they are stiff and painful to move. A lot of people take up yoga to loosen their locked, aching limbs but it looks so strenuous I'm not sure I could manage it, so I just muddle on through, taking each day as it comes. My eyesight is also failing but I don't like to moan or complain. I'm grateful for the small things. I find it the easiest way to live. Setting out unattainable goals only ever ends in disappointment.

Last night I dreamt about the school disco. Do you remember that night, Blake? It was the year we both wore those short skirts and sparkly boob tubes. Gosh, those awful cheap-looking pieces of flimsy material that left little or nothing to the imagination! I recall dancing the night away as if nothing and nobody mattered. We had such fun that evening, our faces plastered with make-up that we had purloined from your mum's dressing table; me in glittery blue eye shadow and you with that garish red lipstick. We thought we owned the world. And for a while we did. That was the night we discovered boys and their unpredictable febrile ways. We were mystified by their idiosyncratic mannerisms. Their sullen looks and monosyllabic utterances. I now know it to be shyness or fear but back then, I saw it as surliness. I think we scared them as much as they scared us.

I realise you thought yourself cautious and awkward but that night you shone brightly, your carefully applied make-up and glossy curled hair attracting comments from everyone in the room. That was before everything turned sour. I know I said we should speak only of good times, but looking back, it's as if everything we did was blighted with some kind of trauma, doom and gloom constantly nudging its way into our orbit. So I'm going to continue unabated because some things should not be forgotten and some things should always be voiced out loud, if only to clear the air. That's all we are doing here, Blake – clearing the air and starting afresh. You have had your say and now I'm going to have mine.

You had had a crush on Gregory Timmons for months and months but he acted as if you didn't exist. Until that night, that is. You were dancing and I was right beside you. There was a glitter ball above us, hastily placed there by one of the teachers in an attempt to try and brighten up a usually drab-looking assembly hall. It lit up your features as you twirled about while dancing to a Janet Jackson song. There was just the two of us, moving and swaying, side by side. And then all of a sudden, there he was, standing next to us – Gregory Timmons. The boy you had secretly fantasised over for months and months. I saw your nervousness, the hunching of your spine, the sudden clenching of your jaw. A rapid transition from a free-flowing soft wave to a block of ice. He saw it too. I didn't mean for what came next to happen. You have to believe me when I say that. It was a moment of madness. Of teenage selfishness. Of utter blindness to your hurt and desires. Because as I have already stated, I wasn't perfect. None of us are. We are all flawed in one way or another. Damaged creatures with a propensity to inflict pain of the highest magnitude on one another, to maim and scar in order to save ourselves. In order to elevate our own crumbling self-esteem.

Having noticed your sudden stiffness and the way you

turned away from him, Gregory smiled at me and took my hand, leading me away from the makeshift dance floor to the farthest corner of the room where he held me in his arms and kissed me. We were concealed in the shadows. But not concealed from you. You saw it all, every little detail.

I tried to extricate myself from his grasp, I really did, but he was bigger and stronger than I was. And at the heart of it, I was weak and also a little bit in love with him. Who wasn't? You weren't the only one who secretly adored and lusted after Gregory Timmons. My heart leapt at the thought of him. Every girl in the school wanted Gregory. But that evening, for some inexplicable reason, he chose me.

Answer me this, Blake – what would you have done if you were me? Would you have turned him away, the best-looking boy in school? Or would you have held him close, flattered by his attention, seduced by his charm and sweet musky-smelling skin? The soft delicate aroma of recently applied aftershave wafting my way and luring me in.

You were convinced I did it to spite you, but that wasn't it at all. I wanted Gregory Timmons as much as you did, and I hate to point this out to you, but not everything is or was about you. Does that sound spiteful? Mean and uncaring? Maybe it is, but we were just kids, Blake. Just a pair of teenagers finding our feet in this big old world. We did what we did to survive, to get as much pleasure as we could out of the smallest of occurrences. It was just one evening out of our lives. One kiss. Nothing more, nothing less. If it makes you feel any better, he went back to ignoring me the following week at school, his sights already set on another girl. But then, you already know that, don't you? You gleaned a lot of pleasure out of seeing me rejected and cast aside.

The silence on the walk home from the disco was unbear-

able, your unwillingness to engage with me cutting me to the quick. I tried to be convivial, to make light of the situation, but you were having none of it, your eyes fixed to the floor as we stumbled through the woods, making our way through the darkness, making our way through the one place we were never supposed to frequent after dark. We were struggling to see, our arms outstretched as we fumbled for something – anything. Fingers trailing through dewy foliage. Rustling behind us, to the side of us. All around us. And then a hard push. I recall the smack as I hit the damp ground, the sodden mulch, wet and squelchy beneath my torso. And then the sense of solitude as I scrambled to get up only to have a hand force me back down into the loam, my face pressed hard against the carpet of cold twigs and leaves. Then came the sound of somebody laughing. A distant cackle as you released the pressure on my neck and ran ahead into a copse of dense trees, leaving me alone in the murkiness of the woodland.

I guess you could say I had it coming. Or it could be argued that your reaction to what happened in the disco was disproportionate. I clambered back up onto my feet after you left, damp, bewildered and exhausted. For some reason, even though we both knew that area like the backs of our hands having used it as an adventure playground as children, I couldn't find my way out and ended up going back the way we had come. By the time I realised my mistake and took a different route, circumventing the darkness of the woods and taking the main road, you had been home for possibly two hours or more. I let myself in, locked the door behind me and crept up to bed, upset and dazed, wondering what would happen the following morning when we met up for our usual walk to school.

As it turned out, I needn't have been concerned. You

arrived at my door at 8 a.m., fresh-faced and ready to take on the world. It was at that point it struck me; we were even. I had taken your man and you had taken my safety and dignity. That was how you operated. Still, at least I knew who and what I was dealing with, how to manage your reactions to difficult or purportedly unacceptable situations. Tit for tat. Even Stevens and all that. We never spoke of it again and as far as I'm aware, your love for Gregory Timmons dissipated and he fell off your radar, another person relegated to the farthest reaches of your mind.

Maybe now we can think back to happier times. Times when we laughed so hard I felt sure my ribs would crack open. They happened, those times, I'm sure of it. We just need to look harder, to delve into our shared history and pluck out the sunshine-filled days, whilst discarding the bad times. I'm willing to give it a try if you are.

Write back soon

Love, Lucy

13

BLAKE

I woke up today feeling brighter. It happens sometimes; life feeling easier and lighter for no apparent reason at all. I slept well, no nightmares, and so this morning I feel as if I can take on the world. After a light breakfast of juice, scrambled egg and toast, I take a walk in the garden. Despite the cold breeze, it feels like a spring day, the sun doing its best to warm the cold saturated earth.

It's as I am bending down tending to my budding roses, that I see her – Sandra. She is standing reading something, a piece of paper clutched between her fingers. I stare at her gnarled knuckles and nails that are bitten to the quick. I watch her features, see how her eyes crinkle with bemusement, how her mouth twitches as she scans the piece of notepaper. And that's when I realise – my letter to Lucy. She is reading *my* fucking letter.

My back aches as I stand up and pat at my pockets. Both empty. It must have fallen out while I was working in my patch of garden. This is the problem with a communal outside space;

everything is shared. *Everything*. But not my letter. My words are private.

Before she can read on, I march over and snatch it out of Sandra's hands, my voice a near snarl. 'That belongs to me.'

Her look of bemusement rapidly morphs into anger. Nostrils flaring, she tries to take it back but already I have stuffed it deep into my rear pocket. If she tries to get it again, she is going to have to wrestle me to the ground. This letter is precious. I will do whatever it takes to make sure it remains with me.

'I found it on the ground. It could belong to anybody.'

I cannot swear to it but it looks like she is smiling, her eyes twinkling with amusement, her yellowing tombstone teeth bared as she tries once again to grab it out of my pocket.

'It's mine and you know it is, you conniving little bitch.' My insult hits home.

I have tried for so long now to be pleasant and tolerant to this lady, and to display all the qualities expected of a middle-aged woman, but somebody reading my private correspondence is a step too far. Everyone has their breaking point. Sandra has pushed me to mine.

My feet twist beneath me, the slap to my face catching me off guard. Before the red mist has a chance to descend, I feel myself being hauled inside, Maya's arms wrapped tightly around my waist, her voice whispering in my ear.

'Come on, let's get you inside, make sure you're not hurt.'

'Seems I'm not the only one with a past, eh? Looks like little old Blake also has her secrets. I always knew there was something about you,' Sandra hollers, her voice laced with scorn. 'People who play their cards close to their chest are always the ones with the most to hide.' Her voice echoes across the garden while my face burns with shame. I've made it thus far without any issues and now one stray letter and the carefully constructed façade I have spent years building is crumbling around me.

Inside, Maya dabs at my face with a damp tissue, her eyes closely scanning my cheek for any damage. 'Looks like you'll have a bit of bruising but apart from that, you're going to be okay.'

'I think my dignity has taken a battering though,' I manage to say, a small laugh escaping in a bid to conceal my embarrassment.

'Sandra is a loud-mouthed nuisance, I'm afraid. She is what she is and nothing and nobody is ever going to change her. Best just to move on and forget it.'

The insult I hurled at her balloons in my mind. I shouldn't have said it. It was juvenile and unbecoming. Next time I see her, an apology is in order.

'Thanks, Maya,' I say as she gently touches my face and leaves me to ponder over what has just taken place.

She's right of course. Sitting brooding over it will only bring anguish. Best to move on, pretend as if none of it happened.

I pull out the letter and re-read it, my past rushing back at me like it happened only yesterday.

1 May

Dear Lucy,

I don't quite know where to begin. How about starting with an apology? I am so sorry for that evening. I think my jealousy and insecurities reached fever pitch and it all came flooding out – my envy and resentment, my bitterness and loneliness. Believe it or not, that disco event slipped my mind until you wrote about it. A lot of things seem to have fallen out of my brain over the years. Maybe that's just as well. Who wants to keep such unsavoury images in their mind? Toxic memories that bleed into our veins, filling us with anxiety and shame. Perhaps you are right and my actions that night, the only way I knew of counterbalancing your actions, helped to erase what I did to you. It clearly didn't leave you and for that I am truly sorry. We were friends and I think we should both have behaved better. Been that little bit more mindful of one another's feelings. But as you said, we were young and lacking in consideration, each of us a little too self-absorbed. It was a blip and we are thankfully over it.

I would like to fast forward a few years, to discuss the day we left school. I was unsure what I wanted to do with my life, whether I wanted to get a job or to enrol in further education. You knew immediately what you wanted to do, your ambitions and life mapped out from an early age. You had a place at college while I wandered aimlessly, uncertain what to do next. Unnerved by what lay ahead. It was you who finally persuaded me to take a place at the same college as you. I could study English and drama, you had said, while you took English and biology. I had visions of us sitting side by side in class, your presence helping to sharpen my thoughts. Turned out we were in separate groups, your lessons in another room at a different time. I was alone, cut adrift without my best friend to guide me in a new and unfamiliar environment.

Breaktimes were the hardest. I watched you work the room, making friends, forming a brand-new social circle, each of them sitting there wide-eyed, mesmerised by your charisma, captivated by your words. Within a week they were eating out of your hand. That was just how you were, Lucy. People were drawn to you, magnetised by your beauty and charm. It was clear from the outset that I was being marginalised. Left out and cast aside. And I couldn't let that happen.

Your new group of acquaintances, your cackling coven,

never took to me. I tried to fit in, Lucy. I really did, but I was an outlier. Whenever they saw me, they closed ranks, shoulders hunched, mouths twisted in disgust. They thought me either deaf or stupid, I was never quite sure which. Perhaps it was both or perhaps, as I suspect, they didn't care enough to think at all about my well-being. I heard the long shuddering sighs as I approached, saw the eye rolls and shakes of their heads. The occasional curl of a perfectly glossed lip.

You were slipping away from me. Despite us being in the same building, despite you sitting next to me in the canteen at lunchtime, you were leaving me, carving out a fresh and exciting life for yourself with a new set of friends. I may as well have been on the other side of the world. For the first time ever, I felt truly alone.

Did you notice the change in me? Did you notice the change in yourself? Your glitter always did shine much brighter than anybody else's, but college took your confidence to a whole new level while mine dragged listlessly on the floor. I should have left college straightaway. I didn't fit; I was a cumbersome, jagged individual in smooth, clean surroundings that were designed for beautiful, effortlessly clever people. People like your friends. People just like you.

Staying on for those extra months and watching you slowly slide away into another world was the undoing of me. Why I hung around to watch you grow into another person, I will never quite understand. Actually that is an outright lie; I do understand. It was fear. Fear of being without you. Fear of being completely cut off and alone. I realise this makes me sound needy, and maybe that's because I was and still am, but it's about time you knew the truth. Losing you was like losing a limb. That's why I left college and applied for that job, the one at the same college. I know it sounds ridiculous now –

hindsight really is a wonderful thing – but I thought that if I held a position of authority in the same environment, it would elevate me in your eyes and the eyes of your newfound friends. Make me worthy of your attention.

But that didn't happen.

I was naïve and inexperienced. I'm not sure why I expected my position of admin assistant to give me any allure or status. There I sat in the small, dated office in my old-fashioned antiquated clothing, my plain knee-length skirt and blouse, complete with lace collar while you and your little gang sauntered past in tight jeans and scanty tops, sweaters slung over your shoulders like budding movie stars.

The titters and snide comments were audible above the ringing of phones and the scrape of filing cabinets being dragged open. I became a laughing stock. A young woman dressed like somebody's elderly relative pulling in more scorn and derision than when I had been a student. With my dignity already in tatters, I sidled up to you one afternoon when you were sitting alone in the library and begged you to allow me back into your life. Your expression was one of bewilderment. My request left you mystified. You acted as if my words were the imaginings of a lost child left to cope alone without anybody to turn to. What you failed to realise was that while you had an array of new friends, I had nobody. All I had ever had was you and that was all I had ever wanted.

I think that perhaps my request scared you, made you wary of me. Begging is undignified, humiliating and unseemly. But I didn't know any other way. And because you are who you are, you took pity on me and allowed me back into the fold. That evening after I got home, there was a knock at the door, soft and tentative. It was you. I knew it before I even opened the door. There you stood, happy and contented, and yet at the same time remorseful and ever so slightly shamefaced.

We hugged. You apologised. I can still feel your breath on my neck, the softness of your skin next to mine as we rested together, arms locked around one another for what felt like the longest time. I didn't want it to end. It was a precious moment; the closing of one episode of our lives and the beginning of another. I loved you like no other, Lucy. We were back together and I had never felt happier. Elation soared through me, blooming in my chest and heating up my flesh.

The following day I resigned from my post at the college. I didn't need a mundane job in a stuffy office. All I ever needed was you, and I had you back in my life. It was enough. You were enough. The feeling of exhilaration didn't last. Nothing ever does. I just wish I had known at the time how cruel people can be. How selfish and uncaring and utterly despicable they can be when given the chance.

I waited for you outside the main entrance of the college. You didn't see me standing alone beside the shrubbery. Your head was thrown back in mirth, your laughter loud and contagious. Around you, people smiled and linked your arm, each of them desperate to be close to you. To be the one. How could that be? I was the one. I was the person who knew your background, your secrets. Things you would rather others didn't know.

That's when it all came out – my festering hatred for them, my isolation and bitterness. A splurge of it directed your way. I'm not sure I can recall what happened after that. Even if I did, I would be too embarrassed to write it down, to see my litany of failures and transgressions written right here in front of me.

I know that I screamed and swore at your group of friends.

Maybe I pushed them out of the way. I can't recall everything, but I do remember the look on your face; the look that said our friendship was over. The look that said you were frightened of me. Of my capabilities.

Of who I really was.

Horror crept beneath my skin as the adrenaline dissipated. I ran home, too humiliated to say or do anything else. I apologised at the time but feel a burning need to do it again. I am so, so sorry for what I did and said that day. You may reply in return that it has faded from your memory and that it was nothing, but you are wrong. It was everything. I made a fool of you and made you look silly and childish in front of your new friends. I also made a terrible fool of myself, and worse than that, I risked losing you forever.

That didn't happen and it is only because you are such a forgiving person that I now have you back in my life. Apart for a while but now back together.

I am so very lucky and I shouldn't ever forget that.

Speak soon

Love, Blake

14

BEFORE

They were here again. Anna and Trevor full of faux happiness and a desperate need to please. There seemed to be no end to their intrusion into her life. Every weekend they would arrive, strolling up to her front door, eyes sparkling with anticipation. With their wide smiles and tidy house, and their perfect baby who never seemed to cry or whine, Isla could barely bring herself to speak to them. Any conversations or contact left her feeling dejected and hopeless. A useless mother and a terrible, hateful person. What did they have that she didn't, these new neighbours who were clearly attempting to replace Martha? She imagined a decent upbringing with loving parents was their starting point, unlike the place she stemmed from as a child. Her home was a place of neglect and contempt. A place she couldn't seem to shake no matter how hard she tried. Every day she would rise from her bed, determined to blow off those cobwebs and be a better version of herself. Fresher, healthier. Happier than the previous day. And every day her attempts were foiled before she even pulled back the covers, flashes of darkness and hatred crowding her mind and pushing her into a tight corner.

She wanted to be more like Anna and poor old Martha, a bouncy chirpy individual brimming with advice and friendliness, but the shadows continually crept in, nudging aside all happiness and tiny shoots of positivity, stamping and crushing them until they were trodden deep into the ground. Flowers rarely grew in Isla's imaginary garden, her patch of green riddled with thorns and spikes, waiting like predators, primed and ready to capture and devour anything in their path.

What she really wanted was to be left alone, and yet still they tried to intercept, these new neighbours, with their eager-to-please smiles and inane small talk. Doing what they could to integrate into the local area and worm their way into Isla's home. She wasn't prepared to let that happen. She would not allow them to be pleasant and convivial in her presence by intruding and muscling their way into the lives of those around them. Isla had lived in the neighbourhood for fifteen years and still knew hardly anybody. That was her preference. All other people ever did was interfere and judge and watch with idle curiosity as Isla stumbled from one catastrophe to another, making it through each day without actually killing her own child. As grateful as she was for their initial assistance, she could do without being held under their watchful gaze. They were the type of people who would see her faults and judge, gossiping to other neighbours about her parenting methods and finding them wanting. Fuck them all. Isla would manage in her own sweet and slightly deranged way. She would cope and her child would survive regardless of how unorthodox Isla's approaches were. Whatever got her through or helped her survive another day in the house with a child who didn't want her as a mother. A child who often scared her, her ability to alienate her own mother something Isla found chilling. Part of her was already beginning to empathise with her own offspring because if she was going to be brutally honest, Isla didn't want her as a daughter. At least they had that much in common.

Things were different when Finn was home. The young girl took to him; she was drawn to his warmth and his affable ways while Isla remained stiff-lipped and unapproachable. In the wee small hours as the baby yowled and cried, Isla wondered if she was actually capable of tenderness and affection, whether she even loved her own husband or would ever grow to love her own child. Jealousy rattled her bones at the sight of Finn and their daughter, how they bonded with ease, like two halves of a whole, while she stood on the periphery of her own life with no simple or straightforward route back in.

'So as we were saying, if ever you need a break, we can take the little one out on a regular basis. These two little girls seem to get on so well together.'

Isla could feel herself stepping away, an involuntary movement brought on by their closeness, by the way her new neighbours stood on her doorstep doing what they could to lighten her workload. Why couldn't she warm to these people? Why did she not have it in her to smile and act in a courteous manner as others did? It came so naturally to other folk. Why did malice and suspicion ooze from her like acid? Martha had known Isla for who and what she was, ignoring her corrosive streak and forcing her to engage, but Martha was gone and there was no way of bringing her back. No replacement. Nobody who even came close to that sort of friendship and implicit understanding. Martha hadn't stood on the doorstep making polite conversation. She had bustled her way inside, doing what she could to coax and cajole and drag Isla into the day before tipping her face to the sun and showing her that there was light beyond the murkiness.

'I'm fine. We're fine, but thank you anyway.' Her voice, a

disembodied strangulated sound that rang around the hallway, caused them to back away from her.

Was she shouting? It was too difficult to tell, her mood and panic levels spiralling. She scared people without even trying, made them wary of her; viewing her as the strange feral-looking woman who rarely spoke or smiled. Fog lingered in her brain. Exhaustion washed over her, a tidal wave of it. Powerful enough to nearly knock her off her feet. All she wished for was solitude. A day on her own. No dishes to wash, no beds to make, no clothes to dry and iron. Nothing except rest and time to do whatever she wanted. Except when she had that, it wasn't enough. Isla wasn't so dim that she didn't know, or couldn't see her own failings. That was part of the problem. She was acutely aware of all of her flaws. They grew in her mind, monsters that clawed at her brain, sucking the very life out of her. Parasites she couldn't shake.

All afternoon the baby whined. One long round of feeding and changing, pacing the floor with her daughter pressed to her breast, had left her feeling flattened and without purpose. What was this joy of motherhood she had read about? Why had it abandoned her when she needed it the most? She craved sleep, the nothingness that it brought. The distance from chores and responsibilities. The distance from her daughter.

* * *

He came home early. That was how he caught her. Isla awoke to see Finn standing over her as she lay in bed, a screaming infant in his arms, his elongated shadow stretching across the bedsheets like the grim reaper. Her daughter was red-faced and sweaty, and her clothes were stuck to her body, the child's sleep-suit darkened by perspiration. Isla should have got up – she knew that – she should have looked horrified, wept and apologised, but her tiredness eclipsed everything. Even her own child. Especially her own child.

'How long, Isla?' Glassy-eyed, a lump bobbing about in his throat, Finn shook his head and waved his free hand about as if he were swatting away a rogue insect. 'How long has she been crying while you've been lying here in bed?'

She had to admire his stoic ways. Even in situations such as this one, Finn kept his cool, his voice and movements calm. Mechanical even. She was the fiery one, the wild one. The person who continually fucked everything up in their tiny little world.

The noise of her daughter's screaming flooded into her brain as she pulled out the remaining earplug. It was impossible to not see Finn's look of disgust, how his chin trembled while their baby howled into his neck.

Before Isla could protest or apologise, he turned and left the room, his footfall as he descended the stairs a muffled sound. Her husband was another perfect being who remained unruffled by the high-pitched crying of a baby. No desperate jerky movements, no wishing he could be anywhere else but glued to a screaming infant whose needs never seemed to be met. She was an insatiable being, always clinging or hungry or tired or wet. Nothing worked. There was no way of placating her. Until somebody swept her into their arms, at which point her cries slowed down, her body responding to theirs like they were taking part in an invisible ritual, a soothing dance routine, their movements fluid and symbiotic.

By the time Isla summoned up enough energy to shower, dress in clean clothes and join him downstairs, their baby daughter was sitting happily on her playmat cooing at the world around her while Finn sat watching, gently sipping at a cup of coffee.

'Yours is in the kitchen. I've also made you a sandwich. You're too thin, Isla. You need to eat something. Food feeds the brain as well as the body.'

And that was the end of the latest episode. Finn's solution was doling out beverages and food to try to mask all drama and upset. Isla sat, a limp-looking sandwich on her lap, a cup of weak coffee in her hand, the days stretching out ahead of her. One after another after another. A pall of grey clouds cloaking her view, pressing down on her until she felt unable to breathe. There was no relief from the heaviness. No end in sight.

She kept her gaze averted, unwilling to look at her own child for fear of upsetting the delicate equilibrium of the moment. Unwilling to look at her husband because despite her befuddled state, despite the thick fog that continually darkened her thoughts and actions, somewhere deep inside, she felt shame.

'She hates me.' In her head the words raged, but here in their home, in the serenity of the recently tidied living room after Finn had put everything away and made it look decent and presentable, her words trailed off, swallowed up by the near silence. Swallowed up by his inability to listen, to really, *really* listen and comprehend what it was she was trying to say.

'I'm thinking of taking her to church with me this evening if you'd like to accompany us?' Finn stood and stared out of the window, his back to her. 'I think we could all do with some solace.'

Isla swallowed, rubbed at her eyes. A painful bony lump in her gullet made it difficult to breathe, to think clearly. The church. As if the coffee and the sandwich and the fucking awful silence wasn't bad enough, she now had the *church* to think about. Looking back, she used to quite enjoy attending mass. Perhaps enjoy was overstating things, but she learned to embrace the quiet and sombre atmosphere. To sit and allow it to envelop her. It was a welcome time for reflection that was occasionally helpful in her battle against the oppressiveness, but once it became a *thing*, a ritual she was forced to endure, it lost its charm, the small smoky tentacles that endlessly circled and swirled in her brain poisoning its initial allure.

'No. You take her if you want, but I won't be going. I'm staying here.' She placed the sandwich and coffee to one side, staring at them as if they were polluted. She had no appetite for food. No appetite for anything. 'I'm just tired, Finn. So damn tired all the time.'

A second passed. Then two, her insides roiling as she waited for a response from her husband. Something – anything – to help her clamber out of the pit of gloom that was slowly but surely squeezing the very life out of her, pressing and pressing until she could no longer breathe properly.

'Right you are,' he said, rising from his chair. 'I'll be home shortly after six. We can pray together when I get back.'

Eyes and flesh burning with anger and frustration, Isla watched him leave, wishing and hoping with every fibre of her being that a bolt of lightning would strike both her husband and daughter dead before they returned home so she could live the rest of her life in peace.

15

BLAKE

16 May

Dear Blake,

Ah, college. I wondered if we would ever speak of that time, and now here it is, out in the open; a period of our lives that both of us would sooner forget suddenly being held under a microscope and studied at length. It was an awkward ill-fitting phase of our existence and neither of us escaped from it unscathed. I lost my friends and you lost your pride and self-worth. We both know your actions did little to help heal our fractured friendship. Sometimes our behaviour is the undoing of us and that day definitely proved to be your downfall.

I'm no longer in contact with anybody from back then and I don't suppose you are either. Best to leave such rot behind us, don't you think? Any kudos and standing I had amongst my recently formed circle of friends was ripped to shreds after that event. I was a pariah, the girl with a friend who was a loose cannon. People were scared of you and in turn because of my association with you, gave me a wide berth. Who can blame them? So I finished my studies, keeping my head down and spending each and every day in the library alone. You got your wish, Blake. You separated me from my friends which was always your intention, wasn't it? I may sound bitter but I'm not. I accepted at that point who and what you were and felt powerless to do anything about it so rather than resist your actions or try to stop your outbursts, I went along with them. I refused to waste energy fighting a battle I couldn't win.

As you know, after leaving college, I went onto university and my ambition was to become a teacher. It wasn't an easy decision and one I didn't take lightly, but I knew that I wanted to work hard at my chosen career and make a difference. I recall you were a little less focused, unsure about your future and rudderless, applying for a variety of jobs without any real success. You even considered joining the army at one point. I was taken aback at that option and questioned you over it, afraid you were about to make a terrible decision, but in the end you didn't go ahead, and instead took a position at the local newspaper offices as an assistant in the classified ads department. After working there for six months, you began a stint working alongside the journalists. It was hard graft, I recall you saying, but stimulating and always busy. Maybe that's where your interest in writing began? It was also where you met your first boyfriend. After the Greg Timmons debacle you retreated into yourself, showing little or no interest in boyfriends, so it was a relief to see you become the person you had always been, stepping out on the arm of Marc Westfield. He was handsome and suave and witty. You glowed beside him, the happiness you felt evident in your features. But it didn't last. You broke up after a couple of months. I never did find out why. I guess we were young and romances simply fizzled out. And then came the surprise revelation that you had a girlfriend. Kathryn was delightful. She was warm and generous and pretty as a picture. But that also didn't last. A couple of months and she too disappeared from the scene. I began to wonder why so few people stayed by your side. I soon found out the answer, although deep down, I think I already knew but wasn't brave enough to think it because thinking it made it real. And I didn't want any of it to be real.

I was busy with my studies at that point in my life. I had managed to get a place at the local university so was able to stay in touch and keep up with what you were doing, although our contact was becoming more and more sporadic. I too had a few dalliances. Nothing serious. A few boyfriends, each of them lasting only a matter of weeks. I think the longest was three months. It didn't bother me too much. My studies were my life. I didn't want a boyfriend cluttering up my days and eating away at my precious time. Maybe I also found it difficult to keep people in my life. Not you though, Blake. You were always around. Whether I wanted you there or not. I don't mean to sound cruel but my comment is a lead-up to what happened next.

Do you remember meeting up for coffee in that little tearoom near the university? It was a small independently run place with shelves filled with exotic spices. You had called, asking if I was free for a chat. I arrived, flustered and red-faced, carrying a backpack stuffed full of textbooks. I slumped into the chair opposite while you in sharp contrast were the picture of calm, smiling at my predicament as I sat and ordered some silly-named tea that made me go green at the gills. I was embracing my student status and being flighty and bohemian while you were a working girl, so serious and focused. Already our differences were becoming apparent. No longer two giggling carefree children, we were planning our futures, putting some structure into our lives. The room was *warm that day, the air thick with the scent of buttered toast and freshly baked pastries.*

I remember asking how you were and then waiting patiently for your reply. I assumed you had something important to tell me. After all, you were the one who had arranged the meet-up. But that wasn't the case at all. I was there to be questioned. Harangued into explaining why I hadn't been in touch. I explained that my studies were taking up a lot of my time but you were dissatisfied with my answer. The exact wording of your criticism that was aimed directly at me has left my memory but the gist of it was that I was purportedly being a bad friend to you; unkind and thoughtless. Selfish and negligent. Tears burnt my eyes that afternoon. I fought them back, too shocked to let them flow freely. I hadn't meant to ignore or disregard you. Time had simply run away with me, exams and assessments, and poring over textbooks consuming every minute of my day. When I replied that aside from arranging the meet-up that afternoon you hadn't actually been in touch with me either, your rage was immediate and forceful. A palpable wave of negative energy in a small friendly café. You had always been mercurial, your moods unpredictable, but even allowing for that, your reaction still shocked me to my core. Your anger escalated within a matter of seconds. You shouted that you were tired of me turning everything around, always pointing the finger at you rather than looking inward at my own failings. I shrank into myself, suddenly afraid of your irrational swell of anger. A hush fell over the room as you screamed at me, the sudden silence drawing attention to your childish meltdown. You had taken centre stage and rapidly became aware of yourself, your behaviour incongruous in a small, quiet setting. You apologised straightaway, humiliation and regret peppering your face and neck, small dots of embarrassment evident for all to see, but your words and accusations had already been voiced, the air heavy with your fury.

The waitress came to our table to see if everything was okay. I nodded and replied that we were just fine. Then it was your turn for tears, blurting out how much you had missed me. How you wished that you had also gone to university so we could see one another every day. I tried to explain that as people grew older, they often took different paths through life, but that didn't mean they would be parted forever. No matter what we did, how we spent our days, we could always meet up and remain firm friends. But that line of reasoning didn't seem to work. I couldn't placate you. You became inconsolable, your tears flowing freely, your hiccupping sobs still managing to draw attention from other diners who were mystified and embarrassed by your strange behaviour. Why was it that bystanders could see what you couldn't? Your lack of insight into your own behaviour has always been your main failure. I'm not telling you anything you don't already know, am I?

The waitress came back and asked if she could assist in any way. I'm sure you remember what happened next. We were asked to leave by the manager after you refused all help and swore at the young girl who was doing what she could to contain a deteriorating situation. It was a repeat of the incident outside college, your temper and frustrations building and spilling out. Scorching everyone in close vicinity.

I apologised on your behalf and took your arm as we left. By the time we were outside, you realised what you had done and mortification pulled you back to normality. You told me later that you had sent a bouquet of flowers to the waitress with a letter of apology, which was the right thing to do. I was proud of you for taking that step and even more impressed when you explained that you had sought therapy for your issues. Anger management is what it is now called. Back then it was simply a way of finding out the root cause of why you felt so upset and furious all the time. Why your outbursts were becoming more and more frequent, your volatility hard to predict and even harder to control.

For the next few months we stayed in touch by phone, me telling you all about my studies and you entertaining me with work-related anecdotes. Every now and then you would tell me of subjects touched upon in your therapy sessions, but on the whole, we spoke little of it. I respected your need for confidentiality and was impressed by your resoluteness, persevering with each session and doing what you could to take on board their advice. That was as much as you told me and it was all I needed to know. The rage that had burned inside you for the past few years seemed to have evaporated and I was relieved to see you happy and serene. On the odd occasion we did meet, you exuded a level of calm that made me feel positive for the future – your future and the future of our friendship, because after all that had happened, I still wanted to be by your side. We had so much shared history, the past a thing that bound us together. I knew it would be a terrible shame to watch it disintegrate. In these so-called enlightened times, people speak of toxic friendships and how everyone should divorce themselves from such situations, but I don't agree. Mixing with people who aren't necessarily the same as we are, helps us to build resilience. To become tolerant and caring. We learn from one another. You and I helped one another to become the people we are now and that is no bad thing. What a boring, dull world it would be if folk surrounded themselves with like-minded people, everyone living in an echo chamber of their own making. It was clear at that point that we had grown into very different people, but that didn't mean we should have drifted apart.

I worked hard at trying to be the best friend I could be, but sometimes doing the right thing isn't always enough. It was sufficient for a while but then things changed, the dynamics of our lives nudging aside all good intentions and the deepest of promises. I will sign off now and let you fill in the blanks on the next part of our lives. You will probably have sharper memories of that era, be better positioned to write about what happened next. Why our friendship nearly came to an end. It seems that with each passing day, my memory becomes more and more blurred, the images that were once so easily within reach now unattainable.

Today hasn't been a good day so I'm going to end this correspondence. The seasons are important to me. Spring is here with its russet skies and early morning birdsong. The temperature still feels wintry which also exacerbates my ailments, and if I'm being perfectly honest, lowers my mood. You've probably picked up on that by the tone of this letter. I shouldn't complain. I'm fortunate in many ways; I have a family and live close to nature. Many aren't so lucky.

It may not sound like it, but I'm relieved we are back in touch and look forward to reading your next letter.

Love, Lucy

'So, would you like to talk about the incident with your neighbour?'

The small bones in my neck click when I shake my head. I do it with such force, the room spins around me. The rattle of glass against wood roars in my ears as Arthur slides a tumbler of water across to me. I take a sip, a trickle running down my chin and dripping onto my jeans. I shouldn't have mentioned the fracas with Sandra. It paints me in a bad light, somebody unhinged and borderline psychotic. My temper is something I hoped I had left behind. I'm a grown woman for God's sake. The spat with Sandra was like something from a children's playground. I'm deeply ashamed and embarrassed about the whole sordid episode. My need to keep my secrets private made them very public.

'Are you ready to speak about your relationship with Lucy yet?'

'No, not yet. We've hit a stumbling block. I need things to turn a corner before I talk about everything.' I sound remarkably calm, which is surprising as my insides are sloshing about like the water in the tumbler that sits in my lap.

I wipe at my mouth and try to smile. In my peripheral vision, I catch sight of myself in the window. An old woman stares back at me. My hair is streaked with grey, my skin weathered and coarse. Where did the time go? I want to snatch it back, relive my life and make a better job of it this time around.

'Perhaps next time you'll be ready to talk about it?' Arthur says, a hopeful glint in his eye.

'Perhaps,' I reply as I stand and leave the room, doing my utmost to ignore the reflection of the embittered woman opposite who mirrors my movements.

16

BLAKE

1 June

Dear Lucy,

Summer is upon us. I should feel happy, ready for that welcome shimmering spread of warmth and those long hot days that are filled with birdsong, and yet, writing this letter feels like some sort of twisted joke. An unwelcome stirring of trouble.

Firstly, I'm sorry to hear about your illness. It must be debilitating, being unable to move without pain. Some of us suffer silently, the discomfort we're forced to endure a private matter. And some of us feel distress and aches in other ways, the agonies we suffer taking place in our minds rather than our bodies. I guess physically I'm fortunate to be healthy, but my mind rarely rests. I spend hour after hour, day after day, going over and over old memories. It's like a form of torture, a constant round of self-flagellation.

Which brings me to what I was about to say. You finished your last letter on a sour note with the mention of how our friendship almost came to an end after we'd reconciled, so I suppose it is up to me to speak about what happened. After all we had been through, anybody would think we would have become inured to one another's ways, desensitised to anything and everything. But we all have our tipping point, don't we? And what happened next almost broke me. I understand why you're reluctant to broach the subject and speak about it. Is it your failing memory that is stopping you, or is it the shame you feel after what you did? You hurt me, Lucy. Just as my life was being stitched back together, you came along with your effervescent persona, your sparkling wit and charm and winning smile, and ripped apart the fabric of my carefully mended life with a jagged blade. Sometimes the damage we inflict on one another is so great, the fissures of the destruction so ragged and irregular, that even when they appear to have healed, they're still there. A break will always weaken a structure even if the cracks aren't visible.

You may have your own interpretation of what happened, and that is your right. Of course it is. However, once you see the facts written down and take the time to absorb each and every word, I'm sure you'll agree with everything I have written. You always were prone to embellishments, twisting and tweaking incidents to suit your narrative. As much as I loved you back then, I also know how you operate, Lucy. You airbrush your life so it matches your appearance. Spotless and stain-free. But I am now about to tell the truth, warts and all. I realise that when we first began writing these letters, I painted you as perfect, an individual without flaws, but as I have begun to dig deeper, I have come to realise that nobody is perfect, least of all you. As a child I was in awe of you, the way you carried yourself. Your confidence. Your exuberance and charisma. As an adult I can now see that beneath that glossy calm exterior, you were as frightened as the next person. A seething mass of insecurities. Or maybe I'm being unnecessarily cruel. A harsh unforgiving woman. I woke up today feeling particularly sharp, my mood low. Outside the skies are grey despite summer approaching and I am the type of person who needs light and warmth to remain buoyant. We all have our off days and you've caught me on one of mine.

Back to our friendship, that fragile connection of ours that has been dented and damaged so many times it's a wonder we are still in touch.

But we are, and now it is time to tell my side of the story. My side as I see it, that is. Feel free to disagree.

After working at the local newspaper, I got a job at a firm of accountants. It was another admin position, my day filled with menial tasks that bored me rigid. Figures and numbers had never been my forte. Words are my real love, so being faced with rows and rows of sums and statistics day after day left me feeling flattened and depressed. I was also still struggling to come to terms with my bisexuality. My parents knew nothing about it and I kept it that way. It was my personal business and I didn't think it necessary to inform them of my relationship with Sara. Like most of my liaisons, it was brief. A few weeks after our split, I met Nigel. The attraction was instant. We didn't meet in the conventional way; we met on a train. I was travelling to Newcastle to attend a course and Nigel was sitting opposite, his gaze never leaving mine as I lowered myself into my seat, flustered and hot, constantly apologising for my clumsiness. I had attempted to place my bag in the overhead compartment and failed miserably, my rucksack landing in a messy heap on his lap. I guess you will smile reading this. I always was the clumsy one. Awkward and cumbersome in any situation.

'Here, let me help,' he had said softly, the gentle yet authoritative pitch of his voice turning my legs to liquid.

And his eyes. Oh my word, Lucy. Those eyes of his. They were a deep shade of green, almost emerald, and powerful enough to cut glass. But you already know all of this, don't you? As the saying goes, I'm preaching to the converted.

We talked non-stop all the way to Newcastle and by the time we pulled up at the station, we had exchanged numbers with the promise of a meet-up when he returned from his conference in Edinburgh. He lived not too far from me in Darlington so distance wasn't an issue. The chemistry was perfect, my skin sizzling with excitement every time I thought of his face, his voice. The possibility of his touch.

My past history and car crash of a love life made me feel certain he wouldn't call. Except he did. Two days after I arrived home from what was quite possibly the most mundane, mind-numbing course I had ever attended, he rang. My nerves jangled like castanets as we spoke, my words jumbled and nonsensical. Undisturbed by my erratic behaviour, he arranged to pick me up the following evening.

'I'll get to yours at 7 p.m.,' he said, his voice, although still gentle and compassionate, edged with something stronger. As if the world would always be at his feet, his commands met without question.

In that respect, he reminded me of you. Some people are born that way, questioning everything and fearing nothing, always assuming that life will always go their way.

I needed that kind of certainty and assurance in my life. Since you and I had drifted slightly apart, I felt rudderless. Cast aside with nowhere to turn. I'm not blaming you for getting on with your life and avoiding me; after all, I had become increasingly unstable, my behaviour questionable. I'm not so dim that I have no self-awareness. But I knew also that my thoughts and actions were triggered by loneliness and having nobody to turn to, so I saw Nigel as my sanctuary. My safe harbour in the midst of a violent storm. He would help save me from myself.

If you think back, it's how I have lived my life; always needing somebody by my side. Somebody stronger. Sturdy and reliable. Someone who could steer and guide me. My low self-esteem and neediness has always held me back. I once read that confidence and ambition always outstrip ability and knowledge. I guess we only have to look at the world of politics to understand that phrase. Nigel was my veneer, the shield I hid behind when the world became too loud and intimidating. Too crooked for me to navigate alone.

That first date, we ate at a restaurant in Darlington, but it wasn't the food that had set my nerves alight. Before dessert, he reached over and placed his hand over mine, his smile melting my insides. I knew then that we were meant to be. His touch felt so familiar, as if we had known each other for the longest time. Familiarity combined with sexual desire. It was a heady combination and one that I craved.

By the second date I knew he was the one. My soulmate. The person I wanted to spend the rest of my life with. He knew it too. His body language told me everything I needed to know. After a bottle of wine at his house, we undressed one another, our fingers dextrous, our movements fluid and seamless. We moved as one, our bodies melding together. My mind was elevated to a new and unexplored level of hunger and urgency. We made love three times before falling into an exhausted sleep, a tangle of limbs on crumpled bedsheets, the scent of sex hanging heavily in the air.

You may be wondering why I'm telling you all of this, why I am giving you intimate details of our life together. But if you think hard, Lucy, and I mean really, really hard, I'm sure you already know the answer to that question. I am trying to demonstrate just how close Nigel and I had become, how we were fused as one, a proper loving couple before you came on the scene. Your appearance in my life changed all that. You altered the trajectory of the only truly solid relationship I had ever had, striding in with your winsome ways and beguiling manner.

I recall Nigel's expression that day all those years ago when you breezed back into my life. I had spoken to you on the phone and tentatively mentioned my relationship, stating how happy I was. How settled and peaceful my life was. You congratulated me and insisted we meet so I could introduce you to the man who had turned my life around. We had arranged to get together in Stewart Park in Marton.

'For a picnic,' you had said. 'Just like the old times when we were kids.'

Like the nearby woods, Stewart Park had been our playground as children and you were desperate to re-create that carefree period of our lives again, even though we were adults. Even though we were very different people who no longer shared any common ground.

A griping sensation nipped at the base of my stomach as we pulled up in the car park that day. Even though the sun was shining and the conditions were perfect – a quiet Sunday afternoon with only a handful of other people around – I had a feeling that something was about to change. Something that was important to me was about to be turned on its head. I could practically taste it; the sour tang of jealousy as you approached us, your long hair flowing behind you, a picnic basket slung over your arm. Everything about you was picture perfect and effortless. Like a vision from a fairytale. An image of beauty I couldn't ever hope to emulate.

I saw it from the first second you met him, how he held your hand for a beat too long, how he watched you when he thought nobody was looking. The twinkle in his eye which, up to that point, had been reserved only for me. The signs were all there from the very beginning. And you did nothing to deter him. If anything you became more flirtatious, revelling in the extra attention, drawing him to you like a siren calling from the rocks.

We lunched on the grass, your picnic an exotic spread of olives, cheese and anchovies.

Do you remember the conversation you had with him that day, Lucy? I do.

'So, what do you do for a living then, Nigel?' you had asked in that low, husky voice of yours that, without fail, always lured in unsuspecting male admirers. You used your charms on the man who, at that point, belonged to me. You already knew the answer to your question because I had told you but you went ahead and asked anyway, making a point of fluttering your lashes and simulating interest in his reply. I realise that people don't own one another but my God, Lucy, you knew how deeply I loved him, how Nigel being in my life gave me balance, made me whole again.

I can almost hear you now, spluttering your denial as you read this, but it's true. You always turned on the charm in the presence of a member of the opposite sex. I wished that just for once, you would hold back, but if anything you went full pelt, determined to reel him in. To keep him for yourself.

That day at the park is emblazoned in my brain as one of the worst days of my life. One of them. But not the worst. We'll come to that later. You weren't at the centre of the worst day, but as always you were on the periphery with your wonderfully polished life. You were somewhere on the horizon of my existence, smiling and sending condolences while I wept uncontrollably for my losses.

'I work in finance,' Nigel had replied, his voice a gravelly whisper as he tried to appear unmoved by your beauty and undeniable appeal. 'It's all very boring really.'

The pair of you smirked and gazed at one another as if you shared some dark secret, one I wasn't privy to. You saw me watching and looked away, shrugging your shoulders and sighing as if what I witnessed was inconsequential. An ordinary everyday occurrence. But it wasn't, was it? It was the beginning of the end for me and the start of something important and life changing for you. As always, you came out on top, trumping me at every turn. Even my relationships were no longer safe when you were around. You took him, Lucy. You took Nigel from me and although I acted as if it didn't matter, it did. It mattered more than anything.

I will let you explain in your next letter how your love for him developed, how the two of you tried to conceal it from me as if I were a particularly dim child, too stupid to see what was going on behind my back. How you were robbing me of the one person who put some meaning back into my life.

I'm out of words now, Lucy, my thoughts and memories like dried flakes, tiny dust motes circling around me, insignificant and meaningless, clogging up my throat and making me retch. Hopefully I haven't dug too deep or been too vocal about how I felt. God forbid I should ever make you feel uncomfortable. That wouldn't do at all, would it?

As upset as I am speaking of that time, I also feel cleansed, liberated even, my bitterness suddenly free to go wherever it wishes. I no longer want it. Carrying it around for so long has been a burden, its corrosiveness causing me untold pain.

Please write back with your version of events. I'm always willing to hear both sides of the story no matter how painful or difficult. I am nothing if not resilient. I've had to be.

Love, Blake

I carefully fold the piece of paper, sliding it into an envelope as if it were a sliver of precious metal. Things are coming to a close; I can feel it. We're nearing an end, Lucy and I. Outside, a bird pecks at the ground, foraging for food. I watch as it pulls an unsuspecting worm out of the soil before hopping into a nearby clump of shrubbery and feasting on its find. Everything on Earth has a function; each living thing has a place. I have known mine for many years now and been too accepting of it. The time has come for change.

17

BEFORE

The passing of time did nothing to change Isla's judgement of her own child. It was wrong to feel the way she did, she knew that, but no matter how hard she worked at it, she couldn't bring herself to smile and coo over her two-year-old daughter the way other mothers did with their own beloved offspring. There was something missing; whatever bond or connection or deep-rooted animal instinct that should have been hardwired in her brain to make sure she loved her child and kept her from harm, was missing. It didn't matter how hard she tried to conjure up any feelings for the product of her own womb, Isla felt nothing but coldness and a deep sense of isolation every time the young girl shuffled her way into the room. And as horrified as she was to admit it, even to herself, the girl scared her. There was something about her, the way she stared at Isla, the way she interacted around other children; pushing and nipping. Whining and screaming when they moved away from her outbursts. Other toddlers didn't act as she did; her daughter was different from them, a coarseness to her. Something savage lurking. Which was why Isla did what she did only a few weeks prior. She hadn't planned it; it was a spur-of-the-moment thing. An impromptu minute of madness that resulted in a near arrest. Isla had taken her daughter to the local park and Anna and Trevor were there with their child. Of course they were. People like Anna and Trevor put effort into their child's day, taking her on outings and picnics, visiting museums and parks where they played and talked at length about the beauty of nature and their surroundings, while making sure their daughter's every need was met. Isla lived five minutes away from a large sprawling play area and that day was her first visit.

'Lovely to see you here!' Anna had chimed, a look of sheer bliss on her face as if she was genuinely delighted to see Isla, which Isla found strange as she couldn't even bear to glance at herself in the mirror. Why would someone as pure and joyous as Anna want to spend time with somebody as cruel and downcast as Isla?

Isla returned the smile and nodded in all the right places as Anna spoke about their new home and the weather and the local school. With her gaze continually switching between Anna and the gaggle of youngsters, Isla watched as her daughter pushed other children aside, yowling when they cried with a ferocity that made Isla go cold, and sneering at them with so much malice, it made Isla wince. Observing her daughter act with such brutality was too much. Something took hold of Isla that day, her own demons rising to the fore. Her desperation spilling out and running amok.

'So as I was saying,' Anna said, the same smile plastered to her face, 'if our girls would like to play together, we should set a date. Neighbours and friends, the perfect combination.'

Isla could stand it no more. She didn't want Anna as a friend; she wanted Martha back. She also didn't want her own daughter. She wanted somebody else's. Any child but the one she had given birth to. It had been hell since that fateful day when she realised she was pregnant, and the only thing that would solve her immediate problem was to take somebody else's child home and leave hers in the park where she could torture other children to her heart's delight. Insanity took hold in Isla's mind that day. Insanity born out of a sense of hopelessness and exhaustion, and a lifetime of being unloved. That was the only way she could explain what happened next.

Without saying a word, Isla marched towards a cute-looking little girl who had rosy cheeks and an infectious laugh and picked her up, scooping her into her arms and striding to the exit at the far end of the field.

'Hey. Hey!'

Trevor's booming voice stopped Isla in her tracks before she reached the gate, his fingers firmly clasped around her upper arm. Snapping out of her trance-like state, Isla dropped the child, who ran back to the swings like nothing had happened. As if a strange woman hadn't just tried to kidnap her in broad daylight. Without another word, Trevor gently led Isla back to a waiting sobbing mother who was standing with Anna, both of them watching Isla as if she were the devil incarnate.

'I'm sorry,' she managed to stutter, her face burning. 'I've not been well.'

Trevor and Anna's persuasive soothing manner was the only thing that stopped the stricken mother from reporting Isla to the police. Their calm manner helped to smooth things out, speaking softly and assuring the woman that it had been a terrible mistake and would never happen again. Isla watched as if in a dream, the whole sordid affair unfolding before her in cinematic glory. She didn't feel frightened or anxious. More worryingly, she felt nothing at all.

When it was all over, Anna and Trevor walked with Isla, their children running alongside until they reached the end of their road.

'We know you were close to Martha, Charlie told us all about it when we first came to view the house. You must miss her terribly.' Anna placed a hand on Isla's shoulder, her touch as light as air. 'We're always here for you, Isla. If ever you need any help, please don't be afraid to ask.'

The house was silent and cold when she stepped inside. She stood at the window and watched her neighbours open their front door and disappear inside. Was life on the inside of that house as shiny and perfect as it was on the outside? Was that even possible, that people lived each day without any drama or anxiety? It wasn't akin to any life Isla had ever known, and she found it hard to visualise.

Her daughter played quietly in the corner, a slow whine building in her throat. Soon the storm would erupt, Isla could feel it; the growing tension, the child's temper stretched as taut as a drum. Isla didn't have the energy to deal with it. Or the patience. It was easier when Finn was around. He more than made up for her icy disposition and dismissal of the child. She tried to affect love and compassion in front of him but when she was alone with her own daughter, the gnawing irritation Isla felt grew a hundredfold every time the girl cried or threw a tantrum or held out other arms for comfort. Isla once visited the local mother and toddler group where she met a gathering of rosy-cheeked infants and smiling, contented mothers who clearly adored their youngsters in a way that Isla knew she would never would. Just like at the park. They were everywhere, those happy families, their inane grins and idle babble about motherhood and how wonderful it was, chipping away more of Isla's self-confidence. One session was enough. She left the gathering feeling isolated and deflated, and made a promise to herself that it would be her first and only visit. Just like the park. She functioned better on her own.

Motherhood simply wasn't for Isla, she knew that, but there was no way out. One time, she forgot to feed and change the girl. It was only when Finn strode into the room and saw their daughter's dishevelled state that it hit her. And the worst thing about it was the lack of remorse she felt once she realised her error. The only emotion that ballooned in her mind was the fear of being found out. She knew that she was a bad mother, but consoled herself with the fact that she had given birth to a bad child. Maybe their genes were identical. Maybe her daughter had inherited the gloom and murkiness that lurked in Isla's brain, obliterating the light and robbing her of any shafts of warmth or happiness. Maybe they were more alike than she cared to admit. Two peas in a pod, their similarities greater than their differences. Isla may well have been a bad mother but perhaps her only child was a bad person too. Speaking critically of children was frowned upon, but to Isla the great nature/nurture debate was one that needed closer scrutiny. Maybe some children were born damaged, their brains incapable of compassion and understanding. Maybe her daughter was one of those people, a tiny fledgling individual who would grow into somebody dangerous; somebody teeming with malice.

Visits from family were infrequent and when they did happen, they were brief. An unplanned visit from Finn's mother ended disastrously with both women hollering at each other after a misunderstanding over a cup of tea. Isla had forgotten to put in two spoonfuls of sugar and was accused of being remiss in her duties as a wife and daughter-in-law. Truth was, she hadn't forgotten and *had* done it deliberately, using what little power she had to anger the woman who had never really taken to her, giving her no or little support through the most torrid of times.

Estelle was bright enough to see through Isla's games and rather than tolerate it, she chose instead to publicly shout and berate.

'Finn keeps me abreast of what goes on in this place, Isla. Your lackadaisical, undemonstrative ways don't go unnoticed.'

The slam of the door as the old woman exited their home rattled the window frames and shook the foundations of the house.

'Isla, this behaviour needs to stop.'

She could feel the heat of Finn's stare, his eyes boring into her back as she stood looking out of the window, her mind already pondering over the next possible disaster. The next bout of darkness that would undoubtedly come her way. Because they would. It was just how her life was. Devastation and ruin trailed in her wake. Finn often accused her of catastrophising but it wasn't like that at all – things happened and she found it difficult to cope, her strategies and resilience non-existent. She had used up all of her reserves during her childhood and had nothing left to give.

'I want you to see a doctor, Isla.'

'And I want you to start taking my side and stop disappearing off to that fucking stupid church every time the going gets tough in this house.'

She couldn't take back her words. She was being unfair on a man who had been unerringly patient for so many years, but then sometimes it was his patient, quiet ways that increased her anger. They were stuck in a viscous cycle and neither knew how to get out of it.

The silence became too much, Isla finally relenting with a promise to try harder.

'It will all work out for the best, Isla, you'll see.'

She had to hand it to her husband, his ability to turn the direst situations into something worthwhile and positive. How lovely it would have been if she could have an ounce of his faith. Just a tiny fraction of his conviction that everything dull and flawed would easily and without too much effort simply turn into gold.

His words were still stuck in Isla's head just two weeks later when she woke to a screaming child that she had locked in a cupboard because it had all become too much to bear, the exhaustion of being a mother draining her of all energy and patience. She hadn't meant to fall asleep; it just happened. By the time she opened the locked door and scooped up the howling toddler, the poor child's face was burning hot, her clothes dripping with sweat.

The first thought in Isla's mind was whether or not any of the neighbours had heard. Maybe they had given up trying to help, Isla's abrasive manner too much for them.

Their daughter was bathed and fed and sitting playing with her toys when Finn came home from work. Isla could see by his expression he was labouring under the illusion that things had turned a corner, that his wife had finally bonded with their seemingly contented daughter. It was only by chance as she watched him put away his shoes in the cupboard under the stairs that she remembered – she had forgotten to clean up the puddle of vomit left there by their daughter. Finn could smell it, his face crinkled in disgust at the rancid odour of sweat and terror that clung to the fabric of the coats hanging on the wall. She knew then that he recognised her plight; they both knew that this thing would go on and on and on. No end in sight. Her husband had nothing and nobody, only God to keep him going, his belief in the good in everyone and everything the thing he clung to. At some level, Isla knew that this was only going to end one way. It was just a matter of when.

18

BLAKE

27 June

Dear Blake,

I honestly and truly don't know where to begin, how to say what it is I want to say without sounding distressed or nonplussed or downright furious. Before you are tempted to screw up this letter or tear it into a thousand pieces, please read on. I am not angry with you but at myself for being so blind and lacking in compassion back in the day. I hurt you and was oblivious to it. Shame was the overriding emotion I felt as I read your letter. I only wish I had felt that same level of shame when I did what I did all those years ago.

I'd like to take a few seconds to explain what happened and perhaps even defend my actions even though I know what I did is indefensible. Firstly, I was young and naïve, driven by emotions and hormones that were whistling through my young body at an alarmingly rapid pace. Also, there were two of us in that scenario. I didn't set out to seduce Nigel. He too played a part in what took place. As much as you would like to think I lured him in and he was manipulated by my what you refer to as wily ways and charm, that simply wasn't the case at all. If anything, he pursued me after our first meeting at the park. I was your friend and did what I could to ignore his requests for a clandestine date, but he was persistent. As you know, Nigel had his own wily charm and spellbinding ways to ensure he got what he wanted. And whether you like it or not, he wanted me. I should have been stronger, told him to go away, leave me alone, but I was weak. I was also deeply attracted to him, drawn in by his looks and sultry voice and his emerald eyes. Neither of us was immune to those eyes, were we? But I should have known better and ignored his calls. He was your boyfriend and what Nigel and I did was wrong. Completely unforgiveable.

I'm glad we're now speaking about it. Keeping something that earth shattering under wraps is too difficult a topic to ignore. If we are to speak without fear of retribution and pick up the pieces of our friendship, then all our troubles need to be brought out into the open. No more secrets or lies.

I'm sorry for that time in our lives and for what happened, but when you look at it logically, everything turned out for the best. Things happen for a reason, and had I not met Nigel, then our lives would have been very different indeed. I realise that not everything was positive, but for a while our lives ticked along quite nicely, didn't they? No swerves or deviations. No bumps in the road. They came later, but let's not look that far ahead. One thing at a time.

After Nigel and I became an item, which I know was devastating for you, I became engrossed in my new relationship, and I should have given more thought to your welfare. I didn't and for that I am truly sorry. More than you will ever know.

Even amidst your sorrow, you surprised us all with what happened next. Despite proclaiming how upset you were over the break-up, you showed up on my doorstep with a new partner.

'Hi,' you said blithely, as if nothing had taken place between us. 'Thought I would call round and introduce you to Melvyn.'

Before I could say anything in return, you strode past me into the house with Melvyn in tow behind you, his eyes lowered, his body language submissive.

I guess it was your way of showing me that you were over Nigel, that you had moved on and carved out a new life for yourself. I was both relieved and happy. Happy that you had found a new soulmate and relieved you were no longer angry at me. I never liked it when you displayed animosity towards me. If I'm being truthful, it frightened me, your edgy ways and sharp glances making me scared and uncomfortable. Your previous outbursts were never far from my mind so I always made an effort to tread carefully in your presence.

It was when you began to see traces of Nigel in the house that your mood changed. I had qualified as a teacher at that point and was working at a school in North Yorkshire. Now financially stable, I had just bought a new house in Norton. It wasn't anything too salubrious; small but cosy, so Nigel's belongings were difficult to hide and easy for you to spot.

'Where is he?'

I assumed ignorance, doing what I could to avert my eyes from your piercing gaze. We hadn't even made formal introductions at that point.

'Sorry, where's who?'

My line of questioning was an insult to your intelligence, I can see that now, but I swear to you I was only trying to avoid any confrontation. Melvyn too felt your growing rage. I could see it by his stance, the way he kept his eyes averted from mine. The timbre and shakiness in his voice when he complimented me on my recently refurbished living room. He was attempting to defuse the situation with idle chatter and compliments. You were a ticking timebomb, Blake, and I had no idea how to avoid the inevitable explosion.

'Fucking Nigel. You know fine well who I'm referring to! How many live-in partners do you have these days, Lucy?'

I could see Melvyn shrink into himself, his shoulders hunched, spine arched as if trying to deflect a possible onslaught. I wondered, then, how often he felt the heat of your wrath, how often he was subjected to your flare-ups for the simplest of transgressions.

I should have been gentler. Seeing Melvyn's crumpled frame, I should have trod a little easier. So if I sounded brusque in my reply, then I apologise. I was aiming for contrite, but clearly that wasn't how you interpreted it.

'Nigel is at work. Why do you ask? And for the record, only one partner, Blake. I don't have time to conduct an affair. It's not my style.'

Your reaction was immediate and explosive. I could practically feel the walls of my house shake when you stood close to me and roared in my face.

'You little bitch! Do not try to belittle or humiliate me. Haven't you done enough fucking damage already?'

It was Melvyn who calmed things down, his soothing voice whispering in your ear, the way he pulled you close and pressed his face to yours that brought you back to a place of calm and peaceability. Had he not been there, I dread to think what could have happened next. I do recall thinking that your therapy sessions had expired and the remnants of any strate-

gies given to you had clearly evaporated into the ether. Either that or you chose to dismiss them and let your inner rage take over. Because anger is something we all experience, it's just that some of us make the explicit decision to not act on it. I recall you once saying that true rage is like a furnace, the flames impossible to control. I don't buy into that theory. The other side of that argument is that when riled, you are totally out of control. Is that really the case, Blake? That you cannot control your own behaviours and responses to certain situations? You may prove me wrong with a valid theory but I don't believe you aren't unable to control your own impulses or anger. I believe you choose to act on them because it's easier than making a concerted effort to regulate your own actions and behaviour. Any fool can break another person's confidence by screaming obscenities in their face and insulting them. But it takes a lot of thought and compassion and effort to build people up, make them feel wanted and needed and loved. If at any time I was remiss in my duties as a friend (and it did happen) you were always quick to point it out, but can you ever recall a time when I hurled obscenities at you or made you feel frightened because my temper flared up to such a point that you felt scared for your safety? I don't think you can, because if ever I was upset or angry, I chose to keep my emotions hidden. Having it done to me by somebody who claimed to be my friend made me realise how it feels to be on the receiving end and so I would never in a million years subject another living soul to such terror and degradation.

But you did, and because I had upset you with my actions, I chose to accept it as a form of punishment, but I want to take this opportunity to let you know how much it hurt. How deeply you wounded me. Your particular skill was sticking in that metaphorical knife and twisting it until it hit bone.

Anyway, after things calmed down, I assured you that Nigel hadn't moved in with me and still had his own much grander place.

'Why would he want to live in my tiny little house when he has a three-bedroomed new build and a huge open plan kitchen?' I had said, my head tipped to one side in faux sympathy as you held back a flood of tears.

Sometimes the unspoken says more than a thousand words ever could. I omitted to tell you that day that we were recently engaged and were planning to marry the following month, that I was moving in with Nigel and selling my house.

But then, you already knew, didn't you? Otherwise how did you manage to find the wedding venue and turn up unannounced and uninvited, screaming at us like a howling banshee as we exchanged rings on what should have been the happiest day of our lives? That scenario is something that will never leave me. Ever.

I look forward to reading your version of events, Blake. To discover why you ruined what should have been the most glorious day of mine and Nigel's life.

Lucy

Her reply sits in my lap, crumpled and sodden after all the tears I've shed. Part of me wishes I'd never started this whole chain of events. And yet another part of me knows that it needed to be done. A clearing of the air is long overdue. So much has been said, so many secrets and shadows plucked out of obscurity and studied at length, that it has been a physically painful experience and one I would not like to repeat.

Summer has finally arrived. It has been a long cold spring and I'm looking forward to tending my garden, feeling the warmth of the sun on my back and the soil beneath my nails.

Those things are real. And I need real now more than ever. I am almost done with the past; mine and Lucy's. The future is what counts. And I'm ready to embrace it whatever it may bring.

I pluck a new fresh piece of paper from my writing box and begin to write.

19

BLAKE

12 July

Dear Lucy,

Oh dear God. How did we get to this? When I wrote the first letter, I never intended to let things sink this low. How have we allowed ourselves to become so entangled and distressed by past events that we are powerless to change?

Please let me explain about the wedding and then we can start again. I had heard through a friend of a friend that you were planning a small ceremony. Was that because you were still slightly embarrassed by how you and Nigel met? Was your informal wedding gathering a way of protecting me from further humiliation and hurt? I hope that was the case but you have to realise that planning a secret ceremony made things worse, Lucy. So much worse. You need to know that at this juncture. To discover through the grapevine that my childhood pal, my longtime best friend, was getting married was a punch to the gut. People you had known for only a short period of time were invited and I wasn't. Me, your greatest friend, left out in the cold on one of the most important days of your life. If you were trying to protect me, to shield me from seeing you both together, it didn't work. I shed so many tears in the lead-up to that day, lying in bed each morning wondering what I'd done wrong. Trying to work out how things had turned so sour so quickly. Nigel was my boyfriend and soon he was to be your husband. I felt as if my life was spinning wildly out of control, everything and everyone I cared about deserting me when I needed them the most.

Perhaps if you had found a venue in another country or even at the other end of the country, that might have been enough to put me off turning up, but you didn't. You chose a small recently refurbished venue in Great Broughton in North Yorkshire, just a short distance from where we both lived. That's the thing, Lucy; you made it all too easy for me. I never was a good traveller and driving to London or taking a train to Scotland or a plane to a remote island in the Mediterranean would have stopped me doing what I did. But you booked a venue within reach of my home and I made the decision to turn up, invitation or no invitation. I couldn't not be there to see my best friend marry my ex-boyfriend, could I? It was like visiting a funeral home to say goodbye to the recently deceased. I had to make sure it was the end. I had to see and hear it for myself, to witness the pair of you place those rings on one another's fingers. To have and to hold. In sickness and in health. Till death do us part.

I had to witness you both say those words to cement the idea in my mind that you were actually a married couple. To cement the idea in my mind that Nigel was never coming back to me. He drifted out of my life as rapidly and abruptly as he appeared.

You need to know that nobody stopped me, Lucy. I was able to slip into your wedding venue undetected. No large, burly people at the door enquiring who I was or why I was there. I didn't mean to ruin your day. I tried to keep my emotions in check. You stated that people who allow their temper to get the better of them are out of control, but that's not true. We are simply more sensitive than others, less able to switch off our feelings. I put it to you that people who keep their anger under wraps are like robots, living their lives devoid of sympathy and empathy, their sentiments and feelings pared back to the point where they feel nothing at all. Anger and happiness are what make us human, make us feel alive. Without them we are half-dead. Our time on Earth is brief. We should embrace every moment and make our feelings known, otherwise what is the point of being here?

Nigel looked so handsome in his navy suit, his eyes sparkling with delight every time he looked your way. That was how he used to look at me, but suddenly it was all reserved for you. I was dead to him. A nobody.

Your dress was beautiful and so were you, Lucy. Your full-length ivory gown looked like it had been made specially for you, hugging your slim hips and waist, the sweetheart neckline dotted with tiny pearls that shone like diamonds beneath the subdued lighting.

Was I jealous? Of course I was. I'm only human. I still can't decide if it was the way Nigel gazed into your eyes and held your hand as if you were the most precious object in the world that did it, or if it was the fact I would never look as glamorous or as beautiful as you did that day, but either way, my envy and sadness were an irrepressible force, a raging torrent of anger and pent-up frustration that was as humiliating as it was vulgar and demeaning.

I was wrong to scream at you both, to tell the guests that you had stolen Nigel from me as you stood in the makeshift aisle of the large, elaborately decorated room. Before arriving, I had drunk a few glasses of wine to steady my nerves, but that is still no excuse. What I did was unforgiveable, screaming that you were deceitful and conniving. My shouts were drowned out by the sound of music playing through the sound system. Somebody was wise enough to turn up the volume but I wasn't about to be defeated, my voice cutting through the dulcet tones of the Lesley Garrett piece of music that was playing, our voices clashing in a discordant thunderous roar.

Fingers dug into my upper arms, two well-dressed men and a female in a wide-brimmed wedding hat doing what they could to lead me away whilst trying to placate and reason with me. I was beyond that. Alcohol had dulled my reasoning skills and made me resistant to the glares of others. Seeing you and Nigel together had been seared into my brain and I was in complete meltdown.

Before I could resist, I found myself stumbling about on the gravel outside, the way back inside firmly bolted shut after my undignified expulsion. My moment of madness was over. I was alone again. Believe me when I say, I considered driving to Huntcliff at Saltburn, leaning over the edge and letting the wind take me to the bottom, the angry waves sweeping me out to sea. I visualised my body hitting the rocks below with a shuddering crash. But I didn't do it. Because deep down, I'm a coward. Instead, I called for a taxi and went home, the four walls of my house a solid protection from the blows of the outside world. There I sat for the rest of the day, watching as daytime bled into evening, then continuing to sit as nighttime descended like a heavy shroud, plunging me into darkness. By the time I had enough energy to stand, I was shivering and dizzy, the floor rotating beneath my feet. The effects of the alcohol had receded, leaving me thirsty and battling a headache. It felt like a vice was being tightened around my skull. Alcohol never did suit me. I drank rarely so the hangover that ripped through my body was ferocious, every nerve ending ablaze, every muscle and sinew throbbing and heavy as lead.

I slept fitfully that night, memories of my behaviour bursting into my brain every time I felt myself slipping into a welcome slumber. I didn't need punishments or admonishments from anybody else for what I did that day. How I ruined your wedding. I was and still am harder on myself than anybody else could ever be, my conscience constantly reminding me of what I did.

A blanket of dappled sunlight lay across my bed when I awoke the following morning. Anybody watching would have thought it like a scene from a fairytale – a young woman arising from a freshly made bed, rays of warmth streaming in through the blinds. But often a snapshot of somebody's life can be highly deceiving. I was falling apart, my mind a snarled tangle of dim, depressing thoughts, my guilt a weighty burdensome thing that I simply couldn't shake. I was slowly falling into a well of despair and there wasn't anybody around to catch me. Apologising to you would have been insulting. I knew you wouldn't ever want to see me again. I was alone, my life unravelling, everything around me falling apart. That's when I knew for certain that I was toxic. Everything and everyone I came into contact with rotted and quickly turned rancid. I didn't have your touch, your ability to glide into people's lives and sprinkle happiness around like confetti.

For the next few days I lay in bed, drinking water and nibbling on dry biscuits, the stink of stale unwashed bedsheets and the odour of my own grimy body filling the room, until eventually I mustered up enough energy to clamber out of bed and take a shower. Every time I thought about what I did, sickness welled up in me, the sharp, serrated lump in my throat making it hard for me to breathe.

I knew that I needed to pull myself round, get back to normal. I had a job to go to, bills to pay. A life to live, although that last part was debatable. My life was empty, a vacuum with nothing and nobody in it that counted. I had lost you and had never bothered trying make friends with anybody else. You were all I had ever needed and suddenly you were gone. The void of your absence was like a huge crater in the very core of me. That was when I began to write about our friendship and everything we had experienced. I had always had a yearning to become an author and found that writing everything down put some brightness back into my life. Each sentence and paragraph I wrote was like having a boulder lifted off my shoulders. Suddenly I was able to function again. Bit by bit I began to feel human.

After work each evening I would write as if my life depended on it. Which in a way, it did. Without it I felt empty, no depth to my days. Seeing those words written down gave me a surge of strength I didn't know I possessed. It gave me the courage to forgive myself for my actions and to forgive you for marrying Nigel.

Melvyn was still in my life, a stabilising force when things became shaky, but he wasn't the sort of man that made me weak-kneed. Not the sort of man I wanted to spend the rest of my life with. That sort of man was gone. He was married to you. Better to have loved and lost than never to have loved at all is utter bullshit. I ached every day without Nigel. But I knew that I had to move on. I couldn't spend the rest of my life wallowing in my own misery so I wrote and wrote and wrote, each word a release. Each word putting a greater distance between you, me and Nigel. The novel didn't take long to write, most of it done in small sections. All it required was an ending; that perfect denouement that would leave readers feeling satisfied and complete. Do you remember the title, Lucy? I called it Strange Little Girl, *something that was befitting of my childhood; a full recount about the way I thought and how I conducted myself. A girl off kilter. An unstable woman.*

Anyway, I fear I've gone on for too long. Dug too deep into my feelings and delved too far into the past. I have undoubtedly made you uncomfortable. That isn't my intention, but you did instruct me to continue telling our story and so I have done just that.

It's been exhausting offloading like this and I am so, so tired. Outside, the world continues with its business while I sit and stare out of the window, wondering what the future holds for me and others like me. I think you know now what type of person I am. We both know, and have always known.

Getting back to nature may help lift my mood. It's been a sombre day and I need to feel the dirt under my nails, to dig and weed and be surrounded by living things that help remind me of how fortunate I am to still be here, telling my story. Reaching out to somebody who has always been there for me. Until you weren't. Until you did a terrible thing by taking Nigel from me and I did a terrible thing by letting the world know about it in a publicly staged outcry.

Of course it didn't end there. I wish it had. How I wish our story had ended that day and we had lived our lives sedately. But as was always the case, life had other plans for us.

And so did I.

Please write back. I need to hear what happened next and I would rather hear it from you. I'm too tired to say anything else, too tired to dig into those darkest of days. For the first time in my life, I am all out of words.

Love, Blake.

20

BEFORE

The two girls became friends. Isla wasn't sure if that was a positive thing or if the relationship would force her even closer to Anna and Trevor, the pair of them turning up on her doorstep unannounced, prying in her business and offering help. Interference from anybody other than Martha was something she could do without. All other people ever did was clutter up her life. Question her motives. Assess her parenting methods.

Isla no longer hated her own child. But neither did she like her. In Isla's opinion, love was an ethereal thing, something people spoke of but rarely displayed. Love was invisible and impossible to pin down; like catching the wind or trying to trap a butterfly. It was better to let it roam free, allow it to find its own path through life.

Finn working away from home so often was either a blessing or a curse depending on how the child behaved and conducted herself. There were days when she and her daughter co-existed without too much anger or trauma, and then there were days when living with her only child was like trying to contain and calm a raging tornado, the intensity of her fury too much for Isla to manage. And those became more frequent the older she got.

The kid loved to roam, the call of the nearby hills or the woods next to Ormesby Hall beckoning her. The house was a much calmer place when her daughter wasn't in it, that much Isla did know. A whirlwind landed every afternoon when she arrived home from school. Isla often dreaded that post-lunchtime lag that preceded her daughter's appearance as she flew into the house all rage and bluster, yapping repeatedly about the latest drama with her friend, how another fallout was lurking on the horizon. The cracks had already begun to appear in that particular relationship, her daughter too stubborn and too blind to the needs of others to see how she was slowly pushing everyone away. Isla could have helped, should have helped, stepping in and comforting her only child, but her own needs were too pressing, her own demons draining her of all energy, leaving her too exhausted to deal with any of her daughter's problems.

Finn's increasingly prolonged absences due either to work or church commitments exacerbated their rapidly deteriorating mother–daughter connection. A connection that was already as fragile as spun sugar. And so Isla meted out her own ways of keeping her daughter in line. She had grown too big for locking in cupboards. Removing her from the house was often the only way Isla could think of to keep her in line. Because she knew that violence would beget violence and her daughter now had the propensity to hit back. When she was younger, Isla had taken the belt to the girl or used a wooden spoon, hitting her where it wouldn't show, but those days were over. The girl was too big for such punishments now. Distance was the answer. Taking her in the car after one of her daughter's misdemeanours and dropping her off somewhere safe yet remote enough to give Isla the time and the space to breathe was the only weapon she had. And she used it regularly. Only once was the girl brought back by the police and it was all too easy to spin a yarn that they believed without question. Isla was the victim. She had a reckless, badly behaved daughter, a husband who was hardly ever home to help. But even Isla knew that she could only push her luck so far. Something had to give.

There was that one time in Whitby when both families hoped for a strengthening of the girls' relationship. That didn't happen. What did happen was dangerous and traumatic and pushed the two of them even farther apart.

It was a relief when the girl began searching for a career after leaving school. A brief suggestion of joining the army as admin or personnel support lit up Isla's hopes. They visited the local recruitment centre, Isla doing what she could to encourage the girl, knowing she would be required to live away from home. Be somebody else's problem. But the thought of moving so far away from all she knew scared her usually brash daughter and the idea evaporated, leaving Isla feeling flattened and desperate.

And so she was forced to watch as her only child staggered from one job to another, one relationship to another, her life descending into a vortex of foolishness and borderline madness. A young woman alone in the world. All those years ago when Isla had silently chided herself for doubting her own child's capacity for love and compassion and the ability to interact peacefully with her peers, all the nights she was unable to sleep, fear and shame consuming her for thinking such thoughts, and she had been proven right. The only problem that continually plagued Isla was whether her child had been born that way or whether Isla's own behaviour towards the girl, and her obvious indifference and lack of love, had caused it. Had her coldness resulted in a female who appeared to care about nobody but herself? Were such occurrences possible? The answer to such questions eluded her. The one thing she did know was that one day in the not-too-distant future, her daughter's behaviour and lies would be her downfall. It was all just a matter of time.

21

BLAKE

30 August

Dear Blake,

I'm not sure I can keep this up for much longer. At some point the truth is going to come out. These letters are beginning to depress me, the thought of penning a reply draining me of what little energy I have. You have probably noticed the length of time it has taken me to write back. Almost two months. It's not as if we have said all there is to say, it's just that you and I already know how this is going to end and it won't be pleasant. So I suppose I had best just get on with it and see this thing through.

Do you still see a therapist, Blake? I believe you probably do, and I also believe that writing these letters is part of your therapy. A way of dipping your toe into the deep and murky waters of your past and viewing your life as an outsider. I hope it has been beneficial. I hope it has helped you heal. For me, it has been a painful process, so I am writing to let you know that this will be my final correspondence. I'm all out of words and ideas. I will leave it up to you to speak about our final encounter. The thing that drove a stake through the heart of our friendship. I use the word friendship loosely and once you really delve into your psyche, and I mean really, really explore the myriad tunnels and passageways in your mind that hide those secrets, you will understand why. We're getting closer to the truth of the matter now, Blake. Closer, I think, than you realise, and closer, I suspect, than you would like to be. Are you feeling uncomfortable yet, Blake? Does the thought of reading this letter make you feel overly anxious about what is soon to be revealed? It should. That is the whole damn point of this exercise, is it not? To examine old fractures and wounds, see how deep they are, to probe for festering infections before administering the necessary medicine and attempting one final repair?

You and Melvyn were an item for quite some time and your life mirrored mine. Although you didn't marry, like me, you also fell pregnant, your ballooning body making you edgy and out of sorts, although how anybody could tell the difference between your hormonal imbalance and your usual behaviour is anybody's guess. You felt nauseous and off kilter. And yet you wanted the baby so badly. You loved it before it was born, when it was no more than a thumbnail-sized foetus growing inside of you. It was obvious by the way you held yourself, how you would place your hand across your swollen abdomen, splayed fingers stroking and caressing the precious cargo nestled safely inside you.

I gave birth later that year after you, my labour relatively easy. If you can call ten hours of excruciating pain that felt as if a scalding branding iron was being inserted into my cervix and fourteen stitches easy, that is. Still, compared to some of the horror stories I had heard, everything went as smoothly as could be expected. No distressed baby, no erratic heartbeat.

No emergency Caesarean or subsequent trauma. Nothing compared to what you endured. I can hear you now saying how typical it is that even in childbirth, everything came easily to me. We both know by now that it simply is not the case, but the idea that life has been straightforward and effortless for me is now so deeply embedded in your brain, it has become a part of you, like the colour of your eyes or the tone of your skin. And it was that one ridiculous naïve notion that led to the next catastrophe.

Think about how we are both now forced to spend our days, living in near isolation. The hours stretch out ahead of us, our lives mundane and restricted. We rarely spend time outdoors, our faces tipped up towards the warmth of the sun. We rarely do anything at all. And that is all because of you.

At the beginning of our correspondence, you hinted that I was the one to blame for our current predicament and I went along with that idea to placate you, but is it really true? Think back to our early years, how we lived our lives. Examine these letters closely, Blake, and try to read between the lines, to think about what has been omitted. Words unsaid say more than a thousand trite phrases ever could.

I'm going to finish now before I say something that cannot be taken back. The rest of the story I will leave up to you to complete. Please try to be truthful in your account of what took place next. Honesty is painful but pertinent. It is an important requirement to make sure you are able to continue with the next part of your life and I with mine. We both deserve dignity and a modicum of solace in our latter years.

I sincerely hope you find peace in your life, Blake, as I have in mine.

Take care.

Love, Lucy

22

BLAKE

15 September

Please Lucy,

This cannot be the end. You have to write back. I'm not ready for this. I'm not prepared for the silence and I am definitely not able to stomach being alone again. I need you in my life. I need to know that you are here, still around. Still nearby. Still my closest friend. My only friend.

I know I've not been a model individual, far from it, but I'm loyal and compassionate. I have done what I can to re-establish our connection. That has to count for something, surely? I'm nothing if not tenacious, but then you already know about that side of my character. Perhaps it's my steely resolve when approaching issues that has led me into trouble in the past. I can change. We all have it in us to change. I truly believe that. I will do whatever it takes, be whoever you want me to be, to keep you writing back to me. A life without you in it is a half-life at best. I'm not about to say or do anything stupid or tell you that I cannot possibly go on living if you don't reply, but I am desperate to hear from you. To know that you forgive me. For everything.

It hasn't been easy, writing these letters, but we've got this far. We have done something of which we should be proud. Why bring it all to a juddering halt? Was it something I said or did? Or is it because we have reached a natural conclusion and our friendship has run its course? It doesn't feel natural to me, but then none of it ever has. All my life I have had to act differently in order to be noticed. To be as good as you. Never as confident or as pretty, never quite enough to keep you by my side. I have had to work hard to keep in line with your effortless ways and elegance, always having to be content with being pulled along in the slipstream of your sparkling presence. And now we are at an end. It's all over. No more you.

No more us.

I hoped to make it to the end of the year with our correspondence still flowing but here we are, only eight or nine months in and it is all over. I suppose I am now going to have to continue my journey into our past without you. I will tread gently in our old footsteps to bring this story to an end. Two people but only one shadow. The story I wrote originally, the one that definitely wasn't lucrative and didn't get a publishing deal, had no end. That was all a lie that I told myself, and you believed it too, didn't you? I was hoping you could help me with the final few chapters of my story but sadly it isn't to be. I won't be completing it unaided, however. I do have somebody in my life who can assist me with what needs to come next. I'm not completely alone. Desperately lonely, but never alone. I'm sure you understand that sentiment and possibly even feel the same way given your circumstances.

I want to thank you for helping me to get to this point. Our lives have been condensed into a few short letters but we both know that we were way more than that. Me not so much, but you were everything, Lucy. My reason for getting up each day.

My reason for living.

At some point in the future I would love to pay you a visit. I realise my presence may be unwelcome but to be by your side just one more time could help stitch the broken, tattered parts of me back together again. But there are things that need to be said first, apologies to be given. Secrets to be unveiled. Lies to be unpicked.

I'm going to say goodbye now. I wish you would get to see this letter, to comprehend the heartfelt emotions behind it. But you won't. And I also hope you can forgive me for never being enough for you. For years and years, I trailed behind you, lurking in your shadow, clutching on to every scrap of attention that came my way. It must have been wearing, dear Lucy, like having a meddlesome puppy that eventually grew and grew into something monstrous. Something uncontrollable that simply wouldn't stop. So I will go now, leave you in peace.

I wish you all the love in the world, Lucy, and hope that you are able to spend the remainder of your days knowing you are cherished and cared for.

Take care, my dear friend.

Love, Blake

PART II

23

Winter has crept in, stretching its icy claws across the landscape, frosting hedgerows and painting the nearby fields in fine white brush strokes. Bare trees stand proud and tall, branches snarled and angry looking. The change of season quietly slid in through the back door as if to remind me of how many months have passed since my final letter to Lucy. Autumn passed in a blur, the russet leaves and whistling wind so subtle I barely noticed its arrival and ensuing departure. I usually savour the seasons, always appreciative of their distinct contrasts, but these past few months have been different. The second half of this year has left me feeling dejected and depressed.

I would like to say it has been therapeutic, liberating even, writing those letters, which in a way it has, but it has also been difficult. Nothing good worth having ever comes easily. Scouring through my past has been like picking at a scab, watching and waiting until it is almost healed before scratching and rubbing at it over and over until it bleeds, the pain both terrible and exquisite in equal measure. I'm not a tortured soul. That's far too dramatic an explanation. I am many things – unbalanced, selfish, impulsive and perhaps even nefarious, but I am definitely not tortured. That word suggests a life of unfairness and paints me as a victim. And I am not that either. What I am is a liar who is still refusing to face up to her past. I have been told it often enough and am doing what I can to rectify that problem. But it's not easy.

My hands are pressed against the large picture window, my face resting against the cool surface of the glass, when Arthur walks in, the sound of his footsteps pulling me out of my reverie. I do a lot of that lately, allowing my mind to wander, dipping in and out of my surroundings before retreating into my own world. It's quiet there, the raging hurricane that has battered my brain for as long as I can remember gradually abating. I doubt it will ever disappear. It's part of who I am, but is less ferocious these days. A little less frenetic. More of a powerful breeze than a full-blown storm.

'Sorry I'm late. I got a little tied up with another patient.'

Slowly, as if in cinematic vision, I turn to face him, our eyes locking. In a second he will glance away, lower himself into his seat and pick up his pen. I know his routine off by heart, his little idiosyncrasies as familiar to me as my own features. Perhaps he thinks the same of me, recognising my quirks and mannerisms from afar. Or maybe not. He has many patients under his care whereas I have only one doctor. Difficult to observe the habits that distinguish one patient from another when you're as busy as Arthur. And in a place like this, he is very busy indeed.

'Take a seat.'

He leans forward, pen already clutched firmly between his thumb and index finger. I noticed a long time ago that like me, he is left-handed. I am perpetually on the look-out for like-minded people, folk whose mannerisms bear a strong similarity to my own. It makes me feel less isolated. Less clumsy and ungainly.

I sit in the faux-leather chair and lean back, my neck pressed against the headrest. I cross my feet and let out a deep sigh before turning to stare out of the window. In my peripheral vision I see Arthur, his gaze fixed on my every movement, his pupils boring a hole in me. This is our little routine, a game we play in the lead-up to him delving inside my head and sifting through the darkest corners of my brain, attempting to prise open those dusty grime-covered chests that contain all my secrets. For years they have lain there, cobwebbed and undiscovered. But I think it's time to find the key and lift the lid, to expose the contents, hold them up to the light and see them for what they really are. It is now time to hold a magnifying glass to my sins.

'So how are things?'

Such an open-ended question. Always the same. I used to answer with 'fine' but soon realised that Arthur had other ways of getting me to talk. And I'm glad he did. So I have decided that I no longer want to play that game. The game of two people dancing around each other, doing what they can to avoid the obvious. I want to speak openly to Arthur, my therapist. The only person I truly trust.

'Okay,' I say quietly. 'And not okay.'

He doesn't ask me to explain, sitting patiently instead, waiting for me to elaborate. The room is silent save for the clicking of his pen that is clutched between his thumb and forefinger. The shrill snapping sound echoes in my ears and crashes in my brain.

When I don't speak, he pushes it a little further, his gravelly intonation forcing me to sit up in my seat and push back my shoulders. His questioning technique is perfectly honed from years of practice. As fond as I am of Arthur, I need to remember that he isn't my friend. I can speak without fear of rancour but am always aware that every word I utter is being assessed, my body language scrutinised. Everything I say and do written down and stored for our next session.

'Are you still writing to your friend on a regular basis?' His eyes travel to the window, as if he is trying to see what I am seeing, an invisible image that will help connect us, help him to see inside my befuddled brain. He's better off living in ignorance. It's a shadowy, dimly lit space that is littered with half-truths and secrets. The veracity of what I tell him is in doubt. That's because I am still not completely ready to show my hand. My trust in Arthur only stretches so far. I learned a long time ago that we come into this world alone and leave it the same way. We are all masters of our own destiny and at this moment in time, I am still unsure of my future and need to protect myself. I want to talk honestly, but still need a little more time.

I nod but there is no need for affirmation. Arthur already knows the answer to the question. After all, it was his idea for me to strike up the correspondence with Lucy. All of it was his doing, not mine.

My mouth twitches; a bubble of laughter rises up my throat. I swallow it down. Arthur always speaks of my friendship with Lucy as if it were a precious, ancient object, something to be revered. To be worshipped and valued like a powerful deity. Every session, we hold it up to the light to study it, its many myriad fissures a telling sign that our past is chequered. For months we have observed those fissures, monitoring them as they grow into an atlas of ugly, irreversible cracks that once opened, can never be closed, the air we breathe seeping into them and damaging them beyond repair.

'The last letter you wrote was the middle of September. Has there been a reply?'

Again, he already knows the answer to that question but asks anyway. The landscape beyond his office is a swathe of white, winter's grip tightening with each passing day. It's been many months since my last letter. It feels like years.

I shake my head and fight back tears, his words a sudden reminder of the passing of time.

'I ruined her wedding day.'

Arthur nods, unfazed by my admission, as if turning up to somebody's marriage ceremony and screaming obscenities at them is an everyday occurrence.

'Why do you think she hasn't written back?' He clears his throat and fixes his gaze on mine. 'Do you think there is a specific reason why the correspondence has ground to a halt?'

I pull at my shirt, trying to loosen my collar. Suddenly this room is too hot, the radiator next to me too powerful. I want nothing more than to leave his office and run out into the rolling countryside, to lie on the freezing ground and stare up at the azure sky. I can almost feel the crisp air as it frosts my skin, biting deep into my bones and chilling me to my core. I could tell him of all the lies I have told, how Nigel was never my boyfriend. How I wished he was mine and therefore made up an imaginary story in my head, a fabrication that allowed me to enter their wedding venue and try to stop them getting wed, but I don't. Lucy and Nigel met through mutual friends. Their mutual friends, not mine. I had no friends and never have. I bumped into them in the local park. We spoke, Lucy her usual effervescent self, Nigel polite and devilishly handsome. I couldn't tear my eyes away from him. Yet again, Lucy had everything I had ever wanted. And so I dreamt up a life where he belonged to me, painting myself as the victim when he and Lucy forged a relationship. Always the victim, never the victor.

'My story isn't finished yet. I have so much more to say.' My throat is thick with unshed tears.

I rotate my shoulders, trying to unhitch them. My tongue is glued to the roof of my mouth. In just a few minutes this session has turned sour, the direction it has taken making me hot and uncomfortable. Arthur knows how to probe deeply without saying very much at all. His light touch approach always leaves me feeling grimy, my sins oozing out through my pores and coating my flesh, the filthy residue apparent for all to see.

'How is your book coming on?'

Humiliation grips me. My book. The one that will never see the light of day. The story of my life.

'It's not finished. It needs an ending.'

'And is that ending incomplete because Lucy hasn't replied to your last letter?'

I shake my head then nod, the complexity of my situation something that always has the power to overwhelm me.

'You know, you can still tell the rest of your story. You don't need to write another letter to Lucy to complete your tale.' He smiles and widens his eyes slightly, his expressions and body language, as always, nuanced and understated. Arthur is as big of an enigma as me. Perhaps his secrets are as monumental and as unwieldy as mine. Although I doubt it. Arthur is a professional, whereas I am... More tears threaten to fall. I swallow hard and rub at my face with crepe-like hands. Suddenly I'm not sure what I am any more. A middle-aged woman who has lost her way? A lonely female with no clear path in life? There are days when I feel imbued with positivity at what the future might hold and then other days, I get out of bed feeling weighed down, as if I am a hundred years old, too tired and too damn confused to do anything except sit and stare out of the window and breathe.

'Why don't you continue to write down the rest of what you have to say and we can speak about it at our next session?'

Arthur is considerate enough to not glance at his watch or

allow his gaze to travel up to the wall clock that ticks away behind me, its movement a solid and silent reminder that my time in this session will soon be over, my allotted slot a brief portion of time set aside to study my beleaguered existence. It is also a sharp reminder that my continuance on Earth is a life half-lived. I spend my days beneath the radar to avoid examination and scrutiny but my misdeeds are about to catch me up and soon everyone will discover the real me. The defective immoral me that I have spent years trying to suppress.

I stand and smooth down my clothes then run my fingers through my hair; all well-practised techniques to avoid looking at Arthur. To avoid staring into his piercing eyes and seeing his assessment of me in those pale, thoughtful features of his that show nothing but tell me plenty.

'Yes, I think that's a good idea. I still have more to say, whether Lucy wants to hear it or not.'

24

Today is a cold one, even colder than yesterday. The thin veneer of frost that coated the landscape has thickened overnight into a covering of snow that has blanketed the entire world outside my window.

I shiver and pull my cardigan tighter around my neck to stave off the chill that emanates from the glass where I rest my hand. I keep it there until my palm becomes numb, then remove it and shove it in my pocket, the pain a refreshing reminder that our bodily reactions to fluctuating temperatures are a sign we are still alive. A misty imprint of my splayed palm on the glass slowly evaporates. Like me, it too is ghost-like. Appearing rapidly and vanishing just as quickly. That's how I live my life these days, softly and quietly behind a cloak of invisibility. My neighbours think me strange but that doesn't bother me too much. All my life I have been seen as an oddball. A Strange Little Girl. Somebody who doesn't quite fit. And I'm too old now to change my ways. All I can do is temper my behaviour, tone it down with softer, quiet movements and gentle words. I'm finally learning how to present myself to others without causing offence. And not before time.

Arthur's words ring in my ears as I sit in my chair and ruminate over yesterday's session. Overcome by a sudden flurry of eagerness, I pull out my diaries and stack of letters that sit in a box beneath my bed. The end of my story will burn a hole in my gut if I don't sit down and force myself to write. If I can get it finished I will take it to show Arthur. It won't be completed in time for our next session. I still have some ground to cover. I don't want to rush it and miss out any important details. Everything needs to be correct. It's important to me that the final part is truthful and accurate. If I am to be judged, then a clean version of events is necessary. I'm not going to address it to Lucy. I am going address it to myself because I am the person who is going to submit it to Arthur. And lying to others is one thing, but lying to myself is stupid and pointless. What is to be gained from such levels of self-delusion? I'm too far down the line for that. Too old and jaded for any more lies. Lies take energy and I am all out of it of late.

Already I feel better, as if a shot of adrenaline has been injected into my veins.

Outside, the snow begins to fall once again, initially a small flurry which soon turns into a white whirling vortex. I shuffle my chair closer to the radiator, staring outside until the words in my head slot themselves into place, and then finally I begin to write.

13 January

Dear Me,

It feels strange writing those first two words, but I promised that I would do this, to get the final pieces of my story down on paper, so here we are, a strange woman penning a letter to herself while winter rages and howls outside my window.

Before I write anything else, I want to say that as well as being liberating and therapeutic, this whole process has also been excruciatingly painful. It's not easy looking inward, seeing one's own faults. Judging oneself and finding yourself wanting. Which is why I have been economical with the truth. Parts of my story are real, and other parts fabricated and embellished in order to protect my sanity. Being completely honest even to myself is akin to slicing open my chest and ripping out my beating heart. Holding it aloft to a watching world and asking if they forgive me for what I have done. They won't ever forgive me. How can I expect them to show leniency when I don't forgive myself? I am a harsh critic when it comes to my crimes; harsher than any judge or jury would ever be.

Nigel was never my boyfriend. He would never look at somebody like me. His affections were reserved for the elegant and the truthful. Somebody like Lucy. So I made up a story and let it run riot in my head. Lucy and Nigel were still on the periphery of my life but after the wedding day incident I was no longer in contact with either of them and could only keep an eye on their lives from a distance. To make sure that distance was as close as it could be, I rented a house near to where they lived.

We're getting to the nub of things now. I'm about to write about how desperate I'd become. How far I had fallen.

Each day after work, I would walk to the end of their road and watch them. They had a lovely house, a new car on the driveway. All the necessary outward signs of a happy family. That drove a dagger deep into my heart. They had everything I had ever wanted. I still had Melvyn, but we were growing apart. I had literally bumped into Melvyn one evening in a pub. I'd like to say our eyes met across a crowded room but that would be a huge lie. While making my way towards some work acquaintances gathered at the far end of the bar, I accidentally came into contact with him, our lives colliding when I all but fell into him. My gaze had been fixed on the group I was meeting; people that weren't friends. Outcasts like me don't have friends. We are invited to such functions begrudgingly because not inviting us would appear rude and churlish, so out of a sense of duty, I was told the time and venue and arrived late and flustered after taking two bus rides and a fifteen-minute walk to get there. Nobody had bothered to offer me a lift. In truth, I don't know why I went. Perhaps I was driven by loneliness and the humiliation of having to listen to everybody talking about the get together the following morning, crooning about what an amazing time they had all had while I would have been forced to sit at my desk, hunched over my computer, my face burning with embarrassment.

Anyway, after our accidental collision, Melvyn managed to keep hold of his beer while I apologised profusely, my own drink lying in a sticky mess at my feet. Even though it was my fault, he bought me a gin and tonic and it went from there. The earth didn't move and we didn't spend each and every moment together, but we rubbed along nicely together. Until we didn't.

It was my announcement of my pregnancy that brought our relationship to a close. I continued watching Nigel and Lucy live their perfect life, hot oil had boiling and bubbling in my gut every time I saw them, while my relationship was disintegrating. But at least I now had something to look forward to. My own child. My baby.

The subject of babies and children had never ever cropped

up in my relationship with Melvyn. We were a casual couple. Easy come, easy go. When I eventually managed to pluck up enough courage to tell him of the child growing inside of me, his face told me everything I needed to know. I would bring up the child alone. It was what I had expected. I always ended up alone in life, so was already prepared for his rejection. Anything else would have alarmed me. I'm not accustomed to closeness or comfort or any of the things that other people take for granted. I'm not asking for pity or sympathy. It is simply a fact of life. My life, that is.

The next part of my story is the most painful segment so I am going to pause. I will pick up on this thread tomorrow when I'm rested, my mind less troubled. And then perhaps you will see why I did what I did. Together, we will unpick the rest of my sorry little tale. We will attempt to tease out the truth and try to sort the fact from the fiction. But for now I am going to take a step back and will return tomorrow with a clear head which is when we will edge closer to what really happened, and why.

Love, Blake

25

Last night I dreamt about my mother. The woman who never wanted me. The information in the letters about me having a wonderful upbringing was all lies, but I'm guessing you have already worked that out. Lucy was the one who had the idyllic childhood while I was left to rot under the care of a woman who never loved me, and a father who was always busy elsewhere, because constant prayers and visiting the house of God was much simpler than attempting to tackle the problems under his own roof. Is it any wonder I turned out as I did? Twisted and badly bent out of shape. It was easier for me to pretend that my upbringing was perfect, and it was definitely a lot less painful than facing the truth: that I was never wanted or loved. Being brought up in a poverty-stricken household is difficult but survivable. Being reared by a mother who doesn't love you is not. Love is everything. And so I projected my damaged past onto Lucy, who grew up surrounded by compassion and devotion while I existed in a house with a woman who didn't want me and a father who tried to intervene, but was feckless and eventually gave up. Writing about what took place was simpler and less traumatic if I pretended it happened to somebody else. That little bit of distance made the whole thing easier to bear. At some point I need to go back to the beginning, to the other discrepancies and secrets, but not just yet. Today I plan on writing my next letter; the one that will detail my suffering. My losses. Not Melvyn. He was no real loss. We were already drifting apart before I informed him of my pregnancy. His absence gave me room to think, to plan the next episode of my life. To prepare for my tiny, beautiful bundle.

My room is cold. I shift closer to the radiator, my hands trembling, my flesh like ice. I spend the next half hour trying to warm up and by the time I have thawed out, I am ready to continue with the next part of my story.

29 January

Dear Me,

Like any decent expectant parent, I did everything my own mother neglected to do. I ate healthily, stopped with all alcohol, something I rarely consumed anyway, and attended all my medical prenatal appointments. I did everything right, so why did it all go so wrong? Why does life reward certain people who breeze through each and every day without a care in the world, and punish others who work hard to succeed? My father was wrong about his precious God. He isn't all loving and caring. Where was he throughout my childhood? Where was he when my mother used to lock me in cupboards for hours at a time? Why didn't he step in when she beat me or bundled me into the car and drove me to remote places, leaving me alone in the middle of the night? I was alone then and am still alone now. That's not such a bad thing. All people ever do is let each other down, and I include myself in that description. People are unreliable and selfish. It's just how we are programmed to behave in order to survive and once we accept that fact, then everything else becomes easier to bear. It avoids disappointment and heartbreak if we expect nothing and it transpires that that is what we actually get. Lack of trust in others builds resilience and self-reliance.

The pregnancy went exactly as expected. I suffered from sickness and chronic tiredness, the likes of which I had never known, but that was simply part of the condition. I was carrying another human being inside of me. I didn't bloom throughout the pregnancy but neither did I wilt. I was a single expectant woman doing what I could to get by. Melvyn had moved away at that point and if I'm being honest, life felt easier without him hanging around. He always questioned my motives when he was there, claiming I should have left Lucy and Nigel to get on with their lives, accusing me of talking about them endlessly. Stalking them even. I suppose he was right but hearing those words spoken out loud made me feel humiliated and anxious. His accusations didn't stop me so in the end his reproaches were wasted oxygen, washing over me like liquid mercury. Being in his presence was akin to living with my mother. His expression and frosty remarks reminded me of the thundering howl of her icy countenance, the scowl of disapproval that was permanently pasted on her face. My mother treated me like an unwanted family pet; irksome and a burden to those around me. Melvyn's attitude was so similar that by the end of our relationship I began to realise that I was the common denominator. I was the problem. But it didn't matter any more because being pregnant had given me everything I had ever wanted: another person to care for. Someone who would need me and love me unconditionally.

My abdomen grew to an enormous size as I waited for my precious addition. It was all I could do to clamber out of bed each morning and dress myself, my centre of gravity weighted down by the baby huddled tightly in there. But I didn't mind. I loved my child before it was even born. I used to sleep with the picture of my scan on the bedside cabinet, waking occasionally and flicking on the lamp to stare at the grainy photograph of my unborn child. The love of my life. My reason for living.

I left work two weeks before my due date. My colleagues were kind, buying me flowers and handing over a voucher for a local shop that sold children's clothes. I think they were relieved to see the back of me for the next few months. The feeling was mutual.

I had no plans for the future, no help with childcare once my maternity leave was over, but I wasn't about to spend the next few months worrying about such trivial matters. I intended to enjoy the next chapter of my life, spending it with my beautiful baby daughter. I had been too impatient and curious to not ask about the gender at my scan and felt my heart soar when they told me I was having a baby girl. It was my chance to right some wrongs, to be the good, loving parent that my own mother never had been.

The pain that woke me the day after leaving my job was excruciating, like having hot greased smeared over my distended abdomen. It was relentless and unbearable, bringing tears to my eyes and making it difficult for me to walk. I had read about how labour pains would begin slowly, building up to a crescendo, but that wasn't how it happened with me. As had always been the case with everything I did, my story of giving birth took a different route; a twisted, rutted path littered with holes and hidden dangers. Peril has always lurked around every bend of my journey through life and by the time I was able to dress myself and book a taxi to take me to the hospital, I could hardly breathe. I knew then that something was horribly wrong. The contractions were ripping through my body, leaving me weak-limbed and weepy with anxiety.

The cab driver was a true gent, helping me into the back seat where I writhed about in pain, doing what I could to mask my fears and tone down my screams. By the time we pulled up outside the double doors of the maternity unit, the poor man was trembling, his eyes wide with horror when he realised how close I was to giving birth.

The rest was a blur. Medics appeared seemingly out of nowhere, swooping in and taking over. I was whisked away to a stark white room where the next exciting chapter of my life rapidly turned into an ugly, grisly nightmare.

I'm going to end this letter here as I need to prepare myself mentally for the next part. Writing about it is as gruelling and exhausting as running a marathon, every written word a gargantuan effort. Each time I think about it, it's like giving birth all over again. The passing of time hasn't lessened the trauma. If anything it has heightened it, made the scar deeper and more painful. A festering wound that will never heal.

Tomorrow is when I will continue with my story. For now I need to rest, to sleep well, arrange my thoughts and sit down to write the next part of my ordeal in a better frame of mind.

Love, Blake

26

The snow has laid again overnight. Outside, a world of crisp white awaits me. Before I continue with my story, I am going to take a walk in my courtyard, feel the bristle of cold against my skin, the crunch of compacted snow and ice beneath my feet. I might even be daring and make a snow angel, lie on my back, sweep my limbs out wide and stare at the sky. Or perhaps not. My neighbours already think me odd, unhinged even but aren't we all a little unbalanced? Maybe they are right. Or maybe I'm just a sad, lonely woman who is still searching for happiness. Even after all these years, it continues to elude me. The joy that many women of my age take for granted is sadly missing from my life. And in many ways it is all my own fault.

After I've written my next letter, I will be having another session with Arthur. We've increased our time together as he thinks I'm close to understanding what is still buried deep inside of me.

The truth.

I haven't yet voiced the facts of what happened all those years ago. That's because the facts and the truth are messy and complicated and uncomfortable. Once I strip away that final layer to reach the reality of my life, I don't think there will be anything left of me. Like a skinned rabbit, all jutting bones and sinew.

I shower and dress and head outside before breakfast. It's the best time to do it, while other people are still eating and staring out of their windows, trying to summon up enough courage to brace the icy weather. My breath clouds in front of my face, the heat of it misting my skin. This is the best time of the day, when the world around me is gentle and motionless, everything and everyone still waking up. There is a hush in the air that pacifies me, reassuring me that everything is going to turn out okay. Even if it isn't, I'm soothed by the possibility of what could be. Calmed by the notion that my life may take an unexpected upturn. It's something that sends a frisson of excitement through me. I'm not so old and jaded that I have completely turned my back on humanity. There is still a spark of hope burning inside of me that things will turn around, a thread of optimism that keeps me connected to the world.

I spend the next half hour wandering around my small garden, sweeping snow off foliage and staring up at the sky wondering if another downpour is due. Then I stand and admire my small piece of heaven before heading back indoors and having breakfast – a black coffee – the only drug I have ever used or needed to help kickstart my day.

Sitting down to write, I am imbued with a sense of something I can't quite name. It isn't joy and it isn't a sense of gloom but something in between. I think perhaps it's relief that I have finally plucked up the courage to write this part; relief tinged with mild dread at what I am about to reveal. Because once the truth has been unearthed, there is no burying it again.

15 February

Dear Me,

Here I am again, delving into my past. A place I would rather not revisit. A place filled with fear and cries for help that never arrived. I have to do this thing if I am to move on with my life. And I want to move on, I really, really do. Many have told me that I am stuck in the past, mired in myriad mistakes and wickedness, but I know differently. I'm simply needy and economical with the truth, but being a liar doesn't mean I deserve what happened next. Even fraudsters and deceivers are worthy of having a tiny scrap of satisfaction in their lives. Aren't they?

I remember little about what happened after I was whisked away once I arrived at the hospital. I do recall the pain and I also remember vividly the erratic heartbeat of my baby as she became stuck inside my damaged womb. Ruptured *is the word they used. Such a brutal and uncaring way of describing the centre of someone's body. The place that held a future life. A future life that was extinguished as my baby daughter finally slipped from between my legs, bloody and silent. There was no time to grieve, no time to absorb the enormity of what had happened and what was about to occur. An anaesthetic was administered and I was plunged into a void of darkness, waking later to discover the tragic news. I had lost both my child and my uterus.*

There, I've said it. I have, for the first time, written down what happened that day. How I lost everything – my baby girl and the ability to have any more children. I was empty and broken. And empty, broken people are capable of the most dreadful of deeds.

My recovery took many months. It was a long and lonely path and I walked it alone. I'm not complaining. Some people function more efficiently when they are left to their own devices and I guess I am one of those people. I was estranged from my parents at that point; they knew nothing of my pregnancy. Judgements from them about being a single parent – a useless one at that – I could do without. My employers were fair, continuing with my maternity pay and then sick pay until I was fit to return. The only difficulty was the emptiness and solitude I felt. I had prepared for a baby and left the hospital with nothing.

That was when the demons returned with a vengeance, whispering in my ear that it was unfair what I had had to endure. I tried ignoring them but they were persistent. Even more so than usual. They nagged and hectored and harangued, waking me in the early hours, reducing me to tears. Roaring at me in the silence of the house that my life wasn't meant to be that way. That it was an erroneous experience and I needed to do something about it.

Which is exactly what I did.

Love, Blake

I'm tired. It's still morning and already I'm dreaming about going back to bed. A lack of energy is something that plagues me these days. My appointment with Arthur is later this afternoon. I need to rouse myself from this inertia so I can be receptive to his advice. His office is warm and often I find myself dozing when I sit facing him in my comfortable chair next to the radiator. Maybe that's one of his strategies, to lull patients into a state of invulnerability, make them feel completely at ease and safe, their underbelly exposed, before he delivers that killer blow and drags them out of their reverie by exposing their darkest secrets.

My thoughts return to Lucy – they always do – of how I would love to visit her at some point. Once I've gained enough courage to venture further than my own little courtyard, I plan on making that difficult journey. Speaking to her, holding her hand. Even if it's just for one last time.

'How's it going, Blake?' I turn to see Maya standing beside me. 'Everything okay?'

I smile and nod, tears unexpectedly biting at the back of my eyelids. Lovely Maya, my neighbour and friend. A kind, thoughtful woman that I continually keep at arm's length. I have no reasons for doing so. Perhaps it is simply how my brain is wired, my awkwardness and lack of social skills continuing to hinder my ability to interact. I try to move on from my past, be a different person from the one I used to be, a better version of myself, but it's as if an imprint of who I once was has attached itself to me and won't depart. I'm not unique in that respect. The past walks stealthily behind many of us, waiting for an opportune moment to strike, reminding us of the real person concealed beneath the façade of normality we wear every day.

'I'm fine, thank you, Maya. Hope you're okay?'

'Very well, thank you.' She stops walking, her shadow interlocking with mine. 'My son is visiting me later today.'

I want to smile, to tell her how wonderful it must be to be able to actually see and speak to her own child. But I can't. Bitterness catches like acid at the back of my throat. I can't remember the last time I had any visitors. My father passed away a few years ago. We began corresponding just months before his death. My mother is in a nursing home, her body bent double, her mind slowly turning to dust. I feel no compassion or sympathy for her. I feel nothing at all. When she dies, I will not be the person who organises her funeral because my mother is the person who made me what I am.

An uncaring individual. A desperate one.

Somebody who will go to any lengths to grasp at a glimmer

of love or recognition from those closest to her. Even those she barely knows or ever knew.

I shrug my shoulders at Maya and manage a half-hearted smile, envy nipping at my flesh as I turn away and head back inside to prepare for my session with Arthur; the only person who has ever had the courage to try to see inside my thoughts. I suspect that even he, as experienced and qualified as he is, is baffled by my behaviour and is longing for the day when he can dismiss me and send me on my way.

27

'I like the snow. It adds to the many reasons I have for not wanting to venture outside.' I am trying to keep the sourness and resentment out of my tone and failing miserably. It appears my propensity for being unhappy is something I am good at. Something that is carved deep into the very centre of me.

The thought of Maya's visitor looms large in my mind, heightening my sense of isolation and discontentment.

'Does the outside world frighten you?'

When I don't reply, Arthur changes his line of questioning to elicit a response from me.

'What is it about the outside world that scares you, Blake?'

I have a hundred answers at the ready but am unable to voice any of them, each one sticking in my gullet like sand until eventually I am able to respond, uttering only one word.

'People.'

He nods as if he understands my predicament. He doesn't. With his probing gaze and easy lifestyle, how can this man possibly ever begin to comprehend how I think? What I feel when I get out of bed every morning?

It is a complete oxymoron that the person who knows my secrets is a virtual stranger to me. I know nothing about Arthur. Whether he is married or single. Whether he has children or a partner or where he lives and what his hobbies and pastimes are. I don't know a damn thing whereas he knows everything about me. We have an asymmetrical relationship and suddenly none of this seems fair, the scales of power firmly tipped in his favour.

'What is it about people that scares you the most?'

This is the question I know the answer to without hesitation.

'Their indifference. The way they can switch their emotions on and off without warning.'

'Why does that scare you so much, Blake?' He is watching me with tapered eyes, waiting for a response when he already knows the answer to his question.

He wants me to spell it out, to say it out loud so my own brain computes what I have just said. I am many things – cruel, thoughtless, harsh and selfish – but I am not stupid. I know his game and today I am too tired to play along.

'I would like to visit Lucy. She's the only person in the outside world that interests me.'

Arthur nods and does his usual habit of tapping his pen against his desk.

'Do you think that would help you to overcome your fear of other people?'

I shrug my shoulders, his question catching me unawares. I have no answer at the ready, and need a few seconds to formulate a reply. A reply that will satisfy him.

'Possibly. Probably. Lucy is my friend and I would like to see her. Even if it's only for one last time.'

'Perhaps we should speak about the letters some more?'

I take a juddering breath, a thought implanting itself in my brain.

'I've got copies.'

'Copies?' Arthur hitches up his eyebrows as if he is surprised by this piece of news.

'I have copies of the letters I wrote. I'd like you to read them, the ones I wrote and the replies from Lucy. I think it would help you to understand me a little better.'

'Would that not feel like an invasion of your privacy?'

I shake my head, wondering why I haven't thought of it before now. Arthur reading the letters would be easier than me having to voice my thoughts out loud. Sitting here week after week, having my darkest secrets plucked from my head, is tantamount to surgery without anaesthetic. I leave this room after every session feeling battered and bruised and am not sure how much more of it I can take.

A boulder is lifted off my shoulders when he nods, the vice around my head slackening a notch.

'I can bring them to our next session.'

I stand. For once it is my turn to signal that our time is up. It feels good to shift the balance a little. It's a small thing but means so much that I manage a smile, my face tight with the effort. Resisting happiness has been my default stance for so long now that being happy feels unnatural, alien even. That needs to change. I want some lightness back in my life. Some warmth and joy. Allowing Arthur to read those letters is the key to happiness. Perhaps happiness is too strong a word. Relief is probably more fitting. A period of respite from me having to speak openly with him, sitting through hours and hours of therapy, watching as he attempts to tease out the slim strands of truth, unpicking and unravelling them from the web of lies I have created to try and protect my sanity. Nobody likes admitting they are wrong. And nobody likes being called a liar. Even if they are one.

And I am quite possibly the biggest liar of them all.

28

'Jesus Christ. She doesn't get any better, does she?' Caren pulls off her latex gloves and throws them into the waste bin. 'I tried being nice, telling jokes, asking how she was feeling, but got nothing in return. Face like a bulldog chewing a wasp, that one.'

'Don't think she's had an easy life, has poor old Isla. She used to talk about losing her best friend but seems to have forgotten about her now.' Darcy slumps down onto the rickety chair next to the sink, weariness evident in her features. It's been a long shift.

'Yeah,' Caren sighs, her voice showing no traces of sympathy, 'now she just sits there as if she's sucking a lemon, silly old bitch.'

'I'd hate to think of one of my relatives ended up that lonely. Must be awful for her, seeing everyone else getting visitors while she has nobody.' It isn't just the labour-intensive graft that has made this shift drag. Working alongside somebody as sour and impatient as Caren takes its toll. Her sort of negativity is draining. Tough on the soul.

'Yeah well, I firmly believe that you get out of life exactly what you put in. There has to be a reason why her daughter doesn't visit.'

Darcy heaves a sigh of mild disgust at her colleague's summary of a helpless old lady and disguises it with a protracted yawn. She's ready for a hot soak in the tub and a lie on the sofa in front of the TV. Twelve hours of changing beds and hoisting frail, elderly people in and out of the bath has left her exhausted. It's as she is visualising her bubble bath and glass of wine that it comes back to her, the thought hurtling into her mind at top speed.

'She did have somebody come to see her a while back. Late last year it was, I think. Said she was an old neighbour. She'd heard that Isla was a resident here and decided to pay a visit. So the poor old dear can't be all that bad, can she?'

* * *

In the next room, Isla lies still, ears attuned to every word that's being said. They think her an imbecile, a tyrant who deserves to live in her own pit of loneliness. That Caren girl has a mouth on her, but maybe she's right. And Isla does recall Anna visiting; the mother of that girl who used to play with Blake when they were children. It didn't last long, that particular friendship. As usual, Blake did what she could to frighten the other girl away. Sweet little thing she was as well. Lucy. That was her name. Why couldn't Isla have had a child like that? Somebody delicate and sensible and thoughtful. Instead she had a child who was too much like her. Watching Blake perform was like holding up a mirror to all of her own faults and shortcomings. A replica of herself. Still, nothing she can do about it now. It was all such a long time ago, and she's too tired to think about the past. About what could have been. Should have been.

She winces, pain creeping up and down her spine as she tries to turn over. She takes a shuddering breath, waiting until it dissipates. More painkillers would help but she can't seem to find the words to ask; besides, she has had her dose for now. The weight that presses down on her is a jagged cumbersome boulder; her thoughts riddled with guilt. This is what Martha experienced. This level of agony is what that poor woman endured all those years ago, and not once did Isla visit to offer any support. She should have gone, seen her friend one last time, but a tangle of knotted thoughts and a screaming baby put paid to that. Too late now for regrets. Too damn late for everything.

Seconds turn into minutes until finally Isla feels it lift, the pain exiting her body with a flutter, like a small bird taking flight and heading off into the sky. She suddenly feels calm, her mind clear enough to think clearly, to go back to Anna's appearance at her bedside.

Isla had woken, the morphine doing more to send her into an unwelcome coma-like condition than it did to deaden the pain of her cancer. She had stared hard at the woman who was sitting there, watching her. Waiting for Isla to rouse herself. Waiting to speak of how she wished both girls had never met, her voice filled with bitterness as she spoke, telling Isla how she regretted with every ounce of her being, ever moving into the house next door but one to her and Finn, and how Isla's daughter with her incessant stalking and anger had ruined her own daughter's life. Lucy was everything to them. Isla's daughter put paid to that. And she hated her for it.

'I just wanted to let you know how I feel about you and your family,' Anna had said as she rose from her chair, her ice-blue eyes boring a hole into Isla's skull. 'I tried to help you in the beginning, we both did; we even let my daughter go on holiday with you and she almost drowned because your psychotic offspring pushed her in the sea. Trevor and I tried, Isla, we really did, but by the end I gave up. Big mistake. I should have reported you instead of ignoring you. You reared a monster, because you are one. I hope you and your daughter both rot in hell.'

She left in a blur, the noise and busyness of the staff and residents, and other visitors drowning out her words, each sentence a poison dart aimed at Isla's heart. Isla had winced as she watched her go, shifting about in her bed, the blistering attack making her heart race and her skin burn, because deep down, she knew it to be true, every word enunciated with laser-like precision. With her estranged daughter no longer around to care for her, and her husband, Finn, long since dead, Isla was truly alone. If there was such a place as hell, then Isla was already in it. And maybe it was exactly where she deserved to be, having entertained such terrible thoughts about her own child for all these years. The fact she had often wished her dead, even trying to stop her life by different nefarious means before it had actually begun. Aside from that nice young lady, Darcy, who often speaks kindly to Isla while tending to her bedsores and bathing her, Isla has nobody.

The pain is back. The effects of the morphine didn't last long. Maybe the cancer has spread. She visualises it like an alien, a grisly entity wrapping its large tentacles around her backbone, pushing hard against her spine and major organs. Soon it will win its battle and kill off its host.

'Everything okay, Isla?'

She shakes her head, unable to stop the tears. It's not the pain; she's accustomed to that. It's everything else. Her life. Her daughter. Her own terrible, awful mistakes.

'I can give you some more painkillers. Here,' the carer says as she lifts Isla up in bed and gives her some medication, 'this should help you to get some rest.'

Isla nods and smiles. She feels herself gradually slipping into oblivion, the rustle of staff members coming through the door to carry out their hourly check on her, infiltrating her dream-like state. She thinks of Blake and Finn but mostly she thinks about Martha, wondering how differently things would have turned out had she lived; had she been around with her gentle yet firm guidance. There would be no Anna and Trevor, and more importantly, no Lucy. And with no Lucy, there would have been no violence, no court case that brought untold shame on their family. Things wouldn't have been perfect but they would have been a damn sight better than they are now. Martha would have sorted everything out, putting Blake on the correct path and steering her in the right direction. She would have been the mother that Blake needed. The mother that Isla couldn't be. The mother Isla never ever wanted to be.

Blackness seeps in at the corner of her vision, her eyes heavy, her body slipping into a drug-induced sleep where nothing and nobody matters.

29

I sit at the desk in the corner of the room, shafts of light filtering in from the window. I love this time of day, the setting of the sun and the promise of another sunrise the next morning. Before I sleep, I'm going to write another letter. I will add it to the collection that I am going to pass on to Arthur. Doctor Leadbitter doesn't know that I refer to him as Arthur. I'm not sure how he would feel about such intimacy. I am, after all, his patient, not his friend. I am nobody's friend. Aside from Maya who is kind to me, I have nobody. Maybe that's why I enjoy using his first name. Friends are in short supply in my life. I need as many as I can get and Arthur knows me better than anybody else. Probably better than I know myself. He'll gain an even greater insight into my existence once I hand over the stack of correspondence I'm about to give him. I hope he enjoys reading about my friendship with Lucy. I'm not sure enjoy is the correct word. Perhaps appreciates and understands is a better way to describe his sentiments. Befitting of a professional like Arthur who has to deal with a headcase like me.

22 February

Dear Me,

This letter is going to prove difficult. Why? Because the words that preceded this particular missive don't fit with what I am about to write. They are like pieces of a misshapen jigsaw, ill-fitting and sharp edged.

I think that the best way to write about what happened next is to simply tell the story as I see it. I will leave it up to whoever reads it to decipher the real meaning. To try to fit together the jagged timeline.

After losing my baby and being given an emergency hysterectomy, the world lost its colour. It had been tinged with sepia before the birth but afterwards I found myself living a monochrome existence, all happiness leaching out of my life at the thought of never being able to have any children of my own. I was due to return to work but couldn't face my colleagues so rang my boss and told them I wouldn't be coming back. Without any income I quickly fell behind with my bills and the rent. A request to my parents for financial assistance went exactly as I expected. As usual, my father was working or at church. My mother railed at me, screaming about how I deserved everything that was coming my way. I had neglected to visit them and at that point, they were tired of my transient lifestyle, continually moving from flat to flat, apartment to apartment, without providing them with a forwarding address. Loan sharks I had been using had somehow discovered my parents' address and had hammered on their door demanding money for overdue payments. Such visits left them feeling raw and distressed, determined to cut all ties with their only child. It was a terrible period of my life. I was unable to make ends meet and in dire straits. Eventually I landed a job with a firm of accountants as an office manager, a position I was wholly unqualified for. Bluffing my way through each day, using the correct terminology and emulating other colleagues in a bid to keep my job was how I operated. And for once, it worked. That job helped me out of a hole that had grown deeper and deeper after the death of my only child.

It was while I was employed at the accountants that I was sent on a course to Newcastle. I took the train and on that train on the way home, I spotted Lucy. She was sitting alongside Nigel. Wracked with nerves, I sat close by, watching them while remaining concealed behind a row of headrests.

They were clearly enamoured with one another, their fingers interlaced, their bodies touching as they sat side by side while I watched, envy boiling inside my veins, my flesh hot with anger.

That was when I spotted it – Lucy's bump. Her pregnancy shone in her eyes, her skin glowing and radiant. My own misery had put a stop to keeping track of what was going on in their lives but seeing them again reignited my interest.

For the next few weeks, I trailed after them, doing what I could to remain unseen while watching their movements. As expected, everything Lucy did, everywhere she went, every item of clothing she wore, was perfect. Her life was a fairytale existence while mine was a lukewarm life devoid of love. I wanted what Lucy had. I wanted happiness and contentment. And more than anything, I wanted a child. Yet again, Lucy had exactly what I would never have. I tried to ruin her wedding day and that memory still pierces my thoughts on an almost daily basis. Standing at the back of that venue, screaming and hollering down the aisle at the bride and groom, was a new low for me. And my God, I have a litany of lows. It was a toe-curling moment of madness, one of many. And yet still her life continued down its blissfully happy path.

And now, Lucy was pregnant, and I just knew that her pregnancy and labour would be trouble free. No hitches, no trauma. No death or destruction. That was when I made up my mind; I had to have her baby. If I couldn't have my own, I would take somebody else's and I would rear and love it as if it were my own. It was a roughly hewn plan but a plan all the same and one that I intended to carry through despite its obvious flaws and defects.

Day after day, I followed in the shadows of Nigel and Lucy, listening to their private conversations. I knew all the details of their lives that they assumed were private. It's surprising how candid people can be, how open and unreserved they are when they think nobody is watching or listening. Or stalking them. And I watched and listened to them all the time. I watched as Lucy was bundled into the car one sunny morning, and I watched her return a few days later with a tiny bundle in her arms. As predicted, her labour had been effortless. Just like the rest of her life. She pushed another human being out of her perfectly lithe body and was discharged and back home in a timely manner, a fact that stuck in my craw and heightened my hatred and jealousy a hundredfold.

For weeks and weeks I monitored the minutiae of their lives, leaving the office and making my way to their house, crouching behind shrubbery in the dying light, observing their movements. Waiting for a chance. An opportunity to take what I felt was rightfully mine.

I followed Lucy and Nigel one dim morning as they took their little one out for an early stroll. Like a ghost, I tiptoed behind them in the half-light, listening to their conversation, catching snippets and trying to piece together their itinerary.

The words 'business meeting' *and* 'New York' *lifted my spirits. I didn't catch the date but I would watch their actions even more closely, make sure Nigel was out of the house when I made my move. Overpowering Lucy would be easy but a grown man was a different matter. I knew my limits.*

For the next week, I was on tenterhooks, every nerve ending in my body sizzling with anticipation. I could practically smell the baby-soft skin of the child, was able to feel her cheek against mine, the memory of my own infant still fresh in my mind before she was removed from me and taken out of my arms to the mortuary. I named her Elise. My beautiful Elise. My baby.

And now I had a chance to get her back. All I needed to do was watch and wait.

One morning before I travelled to work, I saw him – Nigel. He was loading up his car with a large travelling case and a smaller briefcase. New York. This was the date. He was flying for a business meeting 3,500 miles away. Elise would soon be reunited with her mother; me.

My heart pounded in my chest. My flesh vibrated and pulsed, blood surging through my veins as excitement took hold. Everything I ever wanted lay in that house, those four walls containing the key to my happiness.

Later that evening as the sun dipped behind the hills, the horizon a shimmering spread of gold, I took my chance. It was now or never. Nigel was 30,000 feet in the air and I imagined Lucy was still weakened after giving birth. The time was ripe to do what needed to be done.

They were lax and lazy when it came to securing their house, windows left ajar and doors unlocked while an innocent newborn slumbered inside. Some people don't deserve children. I convinced myself that it was an act of mercy, taking that baby from a lazy, uncaring household.

I crept over the back gate and slithered through an open window round the back of the house, my movements stealth-like. I had become an expert at being invisible. For most of my life, people had shunned and ignored me and so I became adept at being on the periphery of everything. Always present but rarely noticed.

Except this time, she saw me. I had glanced through the window before crawling inside but didn't see Lucy standing in the corner by the oven, her pale clothing camouflaged against the kitchen tiles, the low sun hindering my vision.

She opened her mouth to scream but before she could do anything, I was upon her, my hand covering her face, my fingers pressed hard against her lips.

I would like to say the next part is a blur. That would be the easy way out, but it would also be a lie. Yet another falsehood; just one of many.

We thrashed about, Lucy doing what she could to throw me off balance, but I was stronger, my limbs more powerful, my mind funnelled on getting the baby I felt I deserved. Nothing was going to stop me. I've heard it said that a mother can, and will, do anything to protect her child, developing superhuman strength to stop them from coming to any harm, but that would reflect badly on Lucy, making it look as if she didn't care about her child. She did. But I was a mother too and I fought harder. It was simply a matter of luck.

Except at some point, my luck ran out. I had managed to push Lucy away and was planning on tying her up when she staggered to her feet and ran at me, her eyes blazing with hatred and fury. I recall reaching out, my hand connecting with her head. And then the sickening crunch as she slipped and caught the side of her skull on the edge of the marble countertop. Blood sprayed out of her temple and I knew then that it was serious. I hadn't meant to hurt her. I just wanted my baby back. To feel her tiny body close to mine, to see her chest rise and fall as she breathed the precious air around us. I just wanted my little Elise.

I remember thinking at that point, God help me, what have I done?

But it was too late. Lucy lay unmoving on the floor, blood bubbling out of her mouth. I stood and stared at her frail-looking body, wondering what to do next. And then she moved. Panic was a clawing, hissing serpent in my throat. I backed away and as I did so, I heard the sound coming from upstairs. Elise was crying. She needed me. I needed her. Without her I was half-dead. My baby would inject life back into my veins, give me a reason to live.

I darted upstairs to the landing and was stopped by a noise from below. The opening of the front door. The sound of Nigel arriving home. It wasn't right. Everything was askew. Life once again working against me.

It didn't take long for his screams to filter up to where I was standing. A blood-curdling howl that tore at the beating heart of me. I had done a terrible thing and could see no way to escape my crime. Hoping that Nigel would be too distracted by the sight of his wife's bloodied body, I ran into the bedroom and scooped up my baby, wrapping her tiny body in a blanket before heading back downstairs, my feet thundering as I reached the front door and pulled at the handle. I was close, so very close to escaping, to making it out with my daughter held tightly to my chest, when I felt a hand pulling me back.

Before I could resist, Elise was snatched away from me,

her cries echoing in my head and mingling with my own as I fought and clawed to get her back. But it was useless. Nigel slammed me against the wall and locked the front door with his free arm, slipping the key into his pocket while holding Elise firmly against his chest.

The walls of the hallway began to spin, the ground tilting violently under my feet. I felt along the plaster with hot, clumsy fingers, trying to get purchase and failing, before suddenly sliding down onto the cold, tiled floor. My vision grew dim my body was wracked with grief until eventually I felt myself sinking into a welcome oblivion, everything spinning away from me. I knew then there was no coming back from what I'd done. My life as I knew it was over.

From Blake

30

It's been a week since I wrote the final part of my correspondence. The truth is out there now. I've added it to my pile of letters, the ones I'm going to hand over to Arthur. The written word is easier than the spoken truth. It's a solid testament to who we really are. How we think. What we've done. What *I* have done. And my story still isn't finished.

Carrying the truth, or most of it, around with me has been a heavy burden to bear and I'm buckling under the weight of it all. I want to share the secrets of my life with my therapist, otherwise what has been the point of all those sessions? All those hours we spent talking and going over the past, Arthur doing what he can to crack open my head and delve into my thoughts will have been for nothing. I am more than fifty years old. I have more time behind me than I have ahead. What is the point of wasting it by telling more lies and misleading everyone? It's time for a fresh start. I have a life; granted it's not much of a life, but I would like to start living it, doing as others do and facing each day with a smile. I now feel ready to get outdoors and engage with those around me. To shed my fears and begin again. All of a sudden this place feels too small for me, the walls closing in around me. The outside world beckons and I want to be a part of it. Opening up to Arthur is key to the next step. If I can purge myself, admit to my failings, then maybe I can see out the rest of my days as a happy woman. A free woman.

And I want that so much, I really do.

My start in life may not have been as blissful as I would have liked but I no longer want it to define me. I am my own person and able to make my own choices. I only wish I had known it back then when I felt as if the world and everyone in it was set against me.

Once Arthur has read the letters and tells me I am free to live my life how I choose, I will visit Lucy. Just one final time to tell her how sorry I am, how everything spiralled out of control. How my jealousy and grief led me to do a terrible thing. It won't be easy but it's something I have to do if I'm to move on and leave all this behind me.

And I do fully intend to move on with my life, be a better version of me. A sensible, kind me. No longer a strange little girl, I'll be a normal grown woman who is finally able to look up to the sun, appreciate its warmth and smile at the world.

31

'I've read your letters, Blake, and I have also read Lucy's replies. Do you think we should talk about them?' Arthur's eyes search my face, his slightly lopsided smile something he has clearly practised over the years – gentle, compassionate. Ever so slightly alluring. A smile that says, *I am your friend, you can speak openly to me without fear of judgement.*

Our last session was brief. I placed the stack of paper on his desk and backed away, as if I had dropped a ticking timebomb in his lap, each written word a piece of shrapnel that would tear at his flesh and lodge deep in his heart.

And now here I am, a week later, my jugular pulsing, my stomach knotting and unknotting as I wait for his assessment. I knew this day was coming, but it doesn't make it any easier. I feel as if I have failed a friend, even though Arthur most definitely is not my friend. As already stated many times over, I don't have any friends. And that is where my problems all began.

I sit down, my face burning with apprehension at what I am about to say and do. What I'm about to hear. Humiliation and trepidation is a white-hot poker stirring and prodding at my insides. I swallow and place a strand of hair behind my ear, all delaying tactics to put off what comes next.

The truth.

The real truth, not a varnished, airbrushed version of events, but the dirty, sordid facts that brought me to the place where I am now.

I think about Arthur's question and nod, my throat too tight to speak. Chest heaving, I listen to Arthur give a polite cough as if he's addressing a large audience. 'I think the best place to start is, as always, at the beginning.' He gives me a smile as if we have just shared a private joke, then glances down at his notes and the stack of letters sitting next to them.

'Okay,' I reply feebly.

My spine is straight, the skin on my neck and arms stippled with fine hairs and goosebumps even though the temperature in the room is positively tropical.

'Firstly, it's a good thing that you wrote these letters. It's the start of the process of healing.'

'But?' I say, my breath coming in short bursts. I pre-empt him because I want him to know that I know what is coming next.

'But we both know you have been less than economical with the truth, don't we?'

Shame burrows beneath my skin. I want to give my reasons for saying what I said. For writing down certain things that weren't true. For being an outright liar.

'I longed for a happy childhood, for a mother who wanted and loved me. That's why I swapped our identities.'

Arthur nods as if he understands. Perhaps he does. What is the point of all the qualifications that sit in a frame on his wall if he isn't able to analyse somebody like me? And what has been the point of our sessions if he is no wiser as to why I did what I did all those years ago? I pray he is able to comprehend and rationalise my behaviour because it's lonely being me; trying to control the explosion of rogue thoughts and actions that roam freely inside my mind. Thoughts and actions that led me to this place, the place I've called home for so long now I am almost institutionalised; these walls protecting me from the ails of the outside world. I now wait patiently for a panel of people to tell me I am free to leave, to live the rest of my life without being incarcerated by a team of strangers who think me unhinged. They say all the right things, they smile and interact with me, but their true sentiments are evident in their expressions. And they might be right. But I want to leave this place now. I have paid a hefty price for my misdeeds and the time has come for me to be allowed to go home. Wherever home is.

'Let's go right back to the beginning, shall we? To the first time you and Lucy met?'

He's right. To unpick my story, we need to go right back to the start of us, to distinguish reality from fiction. To separate the truth from the lies.

'We met as children. We lived close to one another, but my first real memory of Lucy was on our first day of school. That part of my recollection is real.'

Arthur waits. I take a trembling breath, steeling myself as if I am about to make a lengthy speech to a waiting, eager audience. Arthur's attentive stance makes me just as nervous as addressing any overcrowded venue. More so because of what I'm about to reveal.

'But many parts after that, I made up. Lucy had the perfect upbringing, lovely, considerate parents. Everything a child could ever want. Whereas I had...' The next few words stick in my gullet.

Tears burn at my eyes. I fight them back, determined to continue. My freedom depends on this. I have to muster up enough courage to recount my narrative. The real one. Not a pack of lies, words I told others to protect my sanity. I was, and still am, ashamed of my background. Of who I was. Who I am. So I borrowed Lucy's story, made it my own. Added parts and twisted them. It all felt real. The more I wrote, the deeper it implanted itself in my brain. I actually began to believe it. The lines became blurred the more lies I told until in the end, I no longer knew who or what I was.

'Take your time. We have an extended session today, Blake.' He passes me a box of tissues. I take one and blow my nose, dabbing at my eyes with a ferocious swipe before throwing the screwed-up ball into the bin. Even my own tears disgust me. I shouldn't be crying. I'm not the victim here. Not really. I had a damaged childhood but is that really an excuse for doing what I did?

'I had a mother who hated me and a father who tried to help but was useless when battling against my mother's wilful ways. She would wait until he was out of the house and then she would beat me, berate me, tell me how useless and pathetic I was. How she never wanted me. Many times she would tell me how she wished I had never been born.'

More tears flow. This time I don't try to stop them. They have been building for so many years now that it's a release to free them and stop the corrosive buildup in my brain.

Arthur waits until my sobbing subsides then speaks softly, one of the letters clutched between his large fingers. 'Lucy wrote about an attack that happened to you one day as you were walking to school together. That must have been terrifying. Would you like to tell me about it?'

I press the heel of my hands into my face to stem another

flow of tears. Already my eyes feel as if they are burning and yet our session has barely begun, this conversation still in its infancy. We have so much ground to cover and already I feel empty. Hollowed out by grief and regret and remorse.

'There was no attack. Not on me at least.' My words are muffled, barely audible, and yet in my head they are thunderous, like the roar of a wild animal primed and ready to attack.

Arthur nods as if this is exactly what he expected to hear. Maybe it is. He has the details of my life spread out before him, my life jotted down in the margins of his notebook. Arthur is old school, preferring pen and paper to computers and tablets. He once told me it feels less invasive, makes him feel more lenient and compassionate in his approach.

'Would you like to explain why you made up such a story?'

I shake my head then nod, tears spraying out around me. 'It was me who attacked Lucy. I wasn't the victim. I was the perpetrator. My violent streak was present from an early age.'

The silence in the room pounds in my ears, crashing off my skull with such force I feel dizzy and nauseated. I know what's coming next. Arthur's question is about to blow everything wide open and once that crack takes hold and begins to splinter and grow, there is no turning back.

He makes a show of leafing through the letters, his eyes searching for one in particular. When he glances up at me, I feel myself shrivel.

'It's a bit confusing,' he says with faux confusion. 'If you attacked Lucy, why would she write about the assault happening to you?'

I shrug my shoulders. I'm not completely ready to speak with him about it. Not just yet. I need more time to prepare, to steady my nerves and give a full account of our correspondence. My head is fuzzy and I don't want to stumble over my words or make any obvious errors.

'Okay, let's move on, shall we? What about the incident on the bridge? Maybe it's time to talk about that.'

I pull at my collar, the room now stiflingly hot. Arthur smiles and picks up the glass jug that sits in the middle of his desk. He pours out a tumbler of water and passes it across to me. The sound of my gulping fills the room as I greedily slurp at the cool liquid.

The tumbler leaves a damp ring of moisture on the table when I place it down, and that is what I focus on when I reply to his question. It's easier than meeting his gaze, his direct, penetrative gaze, as he scrutinises my every word and movement. I can practically feel the heat of his pupils as they drill through my skin and bore a hole in my brain.

'I think you already know that it was me who threw the stones and caused the accident. I was alone when it happened and I projected my behaviour onto Lucy. Easier than accepting the blame and looking inward at my own despicable actions.' I emphasise the word 'despicable' to let him know that I loathe what I did and who I was.

He is nodding and raising his eyebrows in acceptance. I can see him in my peripheral vision, his features etched with concern. I have sat at this desk in this room for long enough now to predict how he will react. That much I have learnt.

'There was a mention of a few relationships with' – Arthur makes a show of checking his notes before continuing – 'a Marc Westfield and a lady named Kathryn. Both seemed to last only a matter of weeks. Was there a reason for said relationships ending so rapidly?'

And now here it is; the crux of the matter. My failings as an individual. I shudder as I inhale, a pocket of air becoming lodged in my chest.

'You already know the answer to that question.' I can't help but smile at him, his methods predictable yet strangely rigorous and demanding.

Arthur returns my smile and leans back in his chair, the squeak of leather against leather echoing around us. I wonder which of us will break first. Am I strong enough to sit this out or is it easier to capitulate and give him the answer he wants to hear? I am not stupid. I know that he needs to hear me admit that I have a problem. I have to speak about my issues in order to move forward, make progress and walk away from this place a free woman.

And so I speak, my words sharp. Clipped and forceful. Once I begin to talk, it gets easier, my tone softening. Each syllable sliding from my mouth like melted candle wax.

'I wasn't capable of conducting a proper relationship. I didn't understand the boundaries and Marc ended up taking out a restraining order against me.' I already feel lighter, more buoyant. My mind less clogged up with the detritus that has dragged me down for as long as I can remember. 'And then Kathryn made a report to the police when I refused to leave her house after following her home from work.'

'Were you and Kathryn in a proper relationship at that point?'

My face burns. Humiliation is a jagged icy spear that darts up and down my spine.

'She was a colleague. We became friends. I tried to become intimate with her but she refused; she was repulsed by me if you must know. And I was too dim to take no for an answer.'

Through a blur of tears, I can see Arthur nodding and smiling. We are getting closer. We are almost at the centre of everything; the centre of me, every fault and flaw I have studied at length as if I were a specimen in a research centre.

'So now perhaps we can speak openly about your relationship with Lucy. Do you think you're ready for that, Blake?'

I sigh and bite at my lip before nodding and straightening the creases out of my trousers. If preparation is the key to success then now is as good a time as any to speak plainly about Lucy. If not now, then when?

32

'By the time Lucy and I moved onto secondary school, we had already begun to drift apart, our differences obvious to everyone, except me.' I bite at a loose nail, tugging and ripping until it comes away, bringing a long piece of skin with it. A line of blood appears, and I wince, the pain a small thing compared to what I am about to unveil. 'But I was already obsessed with her and wouldn't take no for an answer. I followed her everywhere and despite not wanting me around, she was always kind and compassionate, never raising her voice or making disparaging remarks like others did.'

'So the part about the school disco and the woods was true? The part where you pushed her to the ground and left her alone? And the incident at college where you waited outside and screamed at Lucy and her friends – that was also true?' Arthur suddenly looks sad, his eyes dewy as if my plight has genuinely moved him.

'I'm afraid most of it is true, apart from the bit about Lucy and me still being close friends at that point. She was already keeping me at arm's length, allowing me to tag along and be in her gang. We didn't share make-up prior to getting ready for the disco but we did walk home together through the woods, and I did knock her over and leave her there in the dark. I also pushed her in the water at Whitby. She hadn't wanted to accompany me and my family to the cottage. It had been the idea of our parents, a ploy to possibly use Lucy as a role model for me. Even my mother behaved herself while we there. Unlike me. Poor Lucy was thrust into my orbit on so many occasions. No wonder she grew tired of me, doing what she could to shake me off. Anyway, while there, Lucy read my diary, all those words I had written about how I adored her father. The truth was that I wanted him as my dad. My longing for him was purely platonic but in a childish rush of affection I got carried away and elaborated wildly, writing about how I wanted to run away with him, have him all to myself. I wish I could say that none of those things happened, but unfortunately they did, as did the incident in the coffee shop when I shouted at her and verbally abused the young woman who was serving us. I saw Lucy getting on with her life, moving away from me, and I couldn't let that happen.'

'So you followed her?' Arthur's voice is low, almost a whisper.

'I stalked her. Let's be honest here. I was Lucy's stalker. From childhood friend to stalker and fucking nuisance in what felt like the blink of an eye. We were never close friends once she realised how damaged I was. Every day, she did what she could to put more distance between us.'

'And you did what you could to stop her?'

I nod, a fresh flow of tears brimming, ready to spill out. 'My inability to see the obvious ruined everything. I can see that now. I just wish I had been able to see it back then.'

Arthur's face shows tenderness, his professional demeanour and composure slipping for a few seconds. 'Don't be too hard on yourself, Blake. You've come a long way. We all have it within us to change, never forget that. You're not the same person you were back then.'

I smile, relieved to hear those words spoken out loud. I never ever thought this day would come; the day when somebody somewhere would have faith in me. Faith I never ever had in myself.

'Why do you think Lucy didn't report you for the first attack when you were children?'

I shake my head and sigh. 'I wondered that at the time but I think it was because she was frightened of me and felt sorry for me at the same time. I was an oddball. Every neighbourhood and school has a kid who's an outsider. Somebody who doesn't fit in. Scruffy, unkempt. So desperate for attention they will do anything to be noticed. *Anything*.'

Arthur smiles and jots down more notes, the sound of the pen scratching at paper screeching in my ears. I think about his background and upbringing, and imagine a large house in a leafy suburb, a house crammed with books and warmth and empathy and love. I doubt Arthur stemmed from a family where beatings were regularly doled out and insults hurled about like confetti. But I bet he sees plenty of people like me who are the result of such upbringings; people from families where poor parenting and neglect is as normal as breathing. Damaged, broken people who just want to be loved and noticed. People who do dreadful things to try to fill the void in their lives.

'It was terrifying, you know, being left alone in a strange place by my mother. She used to say it would make me more resilient, teach me how to behave in a more seemly manner. I was seven years old the first time she did it, leaving me in town amidst a crowd of people while she got the bus home. Everyone thought the time I was left overnight after coming back from playing up in the hills was the first time, but it wasn't. They were all blind to what was going on in that house. None of them cared, not really. Even Lucy's parents started avoiding me when my behaviour became too much for them.'

My chest is tight, as if all the air has been sucked out of the room and suddenly I'm struggling to breathe.

'Remember the technique you've been taught, Blake. Place your hands on the arms of the chair and breathe while counting from one to five. In through your nose and out through your mouth.' Arthur's voice is disembodied, his words coming to me in a low murmur from somewhere far away.

I feel as if I'm underwater, my lungs filling with fluid. My body slowly dying after being deprived of oxygen for too long.

And then the sensation evaporates. The room and everything in it is back to normal. If I can't function here in this place, this familiar environment, then how am I going to manage in the outside world?

My spine clicks when I straighten my posture, a wave of fury swilling through me. 'This is her fault, you know. She made me this way. My mother is the reason I am the way I am.'

Arthur says nothing. He is waiting for me to open up, for all my fears and insecurities to come pouring out. It's not going to happen. I won't waste another breath on that woman. Giving her space in my head is bad enough. I'm sure as hell not going to weep over her. Any further tears I shed will be reserved for myself and for Lucy and all those missed opportunities I had to keep our friendship on an even keel.

'Do you now feel the time is right to speak about the letters? About Lucy's replies to you?'

I knew this moment would come; I just hoped I would be more prepared, less inclined to cry. I nod and rub at my eyes. It's now or never. And truth be told, I will never be prepared so I guess today is as good a time as any.

'Lucy didn't write those letters. I did. Even if she could, Lucy would never write to somebody like me. So I penned them myself as a way of working through that awful period of my life.'

Arthur murmurs and writes something down on his notepad. I presume it's something positive. I've made an admission. An important one. And besides, it was Arthur's idea to write those letters in the first place. He has known from the outset that they weren't from Lucy. He must be delighted that his plan has worked, that he discovered a way for me to own up to what I did.

'Why did Lucy's replies stop when they did? Was that date significant in any way?'

A drumbeat takes hold in my temple, a deep thud that causes the room to spin, for the walls to lean in at a drunken angle. He wants me to say it out loud. All of a sudden the written word isn't enough for him. Arthur is certainly squeezing me dry in this session, getting every last drop out of me before I either clam up or collapse onto the floor, my body an empty husk. Everything I have ever said and done is out in the open. I have nothing left to give.

My fingers inadvertently fly up to my throat to stem the flutter that seems to have taken hold there. Insect wings as light as gossamer scrape at the walls of my gullet.

'Thirtieth August. That was the date of the accident.' Nausea grips me. I swallow and close my eyes before speaking again. 'Not an accident. Not an accident at all. It was an attack. I tried to steal her baby and when she realised that I had broken into her house, she ran at me. I hit her with my fist, and that was when she fell. There was so much blood. Too much.'

I'm gasping now, tears and snot sliding through my fingers, running down my chin and dripping onto my lap.

'I just wanted to see the baby. I wanted my baby back. I wanted my Elise.'

'And...?'

I know what to say next, how to play this game, to say the words that will help free me from this place. Each syllable comes out like rapid gunfire, my breathing a staccato rhythm as I speak. 'And it wasn't Elise at all. It was Lucy's child. Elise is dead. I can't have her back. I'll never see her again. I'll never see or hold my baby daughter ever again...'

The room spins around me, my vision diminishing before everything turns black.

33

SIX MONTHS LATER

I can't quite believe it. I never thought this day would ever come, but here I am, standing in front of the building that has been my home for a good portion of my adult life, but this time I am on the outside of the gates. Freedom beckons and it smells and tastes heavenly. I glance up at the haze of blue that is streaked with snow-white clouds and let out a trembling sigh. The sun has decided to show its face and it feels so damn good. Everything is perfect. It is also terrifying. Freedom is a huge thing, the world suddenly big and frightening, the scaffolding around me that has propped me up for so long now, stripped away. Who will catch me if I fall?

'Ready?'

Melvyn takes my case and carries it to his car. We're not back together and are far from being an item again but in the last few months we have been corresponding, me out of a sense of loneliness and mild fear at what my future holds, and him most likely out of a sense of pity for his ex-partner who was never quite fully balanced.

I took a chance when I discovered I was going to be released and wrote to him. Fortune smiled on me that day when it became apparent he was still living at the same address. For once I got lucky. I expected a rebuttal, to be told in no uncertain terms to fuck off, but Melvyn is a better person than I could ever hope to be and he replied, stating how sorry he was for abandoning me all those years ago and that he would help me to get back on my feet. I'm fortunate in so many ways. I have my freedom and I have Melvyn. He's not going to be by my side permanently, but the next few weeks and months are going to be rocky and knowing he is close by and ready to help is reassuring. I don't mind admitting that I'm more than a little scared. I have no routine, no family, no secure base to call home.

I stop walking and sniff the air, thinking of the small courtyard of plants and flowers that I'm leaving behind. For the next few months I will be residing alongside other people who are like me. Assisted living, they call it. I don't need any assistance but I guess it's their way of keeping an eye on me, making sure I don't do anything stupid or reckless.

'Here we are.' Melvyn unlocks the car door and opens it for me to climb in. 'You get yourself belted up while I load your bags into the boot.'

The seat feels cool against my hot skin. I glance at the interior, trying to take it all in. Everything feels smooth and clean, the scent of air fresheners filling every pocket of space. It occurs to me that I have no idea what Melvyn does for a living. He is a different Melvyn to the one I used to know. In a previous life, he worked at a local food packing factory but as I look around, I can see levels of comfort and luxury that would not be affordable for his once meagre wage.

I wait while he arranges my belongings and then slams the boot shut. It's as he slides into the driver's seat that I pluck up the courage to ask. 'So where do you work now then, Melv? This is a lovely car by the way.'

He smiles and shakes his head. 'Yeah, so you've clearly realised that I left the factory a while back and I no longer drive that battered old Toyota.' I can feel the power of his gaze as we swing out of the car park onto the main road. 'I did a university course in my spare time and qualified as an engineer. This is a company car by the way. I don't earn enough to buy something this swanky but I do now own my house instead of renting it.'

I smile and gulp back the lump that has risen in my throat. I should feel happy for him, elated even, so why is my old friend misery rearing its ugly head?

'That's great, Melvyn. Well done,' I say, managing to muster up enough energy to sound happy.

The contrast between my life and his is stark, Melvyn's trajectory on an upward curve while mine is down in the gutter.

I swallow down my jealousy and stare out of the window, amazed at the level of heavy traffic on a road that doesn't feel much wider than a country lane. 'You're getting on and improving your life, while I—' Tears mar my vision. I swipe them away. I need to stop this. I'm a grown woman, a free one at that, and here I am, feeling dejected and sorry for myself; balking at somebody else's hard work and good fortune. Everything I don't have or desire, and in all probability will never have, is my own fault. I behaved irresponsibly and this is the net result. Except of course there is another person who has never been held responsible for what she did. My mother for years has slipped beneath the radar of accountability. She has lived her life free of blame while I have paid a hefty price for my own actions and her inadequacies as a parent.

'Hey, hey!' The light touch of Melvyn's hand on my shoulder is enough to drag me out of the shadows of my past. 'You're doing great, Blake. This is your chance to start again, be whoever you want to be. The world is your oyster as the saying goes.'

He's right, I know he's right. Perhaps relief at being free and untethered is warping my emotions. Every day is going to be a new and different step forward. There will be many stumbling blocks, plenty of hurdles littering my path. I'm over fifty years old and am going to have to learn how to live independently. I should feel excited yet all I feel is scared. I have dreamt about this day for so long and yet now it's here, nothing is as I imagined it would be. The sun is shining but there is a thick pall of mist inside of me, swirling fog that continually lingers without purpose. I need to banish those feelings, set them free and be my own person. Not the girl I used to be. I'm different now, a sensible, rehabilitated middle-aged woman. The panel who deemed me fit for release trust me. So why am I unable to trust myself?

The journey passes quickly, Melvyn and I sitting in companionable silence, the whispers of music doing little to soothe my agitated mind. I kid myself that I don't know what it is that is bothering me. Because I do know. Admitting it forces a rock into my throat. Melvyn has made something of himself while I am still on the bottom rung of the ladder of life. And from where I am standing, it feels like a long way up and a difficult climb. And I have to do it alone. Melvyn and I aren't together. We will never be together and I had better get used to it.

We pull up outside a small apartment block, my nerves jangling. Before I can do anything, Melvyn leans into the back seat and pulls something out of a bag.

'Here,' he says softly. 'I thought this might come in handy. I can show you how to use it if you like?'

It's a phone. I stare at it then glance at Melvyn, suddenly happy and relieved that he is here, with me. Rooting for me. I don't deserve him and yet here he is, offering support. Being kind and generous. Many people don't have a Melvyn in their lives. They don't have anybody.

'I'll work out how to use it. Thank you,' I say, fighting back more tears. 'For everything.'

'I've already put my number in there. Give me a call if you need anything at all. Allison works nights at the hospital so feel free to ring me if you have any nightmares or just fancy a chat.'

Allison.

Melvyn has a partner. Maybe even a wife. It never occurred to me that he would have somebody else. Ours was a brief, loose relationship. I'm lucky he is here at all. A surreptitious glance at his finger and I can see it is bare, not that that is any indicator of his married status. Not all men wear wedding rings.

I step out of the car thinking how stupid I was to let him go all those years ago. The thought of being a father terrified him, but maybe if I had worked a little harder at keeping him, tried to be a decent person, been more predictable and robust, then maybe, just maybe, we could have had a future together. Our break-up was my fault. I drove him away. He could see my flaws and didn't know how to manage them. We all have our faults. Melvyn's was fear of my instability. Mine was everything else.

I fumble for my keys, images of Elise and how she would have looked had she lived, in the forefront of my mind. Would she be the image of me with my plain, forgettable features and small eyes or would she look like her father, with his more handsome, angular cheekbones and full mouth?

No.

I have to stop it. Thinking of her rakes up raw, painful memories. Life goes on. The grief doesn't get any easier but I have had a lot of time to come to terms with it and I need to learn to live without my beautiful baby girl. Today isn't the day for dredging up the past. It's the future I need to focus on. I wave goodbye to

Melvyn, pick up my bags that contain everything I own, and step over the threshold into my new home.

The flat is basic. It has a certain unlived aroma to it and a few items of cheap-looking furniture strategically placed to make it look more appealing than the square boxy place that it actually is. In the corner of the living room is a small flimsy-looking bookcase and next to it a two-seater sofa. It's exactly as I expected. And it's exactly what I deserve.

* * *

Melvyn's words were prescient. The nightmares are frequent. Vivid and frequent. I have no idea why they have come back with such alacrity after dissipating while I was inside, but they have and by the third night I am sitting up in bed, panting and gulping while waiting for my pulse to slow down. A sheen of perspiration covers my neck and chest. Rivulets of sweat course down my back and abdomen. I shiver and step out of bed, padding to the bathroom in the darkness where I wash myself down, the scent of the soap hitting the back of my nostrils and snapping me awake.

It was Lucy. She was there in my dream, teeth bared, anger oozing from her as she launched herself at me. Except of course it can't be Lucy. And yet it felt so real, her expression so familiar, as if she were here in the room with me. An unhinged, horribly angry version of the Lucy I once knew. Before I did what I did to her. Before her head split open and blood splattered across almost every surface of the kitchen, the tiled flooring a pool of deep red.

I creep back to bed, the moon between the blinds silvering the room and highlighting the cheap-looking sticks of furniture. Beside me on the bedside cabinet sits the phone that Melvyn gave me. I snatch it up, the image of the nightmare still vivid in my mind, and then throw it across the bedsheets. It's 3 a.m. I can't call him. This is something I need to get through on my own. I'm a grown fucking woman for God's sake, not a child. So why do I feel so frightened and rudderless? Cast adrift with nowhere to go, nobody to turn to.

Tomorrow I start a new job stacking shelves at the local supermarket. I should feel grateful, excited even for a chance to begin a new life. To wipe the slate clean and start again. Something jolts inside my stomach every time I think about it, strands of barbed wire snaking around my intestines and cutting into the soft flesh of my innards.

I lie back on the pillow with an aching head, willing sleep to envelop me. I need to be ready and alert in the morning. Refreshed and ready to face the world. It doesn't take too long for me to slip into a welcome slumber and I wake at 7 a.m., my phone buzzing and vibrating as a message from Melvyn arrives wishing me good luck for the day ahead. He's a decent man and I was an idiot for not appreciating what I had and trying to keep him in my life. He is now somebody else's partner while I spend my nights steeped in loneliness and anxiety.

Even now, after I have paid a hefty price for my sins, I am still being punished.

34

'This is very kind, but you didn't need to pick me up.' I sigh deeply, still in awe of Melvyn's car, the sheer size and luxury of it, the soft leather swallowing me when I rest my head back.

'No problem at all. Just thought I would make sure you get home safely until you manage to work out the bus timetable to get to and from work.'

I suppress a smile. Poor Melvyn, still the master of nuanced remarks, doing what he can to soften the blow and make sure I don't get too used to his kindness. Many would hand over a copy of the local public transport times or send a link. Many wouldn't have turned up at all. But he has and for that I am eternally grateful.

'Have you been sleeping okay?'

An offhand question that has the power to root me to the spot.

'Kind of.' I bite at the inside of my mouth and rub at my face, weariness after a long shift on little sleep suddenly hitting me. 'Actually no, not really. I've been having terrible nightmares.'

My eyes follow the passing traffic. I am now a keen observer of the hustle and bustle of everyday life. It is a world that for so I longed to be a part of, but a world that now seems overwhelming, everyone rushing and pushing, desperate to be somewhere other than where they actually are. At the edge of my vision I see Melvyn watching me, waiting for me to elaborate, before turning his eyes back to the road.

'I have nightmares about Lucy. About her trying to exact revenge.'

Do I imagine the small sigh? Is Melvyn already exasperated by my behaviour? By the fact I've been insensitive enough to mention her name? I have never been good at reading other people's thoughts or taking social cues, and more than a decade spent in a high security unit hasn't helped develop what was already lacking.

'I guess that's to be expected. Once you get used to your new environment, things will begin to improve. You just need a bit of time to adjust is all.'

I nod, hoping he's right. Time is purportedly a great healer, although I have my doubts about that particular idiom. All time ever seems to do is highlight my many failings, each passing day putting a greater distance between who I am and the person I would like to be.

'I can still see their kitchen, her face. The horror of it all.'

A brief silence, then, 'He still lives there as well, at the same house. I thought he would have moved but—'

A sudden hush surrounds us. I can feel the vibration of Melvyn's regret. It shimmers and pulses in the air between us. The terms of my probation prohibit me from going within a two-mile radius of Nigel and his family. If I want to remain a free woman, I must abide by that rule. And I do want to be free, to live my life in my own way. But the idea of seeing Nigel again is so tempting. If only to bring some closure to that period of my life. If only to see his handsome face again, to stare into those piercing green eyes.

'You can drop me here,' I say, the words leaving me in a hot rush. 'Easier than trying to get parked round the back of the apartment block.'

The engine idles as we pull up and I unfasten my seatbelt. There is a new awkward atmosphere hanging between us and I don't know how to dispel it. A sourness has formed, the stench of it clinging to the back of my throat and my nostrils.

'Thank you for everything,' I murmur as I slide out of the car and bend down to look at Melvyn, who is staring straight ahead, his features frozen, his spine rigid with guilt. 'And don't worry, you haven't said anything untoward. Things are different now. *I'm* different.'

His smile warms me as he turns and looks my way. I know at that moment that things are going to be just fine. I am going to make it through life in my own strange, sweet way.

* * *

It's 2 a.m. The witching hour. I toss my phone back onto the floor, the image of Lucy's raging expression ballooning in my mind, then head to the bathroom where I splash my face with cold water until it turns numb. I stick my head under the tap and gulp down a few mouthfuls of water to try to alleviate the gravelly sensation in my burning throat. I woke up crying, my mouth as dry as sand. Maybe I deserve this. I had nightmares when I was inside but nothing on this scale. Now I am a free woman, my dreams are filled with Lucy's fury. Fury she didn't display when we were friends. Every night, all I can see is her face twisted and crooked with anger. Perhaps it's because I am living close to where it all happened. Or maybe it's just because I deserve to lose sleep over what I did. When I was inside, although I had vivid night terrors, I still slept soundly knowing my needs would be met. I had three square meals a day and a warm bed at night. I am now on my own. The responsibility for my own welfare lies with me, and it is utterly terrifying. Nobody around to pick up the pieces of me when I start to fall apart.

I'm tired and need to sleep but a thought slowly edges its way into my brain. An unwelcome, dangerous thought that, if acted upon, would see me returned to the place I have just left. My mind is a dark, savage place. It presents me with ideas, notions that are laced with menace, and because I am weak and reckless, and downright stupid, I act upon them. But not this time. I risk losing everything should I make such a move. My life isn't brilliant but at this juncture it is on an even keel. I have my freedom, the thing I have craved for the longest time. To rupture my life and lose my liberty by paying a visit to a person who doesn't want to see me would be idiocy. I lie back, close my eyes, banish all thoughts of Nigel from my mind, and wait for the darkness to descend.

Two hours later and I'm still awake. A cup of tea hasn't helped to quell my restless brain. In only three hours my alarm will go off. I will pull back the covers and get up for work. And all the while Nigel's face will haunt me. Seeing him is out of the question. Setting foot near his home is high-risk. And yet I can't seem to shut any of it out of my mind. The idea that I could stroll past his house and catch sight of him has my nerves blazing with excitement. To see his and Lucy's house just one more time may help drive away the thoughts that are keeping me awake at night. Catching sight of him one last time could be all that is needed to stop these nightmares and help me settle into my new routine. And the only way I will ever find out is to take that step.

I slide down under the quilt, a lightness taking hold. My anxiety-fuelled headache lifts. For the first time since getting my freedom back, I feel at ease. All I need to do is be careful, make sure nobody sees me. Be furtive and secretive. That's not so difficult. Is it? Being furtive and secretive is who I am.

* * *

The light cuts into the room, forcing me awake. I glance at the bedside clock and groan. I've overslept. Breakfast has always been my least favourite meal of the day. Missing it won't kill me. A quick shower followed by a sip of juice and I am out of the house and running to the bus stop. I pray I haven't missed it. My new team leader is a stickler for punctuality and punishes any tardiness robustly by cutting breaktimes. The roar of an engine pulses in my ears. I turn to see the bus rushing past me before grinding to a halt ten yards ahead. I pick up my pace and hop on with only seconds to spare. The emptiness of the back seat calls out to me, the expanse of vinyl and lack of passengers an inviting sight. I drop onto it, wearied by my sprint, and stare out of the window, my mind blank, my head aching from a lack of sleep.

In less than fifteen minutes I arrive at the supermarket, flustered and fatigued. I have already erased all thoughts of Nigel from my mind. Visiting him is stupid and dangerous. I was exhausted and overwrought and entertained thoughts that should never be entertained. I have a job now, my own place to live. I also have a probation officer and social worker who would both file reports about me if I broke the rules of my probation and visited Nigel, advising their superiors about my behaviours and recommending that I be incarcerated again. And I don't want that. I want to revel in my freedom, to learn new things and immerse myself in this fast-paced, competitive world that has expanded in my absence.

Promising myself that tonight and every night hereafter will be different, I get off the bus and take the short route into work.

35

The weekend arrives, allowing me the time and space to think. The nightmares have lessened but they haven't stopped completely. I'm exhausted by the physical graft of carrying and lifting, and stacking shelves at the supermarket, but fatigued mainly because of my fractured sleep. Hour after hour, I lie in bed, drifting into a slumber only to wake minutes later, terror ripping my eyelids open and forcing me upright, Lucy's face leering over me, saliva gathering at the corners of her mouth as she hurls abuse my way. They are images that will stay with me.

Ideas of how to make peace with my past sidle up to me as I carry out menial tasks around the apartment. Things I wasn't able to do while I was inside. Some good, some bad. And some of them deeply disturbing.

I spend all morning trying to brush them aside, telling myself that they are rogue thoughts I can easily ignore, but they are persistent, sliding back into my brain, tapping away in my subconsciousness and making themselves known. They refuse to leave, like unwanted guests at a dinner party. I need to clear my head, get out of the house and walk off my demons. I decide to wrap up against the sharp breeze, take the two-mile round walk to the churchyard and visit my father's grave. I own no gardening implements, nothing with which I can tidy his small final resting place, and instead call into the florist on the high street before I head to St George's where he is buried.

The cost of things has clearly skyrocketed while I've been living in another world. Having been subjected to an austere way of life in the unit regarding limits on my freedom, I've also been protected from the practical aspects of day-to-day living, and inflation is one of them. I buy the smallest bunch of flowers available after trailing my fingers over the larger sweet-smelling wreaths, and then make my way to St George's where life is less intimidating, the atmosphere still and calming, the air fresh and clean.

I silently scan the names on each headstone, row after row after row, until I finally spot my father. He resides in death as he did in life, in a quiet corner where birdsong filters down from nearby trees. He is far from everything and everyone. Including my mother. I'm relieved he is alone. When he was alive he ignored her, exasperated by her inability to change and his inability to make her, and in death he has carried on in the same vein. Alone in his own space. Hidden in the shadows. I think about how professional help may have altered all of our lives, how my existence could have had a different outcome had somebody stepped in and tried to help my mother. Taught her how to parent, how to nurture and love. Tears threaten. I blink them away. Weeping is wasted energy. It is also a waste of time, and right now my time is precious. Why weep for things that cannot be changed? And yet still I am plagued by memories. Memories of Lucy, of my parents. Of mistakes I made that ruined so many lives.

I take a shuddering breath and glance around, acutely aware

of the fact that Lucy is close by. A visit is out of the question. For now. Maybe in time, I will summon up the courage to step into her place of care and sit by her bedside. Grasp her hand and tell her how sorry I am. How much I miss her; her laughter and her smile. The way she used to hold people captive with her sparkling wit and winsome ways. The thing is, Lucy isn't dead. She's still alive. Just. Her care home is close by, only half a mile from where I am standing. My actions that day didn't strip her of her life. What I did was strip away her ability to walk and talk unaided. Lucy suffered massive brain damage and requires round-the-clock care from a team of medical staff who diligently tend to her every need. Lucy's current condition is the result of my thoughtlessness and stupidity. She will never recover. And it is all my fault.

I kneel at my father's grave and try to picture Lucy's porcelain skin and elegant posture. Her sparkling eyes and magnetic personality. I try to remember her as she was, not the poor, debilitated creature she has become. Even though shame consumes me, there is a small part of me that feels buoyed up by her condition. No longer the lithe, leggy beauty, Lucy is now a bed-ridden woman who lives a half-life. If it were me I would rather be dead. It took a hideous crime for me to overtake her in the beauty stakes and stride ahead in the world, while she lies incapable of doing anything unaided. Her toileting habits, eating, drinking, washing and dressing are all carried out by other people. I may not be fully independent but at least I'm not being spoon-fed by a team of strangers.

My knees creak as I finish arranging the flowers and stand. It wasn't Lucy's fault that I lost my baby, and she doesn't deserve to live as she does, and yet I can't help the feelings of superiority that bubble inside me. For the first time in my sad little life, I have the upper hand.

The walk to the gate gives me some breathing space, just enough to shake those awful thoughts out of my head. Is this what I've become? What I really am and will always be? A bitter, twisted individual with no moral compass or compassion? All those therapy sessions with Arthur and yet here I am, still thinking terrible thoughts about an innocent woman whose only wish in life was to have a quiet existence surrounded by her loved ones.

The air feels clean on the walk back to my apartment. I call it an apartment because it sounds glamorous and elevates my self-esteem, but in truth it's a small space in a building complex that houses other people like me: deranged, damaged individuals who need to be monitored because we're incapable of taking care of ourselves without supervision. Hardly a superior lifestyle and definitely not something of which I am proud, but my choices are currently limited and I have to seize the positives.

The high street is busy, filled with shoppers, people keen to browse and part with their hard-earned cash. I enjoy the sensation of getting lost amidst the crowds, of being invisible and feeling the sun on my face and the chill of the wind as it passes over me like a gentle caress. It's been a long time since I've known love or been touched or hugged. I'm not entirely sure how I would respond if anybody were to step into my personal space. As a child, affection was something I rarely experienced, the occasional embrace from my father breaking the long dry spells of simmering hatred displayed by my mother. But those embraces grew less and less frequent, my father spending more and more time out of the house until in the end, he was hardly there at all. I don't blame him for that. I would have left too if I could. Being around somebody like my mother was a draining experience, her misery and anger sucking the life out of everything and everyone around her.

And now my mother is in my head and I can't seem to block her; her twisted grimace, her wild cackle. Her screeching voice and the stream of obscenities she would hurl at me simply for existing. Most children need to misbehave to feel the heat of their parents' anger. I simply had to be alive and in the same room. Being born was my first offence. Breathing the same air as her was my second.

At my front door, I'm speared by panic. I can't find my keys. I check every pocket, rummage through my small shoulder bag, but they are all empty. Turning around, I retrace my steps, my eyes glued to the ground. I would have heard them drop, but the high street was busy, swarms of people heading in every direction like a cloud of insects. My heart bangs against my ribcage. My throat tightens as I walk back, keeping my gaze lowered. I have no idea what the ramifications will be and I don't want to find out. Images of an irate probation officer fill my head. I need to find those keys. I need to do better, to be better. This is a wake-up call to get my act together. I'm a grown woman acting like a spoilt child and it needs to stop.

I scour the pavements and trail my eyes along the roads and guttering, even peering into leaf-clogged drains, but see nothing. Anybody could have scooped them up. Anybody at all. I try to stay calm but by the time I get to the gates of the graveyard I am bathed in sweat and panting hard. Only a few days of living on my own and already I'm losing my grip and coming undone.

My legs are liquid as I slowly tread the same path that leads to my father's grave. I can see a flicker of a movement, somebody standing close to his headstone. It's an elderly woman, her silver hair glinting beneath the glare of the sun. I watch as she bends down next to my father's grave and picks up a small metal object, holding it in the palm of her hand and studying it closely. My keys.

'Excuse me!' I run, catapulting towards her, fuelled by relief and confusion.

Perhaps she's the verger, or somebody who tends to the graves, or maybe even a member of the local community, a person who regularly walks this area, hoping for a moment of calm amidst the storm of shoppers outside the gates.

'I think you have my keys,' I say as I approach, my breath coming out in short bursts. 'I was here a short while back and only realised I had mislaid them when I got back home and couldn't find them.'

I can feel her scrutinising me, this elderly lady who holds on to the fob as if it were gold bullion. She continues to stand in front of my father's headstone, unmoving. Watching. In her other hand is a small bunch of flowers. She glances down at the bouquet I placed there, and I see the look of puzzlement in her expression.

'This is my father's grave,' I say quietly. 'I put those flowers there.'

I'm aware that I am gabbling, giving personal details to a stranger. I should stop, rein in my panic and start thinking clearly, but her presence coupled with my own carelessness has got me twisted with anxiety.

Her eyes cloud over, her mouth closing into a thin, tight line, and I see that something is happening here. Something I would rather not be a part of. A thought jangles at the back of my mind. I feel as if I have seen her before, and yet I can't have. It's impossible. A woman like this won't have spent time in the sort of place where I have been for all these years.

'And you are...?' The words are out before I can stop them, my curiosity piqued by her, the fact she is standing so close to where my father is buried, refusing to step away from his personal space. I am also vexed by her scrutinous gaze that has me hot and bothered while she remains aloof and unruffled.

I think that perhaps I already know the answer to my own question, my father's prolonged absences suddenly making perfect sense. Why did I not think of this before?

'I'm Harriet,' she replies, her voice a soft murmur, barely more than a whisper.

'My father's partner?' I feel the blood drain from my face when she nods and sighs.

I remember it then, her features and cool composure registering in my brain. I saw her at my father's funeral. She was there, standing alone at the back, her demeanour detached and dignified while my mother's manufactured cries echoed around the vaulted ceiling. I had been allowed to attend, a heavy presence with me at all times. I watched as Mother's carer held on to her wheelchair, passing her a tissue to dab at her faux tears. She tried to catch my eye as everyone filed out afterwards, but I looked away, too immersed in my own grief to feel any pity for a woman who never loved me. I left straight after the service and haven't seen her since.

'Your keys,' Harriet murmurs, handing them over to me, her words slicing through my thoughts.

Her hands are small, the skin stretched across them liver spotted and as fragile as parchment. I guess she is probably in her late seventies, maybe early eighties. And she is the person my father spent his days and nights with when he wasn't at home with us. Another woman. Another life. I wonder if my mother knew and chose to not tell me. Maybe she was ignorant of it all, or maybe she knew but didn't care. I think probably the latter. She was distant and loveless enough to accept his motives. Perhaps it was a blessing, affording him a few happier years with a woman at his side who actually cared for him.

'Thank you.' I begin to walk away then stop and turn again to speak. 'Can I ask how you met my father? Was it through the church?'

A quizzical look is etched into her expression, her brows knitted together in confusion. 'The church? Goodness, no. I was a work colleague.'

'But you must have accompanied him to church every now and again? He spent such a lot of time there.' A breath is trapped in my throat, the air around me suddenly sparse. I press at my breastbone as if to try to massage my airways to manipulate more oxygen into my system. Everything feels skewed, the world suddenly pushed off balance by her revelation.

Harriet's smile, the sympathetic tilt of her head, sends a dart of annoyance through me. She stares at me as if I'm a particularly dense child, incapable of nuanced thought or reason.

'Darling, your father stopped going to church a long, long time ago. Shortly after you were born, actually.'

A pounding sensation pummels at my temples, a small drumbeat of dread at what I am about to hear. Any second now, my father's litany of lies will come slinking out. Seems like I'm not the only family member capable of deceit. I appear to have inherited the worst of both of my parents' genes. An inability to love and a propensity to lie all wrapped up in one misshapen ugly package.

I nod, my voice temporarily absent. All those times he was elsewhere, both my mother and I thinking he was at church when in reality he was in the arms of another woman. In the arms of Harriet. I understand why he did what he did. My poor father, being lumbered with a woman like my mother; a cold, undemonstrative individual with all the emotional warmth of a cold-blooded lizard.

'I understand why he stayed out of the house so much, why

he chose to spend so much time with you. I know that he grew tired of my mother's behaviour and her strange ways. Her cruelty and lack of care and compassion.'

Harriet's laugh is caustic. She throws back her head for dramatic effect, her slightly yellowed teeth and lined skin giving her a look of somebody marginally unhinged. A deranged, frail old woman.

'Oh, you are so blind, my dear. So very stupid and so very, very blind. Finn didn't stay out of the house because of your mother.' She narrows her eyes, fixing them on me, drilling them deep into my face, causing me to shift about, discomfort twisting my innards as she fires her poison invectives my way. 'You're the one who dented his faith in God, my dear. He stayed out of the house because of you.'

36

She's lying. She is also enjoying her moment, savouring every second of it and relishing seeing my face crumple as her words hit home. I straighten my posture, pushing back my shoulders. Doing what I can to appear unmoved and unhurt by her claim, even though every part of me has turned to liquid, my bones crumbling into dust.

Harriet smiles, her lopsided grimace reptilian and disingenuous. She's waiting for me to reply. I imagine she is expecting a denial, a booming, vociferous rebuttal. Instead I say nothing, unwilling to get drawn into a conversation that is designed purely to cause me anguish. I wonder how long she has waited for this, if she has dreamt of this moment for many years. And now it's here she is going to make sure she gets her fill.

I think of Arthur and how he would advise me to respond, Which is why I smile benignly, then turn and walk away, my thoughts focused on leaving this place far behind, but Harriet has other plans, striding alongside me, craning her neck to catch my attention as she spews out her bile.

'Your mother was bad but you were the one who ruined your

father's life. He had high hopes for you, but you threw it all away. Your actions and behaviour put him through untold stress. He lost so much sleep because of you and what you did. And when you got locked away – well, he just went downhill rapidly.' Spittle has formed at the corners of her mouth, white foamy flecks that rest in the deep grooves around her wizened lips. 'You're the reason his heart gave out. You killed him, Blake. You actually killed your own father!'

As frail and elderly as she is, I have no qualms about grabbing Harriet's arm and pushing her up against a nearby wall, the crunch of her spine as it meets brick sending a rush of satisfaction through me. I can't believe my father chose to spend his time with a woman like Harriet. My mother was a cold, heartless individual but this vicious foul-mouthed creature is on another level. Maybe it was part of who he was; a man drawn to dark, damaged females, the type of people who enjoy inflicting pain and misery on others.

I will have none of it. Not any more. Harriet can go fuck herself.

I lean into her, our faces almost touching. I can smell the fetid stench of her breath as she gasps and writhes while I attempt to hold her still.

'My father loved me. You had no hold over him. He didn't even leave his wife for you. You were just his bit on the side. The other woman. His dirty little secret, nothing more, nothing less.'

My words hit a nerve. Harriet's narrowed eyes turn to ice. She tries to push me away but I'm younger and stronger.

'Get your hands off me. If you don't let me go I'll scream and tell everyone you attacked me. You'll be back inside in no time. Right back where you belong. People like you shouldn't be out on the streets. You'll—'

My actions are instinctive. I grab hold of her hair and slam her head against the wall over and over and over and over, watching in horror and yet unable to stop as blood runs down the bricks, her clothes a glutinous smear of ruby red.

Dazed and horrified, I drop my hands by my sides and step back, watching as she slumps to the floor, her neck and spine twisted at an awkward angle, her eyes closed. What have I done? Oh dear God, what the hell have I done? This is exactly like last time. Except last time was an accident. Wasn't it? I try to think back to that day in Lucy's kitchen, her head catching on the countertop, blood spurting out and coating the walls and floor. I try to remember the details, but it's all a blur. I thought I pushed her, could have sworn I did, but what if my mind is deceiving me, playing some kind of cruel trick and it was the same as this incident? What if I actually held her tight, a thick clump of Lucy's hair wrapped around my fist while I slammed her head onto the marble top over and over and over?

Sickness wells in me, rising up my throat and burning my gullet. I swallow and rub at my face, terror shredding my guts. I need to get out of here. But first I need to move Harriet out of view. With no idea if she is alive or dead, I grab her arm and drag her body behind the wall into the undergrowth, a trail of blood on the grass snaking a path to where she lies. I have to clean up, cover my tracks. Grabbing a handful of leaves, I do what I can to wipe away the red stains, rubbing repeatedly and throwing the foliage under nearby bushes that cover Harriet's groaning body. She's alive at least. I haven't killed her. I am suddenly incredibly grateful for the smallest of mercies. I've only assaulted an elderly woman. I haven't murdered her. My head spins and pounds. Oh dear Lord, what have I become? What sort of a person am I? What sort of person have I always been?

I swallow and take a deep juddering breath. At least the graveyard is empty. I glance around, quickly scanning for cameras, and see nothing. No witnesses. No footage. Maybe she'll be too dazed to remember what came before the attack. And even if she does remember, it's my word against hers.

Or maybe she will die soon.

I walk to the gates, my limbs wooden, every breath an almighty struggle. Outside the graveyard, the path is empty of people. If I'm lucky, I might be able to walk away from this situation unscathed. I was goaded, that hideous old woman doing what she could to berate and insult me. I didn't mean for any of it to happen. Except it did and now I need to get away from this place as quickly as I can.

I'm on autopilot as I walk back to my apartment, navigating my way through the high street, deftly weaving past shoppers and slicing through crowds of people like a hot knife through butter, until I eventually arrive at my front door. Fingers trembling, I shove my key in the lock and let myself in, then lean back on the wall and shut my eyes tight, my head swimming. It takes a few seconds to calm down, for my legs to stop shaking and for the fog to clear from my mind. I've made it home. Nobody saw me. Everything is going to be fine. It has to be. If Harriet does recover and remember, I will deny all knowledge. She's a confused old woman who hates me. That's the line I'll take. A confused old woman who had a long-standing affair with my father. She has every reason to despise me, to tell lies about me. To see me readmitted to the one place I don't want to go.

A small voice nags at me, whispering in my ear that I'm being naïve and that everyone will believe the word of an elderly woman over my statement. Why wouldn't they? I've been locked away for years. I'm a dangerous person. A criminal recently released from a high security psychiatric unit.

I wander around the house, doing what I can to forget the horror of what I've just done. I pick up a magazine and throw it back down. I pace the room and turn on the television, the content no more than static in my head. Nothing works. The notion that I might have killed somebody combusts in my brain, sending white-hot sparks through my veins. I lean over the sink and retch, my body convulsing with the effort. If I were a true psychopath then surely I wouldn't be feeling this dizzy and nauseated. So if I'm not a psychopath, then what am I?

The reek of vomit and stale blood emanates from my body, the heat of my fear and my own sweat a rancid odour that catches at the back of my throat. I shower and place my clothes in a black sack, dumping them in the bin outside. I'm not putting a great deal of effort into covering my tracks but have limited resources at hand to conceal my crime. And it is a crime. I have done a terrible thing. Harriet is an old lady. I'm not so devious and damaged that I don't recognise the gravity of my actions. I lost control momentarily and have to hope and pray that nobody finds her. I also hope that any DNA I left behind is washed away or rots into the soil. I know that such a wish is unlikely but it's all I have left. All it takes is a miniscule fragment from my clothing, the tiniest of fibres to be recovered from the scene, and it will lead the police straight to my door.

I spend all afternoon cowering in front of the television, watching as dusk settles over the rooftops. Every hour that passes reassures me that she hasn't been found. I visualise her body bleeding out and growing cold. Or maybe she has survived and has staggered home, her thoughts clouded, her recollection of what took place hazy. I pray repeatedly for memory loss. The alternative is unthinkable.

Darkness eventually descends and I sit, waiting for a knock at the door. When it doesn't come I head to bed, pulling the covers over my head to try to blot out the horror of the day.

I sleep soundly, no nightmares. No visions of Lucy. I wonder if I've become worryingly inured to violence and death. I also eat a hearty breakfast and afterwards, just as I dare to allow myself to relax, I hear it – the knock that I've been expecting. The sound that tells me my freedom is short lived and I am about to be put in handcuffs and escorted to the nearest police station. Which is exactly what I deserve.

Keeping my breathing in check, I shuffle to the hallway, brace myself and open the door wide, prepared for the worst.

37

'You got any smokes?'

A skinny, ragged-looking man stands at the door, his feet shuffling from side to side, limbs twitching as if ants are crawling over his flesh. His acne-pitted face is gaunt and ashen, and a straggly wispy beard clings to his chin.

'No, sorry,' I reply, my voice gravelly, my eyes travelling over his grimy-looking clothes.

I make to move away and close the door, but he steps forward and rests his hand on the frame, his grimy, pale fingers curled around it like the talons of a bird of prey hooked around a perch. Crescents of dirt sit beneath his nails. He reminds me of a cartoon character, his wiry body and movements exaggerated. His voice a low drawl. 'I saw you earlier out the back. Dumping a bag in the bin. You new round here?'

Blood thunders in my head, roaring in my ears. This building has a shared courtyard. No escape from prying eyes. Every move I make, every single thing I do is being closely monitored. Any ideas I had about escaping from yesterday's debacle undetected, vanish like specks of dust.

'Yes, I am. Sorry, got to go. I need to get to work.'

I step back and push at the door but he's persistent. 'You got a job? Keeping you busy, are they? They do that so we don't get into any more trouble.'

His throaty cackle disgusts me. I am nothing like this guy. We share no common ground. And yet here I am, living in a building complex alongside him and others like him. We are a clique whether I like it or not. A gathering of broken people who need constant support and guidance.

'Sorry,' I say, backing away from him. 'Really got to get going.'

I'm acutely aware that he will be watching and waiting for me to leave the apartment. I give him a curt nod and close the door, praying it is solid, not a flimsy piece of wood that will shatter with one swift kick. For years I lived in a secure place surrounded by dangerous people and now here I am, living in a less secure place and yet still surrounded by dangerous people. People who are just like me. I swallow and run my fingers through my hair, thinking of Sandra back at the unit, and how this living arrangement is more suited to somebody like her. Sandra, with her abrasive ways and callous manner. Sandra, who pried into my letters and mocked me. I think of the man outside my door and stifle a sob. I am nothing like this man and I am nothing like her; I have compassion rooted deep inside me and yet here I am, mingling with criminals and ne'er-do-wells.

I swallow down the solid lump that is wedged in my throat. Right now, I need to focus on getting ready to leave this place. Today is my day off, but I'm not about to stay here in this squalid little apartment knowing people are watching me. People like that guy, a man brazen enough to knock on the door of a stranger and ask for cigarettes. I'm better than this and I'm better than him. I snatch my jacket off the newel post and pull on my boots, ignoring my reflection as I pass the mirror hanging in the hallway.

* * *

The air is cold and fresh when I step outside. It bites at my face and hands and sneaks beneath my flesh, numbing my bones. I inhale deeply, eager to feel the rush of it, to savour its deep chill as it brushes over my skin. I know where I'm headed. I have to go there, just to be certain. The only way I can stay in control of this situation is by keeping on top of what is happening out there. Be one step ahead of any possible police involvement. The day after tomorrow I have a meeting with Jilly who wants to make sure I'm managing since my release. I don't want to lie to her but I will if I have to. I will do whatever it takes to survive. I'm not going back to that place. No more Arthur. No more of those four walls with people probing inside my head to see if I'm fit to be around other people. I'm not a fucking child.

It's early and folk are just starting to venture out to the shops, bags slung over shoulders, determined expressions on their faces as they thread their way past me. Nobody gives me a second glance. I'm invisible. A nobody. Relief unfurls in my chest, blossoming and warming me through. It feels good being a nobody. Yesterday was a mistake, an aberration. Today will be different.

In my pocket, my phone buzzes. I stop and stare at the screen. It's Melvyn. Of course it is. Who else would it be? I have nobody in my life but him.

> Just checking you're okay x

I smile at the added kiss. At some level, Melvyn still cares for me. His message is brief but it's enough to give me a warm glow.

Who knows, maybe if our daughter had lived, we would have got back together, been a proper couple. He left because he was scared, a young man frightened of the future. People change. They do it all the time. *I* can change. I have the power and the drive to be better than the person I've always been. My distortions run deep but not so deep that they can't be bent back into shape.

I send back a thumbs-up and slip the phone into my pocket, then make my way towards the graveyard, my footsteps suddenly tentative, my body vibrating with apprehension as I round the corner and spot the blue crime-scene tape pulled across the gates.

A volley of beats pulse behind my breastbone. They've found her. Shit, somebody has found Harriet. Maybe she got up and staggered home then called the police? Maybe this is just a routine procedure. I'm not sure which is worse – Harriet dying or Harriet being alive and pointing the finger of suspicion at me. A thousand thoughts slice through my brain like sharpened knives. If Harriet was still alive, she would have already told them it was me and I would have woken this morning to a team of police officers hammering at my door. Best-case scenario is that she is unconscious and stays that way for the longest time.

Just like Lucy.

A wave of nausea rolls over me. I rub at my eyes, pressing the heel of my hands into my sockets. Harriet was a malicious woman, goading me, taunting me. Firing insults at me until I cracked. I didn't mean to hurt her. It was a moment of madness that ended catastrophically.

I head past the gates of St George's and am tempted to peer in. I don't. I have to keep walking. There is no noise coming from beyond the entrance and I pray they are finishing up, that they have done the detective work and are mystified by the old lady who was found in the bushes, blood oozing from her head. They will find no motive – no signs of robbery or a struggle. Maybe for once, fate will look kindly on me and allow this one past. Far worse things happen. Drugs, hit and run, rape, murder. What I did to poor old Harriet ranks so low on the scale of crimes that it hardly warrants an investigation.

What if she's dead? What if you killed her?

I end up jogging past, my calves and thigh muscles burning from the exertion. By the time I slow down, I'm at the end of a stretch of wide road that reduces to a country lane. Beyond that, the path disappears into a grass verge and I will be left with nowhere to go. Either I cross over and take a right turn, which will lead me to God knows where, or I turn around and head back the way I came.

Behind me, a stream of cars come hurtling past, their speed a wake-up call to the dangers of the traffic I would have to face should I keep going. With my options limited, I spin around, keeping my head dipped, and make my way back towards the high street, trying to remain unobtrusive and undetected. Just an ordinary woman taking a brisk walk is all I am. If I say it often enough in my head, I might actually start to believe it.

My heart jackhammers its way up my throat as I spot the graveyard in the distance. Still no sign of any police, just a blue tape flapping in the breeze. That's got to be a positive thing. If there was anything awry, the place would be swarming with detectives and forensic officers dressed in Hazmat suits. There would be a line of patrol cars parked up outside, but instead the road is empty. This occurrence is nothing in the grand scheme of things. Just the fall of an old woman who stumbled; a fall they are duty-bound to investigate.

I'm able to hear the murmur of voices at the far end of the graveyard as I approach. It happened at the bottom near the perimeter hedge. That's where everybody is gathered. Not up here near the gates. Not where the general public can see them. My pounding heart continues to crawl up my throat. Every nerve ending in my body blazes with fear and dread. I need to remain calm, appear composed, Curious even. An innocent passer-by would stop and stare, intrigued at this unusual turn of events. A polite passer-by would keep on walking, refusing to peer in to help preserve the dignity of any possible victims. What is the protocol in such situations? Am I supposed to appear unnerved or should I stop and peer through, affecting horror at what might lie beyond those wrought-iron gates?

I spend the rest of the journey tying myself in knots, wondering whether I've done the right thing by passing by at all, wondering if I should have turned and walked in the opposite direction as soon as I saw the police cordon. I don't know what any normal, innocent person would do because I am anything but innocent, and as my past actions have proved, I am also anything but normal.

The thought of going back to face the rest of my dysfunctional rough edged neighbours flips my stomach. Instead I sit on a bench in a park that was once a haven for wildlife and local people seeking solace from the busyness of the town and the roar of the traffic, but which is now a square of green that attracts all manner of and lowlifes. Including me.

Discarded needles and litter blow around me as I sit, taking deep breaths while trying to slow my pulse. The area is empty. I'm alone with my thoughts, everyone either shopping or working or sitting at home in their rundown flats and apartments, injecting or snorting drugs, or drinking themselves half to death to escape the harm and the horrors they have inflicted on themselves just by being who they are. I don't want to be one of those people but I can't seem to be able to get off this treadmill of self-destruction. I have enough awareness and insight to recognise who and what I am. I just don't know how to stop it or how to change. The much-improved version of me is in there somewhere, but she is stuck. Locked inside the vaults of my own mind with no visible means of escape.

The walk back to my apartment seems to take an age, misery and hopelessness weighing me down. I round the bend to a huddle of people gathered on the street corner, a cloud of cigarette smoke swirling above their heads. An empty beer bottle rolls about in the gutter at their feet. They're all too immersed in their conversation to notice me approaching, their loud, serrated cackles bursting into the air like a clap of thunder. I can see the guy who knocked on my door begging for cigarettes. He is standing amongst them. I don't want to be spotted and drawn into their dishevelled-looking circle so instead turn back the way I came, letting my feet and heart lead me to a place I know I shouldn't visit. A place that although isn't strictly forbidden, is somewhere that will prove difficult to enter. Not because of where it is, but because of who it contains. I pull my collar up as protection against the sharp wind and make my way to the other side of town to visit my mother.

38

I use a pseudonym when I sign the visitors' book. A care home of this size probably has cameras but if I keep my head lowered, my movements muted, I might just evade detection. Ordinarily, I'm not neurotic or paranoid but my nerves are screaming at me after seeing the police presence at the graveyard, my senses heightened and as sharp as broken glass. Every part of me is primed for something traumatic happening. I'm not a fan of surprises. If life has taught me anything, it's that vigilance is key to survival.

A sea of faces sail through the corridor, everyone too busy to take any notice as I stroll past. Nurses and carers stand at a desk checking paperwork, and beyond that I hear a metallic clatter, the distant grating echo of residents as they eat, their voices discordant, the scrape of cutlery against crockery a high-pitched clatter that causes me to shudder.

My mother's room is at the far end of the care home. I step inside, her view of the nearby hills something I doubt she even notices. Her state of mind is too far gone to appreciate the beauty of nature. The outside world was something she always saw as tainted and toxic. Filled with peril. The irony is that the real threat resided within that house. It was her. It was always her. Am I foisting the blame for my failures onto my mother? Absolutely. I refuse to let her escape justice. I've been held to account for my crimes and so should she.

'Hello, Mum.' I close the door behind me and march over to her bed, anger and resentment fuelling me. Hatred pummels at my chest.

Seeing her emaciated body is like a punch to the gut. I didn't expect this. The woman I once feared now lies in a bed, her tiny frail body swamped by blankets. A tube is hooked into her arm and her features are pinched and skeletal. But looks can be deceiving. She is fooling no-one. Beneath that fragile exterior lies a heart of solid stone. My mother cares for nobody but herself.

Her eyes flicker when I sit down beside her. A certain stale aroma is leaching from her pores. I try to not gag, to keep my disgust at her current condition under wraps. I feel no pity or sympathy for her plight. No care or compassion for the woman who raised me. I feel nothing at all. This dying woman is a stranger to me. A stranger who, for so long, made my life hell. I lived in fear of her beatings, her acerbic insults and cold dismissals. So often she would hide what she had done to me, concealing it from my teachers, from neighbours, even from my own father. They were all complicit in her actions, refusing to see what was right in front of them. Was my father really as dumb as he appeared or was it easier to believe her lies because getting her to change her ways was impossible? I guess I'll never know. None of it matters any more. I can't modify the past but I can alter the future. I can make amends for the hurt she caused me. If I can inflict the same suffering on the woman who ruined my life, and tip the scales back into position so we're even, then maybe life will start being a little kinder to me.

Voices filter into the room from the corridor outside; all the usual sounds of the coming and going of nurses and carers as they go about their daily business. I wonder if my mother has been kind to them or if she still has a wicked tongue and a propensity for hurling insults. Her days of violence are behind her, her body now too weak and frail for physical altercations. But she would if she could.

I think of Harriet and her sickening assertion that my father stayed out of the house because of me, but I don't believe that. My mother was the reason for his absence. I was a child for Christ's sake, a kid who acted up because my mother showed me no affection. A child starved of love will look elsewhere for it. I hooked onto Lucy because I had nobody else. She filled the void in my life, guiding me through torrid times when my home was a cold, loveless place filled with violence and malice. Harriet is wrong. My father loved me, but he was weak. His quiet ways were no match for my mother's iron will. So he gave up, staying away from the family home to avoid the conflict, thus giving my mother the freedom to destroy me in hundreds of unseen ways. Neglect is a form of abuse, and he neglected me, negating his responsibilities as a father, choosing instead to have an affair with an old harridan while my mother acted as if I were the scourge of humanity. I was her only child and she hated me like no other.

The door opens and I freeze, my shoulders locking into position.

'I'm just emptying the bins, love.'

A cleaner. I relax and spin round to face him. A ruddy-faced middle-aged man is bent beneath the sink in the corner of the room but as I turn, I see it – the sudden change of expression as he moves his gaze away from my mother. That look of weariness that tells me my mother is still as difficult as she has always been. Joyless and challenging. Her behaviour tough and unrelenting.

'She's a distant great-aunt,' I say softly, hoping my tone conveys kindness and understanding.

I imagine he does a demanding, thankless job for very little remuneration. And I am willing to bet that my mother has been rude to him on more than one occasion.

'I hope she's been behaving herself.' I keep my tone light, intentionally upbeat. I want to get this man on my side. I purse my lips, hoping to appear exasperated and lacking in patience at the elderly woman who is lying as still as death, her body unmoving, eyes sealed shut.

His smile is infectious as he scoops up the bin bag. He says nothing, ignoring my comment and continuing with his duties. A true professional, refusing to get embroiled in tittle tattle about patients.

'I like to visit,' I say brightly, trying to lure him in, 'even though she was rude to me when I was younger. I guess we have to forgive and forget, don't we?'

He nods and then stops, looking at me as if trying to assess my intentions, determining whether I'm trustworthy or whether I'm the type of person who would file an official complaint about his conduct if he speaks out of turn. 'She's okay in small doses. Called me a fair few rude names over the past few months but I'm used to it. She isn't the only one. We have lots of patients like her in this place. I guess they can't help it. They're all suffering and we're here to help.'

And with that he is gone, disappearing through the door is if he was never here at all. I hoped for more, for him to tell me about the years she has spent railing against everything and everyone while I was locked away. The crushing silence forces me to speak.

'You've been rude to the man who cleans your room?' I say to my mother, her wispy pale eyelashes flickering in response to my statement. 'Even when you're ill and close to death, you just can't help yourself, can you? I bet you came into this world fighting and it looks like you'll leave it in the same way.'

I jump back as her eyes snap open, pale rheumy irises glaring at me. Blue with flecks of white, the colour of ice. No signs of love there. No long hard stares of anguish or regret. Her appearance nauseates me. She looks as if she is already half-dead, her translucent skin riddled with snaking veins. Her fusty breath hits me as her cracked lips slowly part. She licks them in a swift lizard-like movement and tries to speak but her voice is no more than a whisper.

'What?' I say, my tone shrill and exacting.

Thin bony fingers beckon for me to get closer. I lean in, our proximity a painful, awkward encounter. I don't ever recall a time when my mother cuddled or held me. A time when she consoled me or made me feel better about myself. If she's hoping for a reconciliation at this late stage then she is going to be sorely disappointed. I would rather gouge out my own eyes than forgive her or attempt to reassure her in her dying minutes that she was a good parent just to salve her conscience. This woman is nobody to me. She isn't my mother. She is a monster.

And monsters should be destroyed.

'I don't want you here,' are the words she whispers into my ear. The heat of her breath on my face brings a rush of bile up my throat. I swallow and rub at my eyes, my vision hazy with hurt. Even at this late stage, part of me hoped for kindness, for acceptance and perhaps even the tiniest scrap of compassion. I should have known better. I should have been ready to hear what she is about to say and yet it still hits hard, catching me in my solar plexus. 'I never wanted you. Not now or ever. You were a terrible daughter. I tried with you but you never cared for anybody but yourself.'

Beyond the room, all is silent. We are completely alone. No muffled footsteps, no murmurs of people passing by. I take a long shaky breath, pluck a pillow from beneath her head and place it over her face. Using both hands, I press down, watching dully as her feet thrash about. It takes no effort from me, her resistance minimal. She is too weak to claw at me, too emaciated to try and prise my fingers off the thing that is killing her. It's almost as if she wants me to do it. In a matter of seconds she stops her weak-willed writhing. I remove the pillow and look into her face, half expecting those cold eyes to snap open and for her to give me one of her judgemental looks, one of those hateful gazes that I became accustomed to when I was a child. I longed for love but only ever received hatred.

She looks more serene in death than she ever did in life, her skin smooth and pale, her mouth lifted in a half-smile. Maybe she is at peace now, all that badness ebbing away. I hope so. I hope that wherever she is now, she is happy.

My movements are fluid and effortless. I stand and sling my bag over my shoulder, then replace the pillow, pushing it under her head before turning to leave. I don't look back. There is nothing to see. I feel no remorse or sickness. All I feel is relief. She is gone. The woman who spent every waking moment hating me is finally gone.

The corridor is empty when I head out. I sign the visitors' book to mark my departure and stride out into the light. Clouds part and the sun appears as if to welcome me, its golden hue a sign that everything is going to be okay. My breathing feels easier, the air warm on my skin as I make my way back into town.

39

It's peaceful down by the river, everyone at work, children all at school. Being here is therapeutic. It gives me time to think about the past and the future. About what I've done and what comes next. In the distance I hear a siren. I glance up to see an ambulance racing over the bridge, traffic parting to allow it through. My heart races. This area of town is close to the hospital. It could be for anybody. Besides, my mother is already in a nursing home. She has all the necessary people and equipment around her. There is no need for me to panic. Not just yet. The fear and panic will come later, as will a visit from the police. I'm not an idiot. I've lived within the system, I know how it works. Everything is closing in now, my options limited. All escape routes sealed off. I have no money, no resources to help me out of this mess. A mess that I created.

I sit and stare at the water, watching the ripples, overcome by the enormity of my situation. I wonder how deep it is out there? How long it would take for me to sink to the bottom and become lodged in the silt and the mud. Nobody would miss me. I think of Melvyn and check my phone. Nothing. Just a blank screen. Even he has given up on me. I don't blame him. I would give up on me if I could. I'm just too cowardly to take that leap, to fill my lungs with muddy water and gasp my last beneath the murky waters of the River Tees.

I don't want to return to my ghastly apartment and instead take a walk along the river path. It feels strange knowing my mother is dead. I hoped for euphoria, a dazzling explosion of happiness or a renewed sense of freedom, and am dismayed to feel nothing at all. Maybe placing that pillow over her head wasn't the answer after all. Maybe there is something else that is pressing down on me, something I need to do that will help fill the emptiness that sits at the base of my stomach. Because I do feel empty. Lonely and hollow.

I think of Melvyn; good, kind, thoughtful Melvyn. Even he can't help me now. Nobody can. I'm alone. No-one around to steer and guide me. No Lucy telling me in that soft welcoming voice of hers that everything is going to be okay. I rarely took notice of her words. Is it any wonder she distanced herself from me once we hit our teenage years? She had enough common sense to know trouble when she saw it. And she saw it in me.

On instinct, I raise my arm and throw my phone into the water. I don't need it and I don't want Melvyn to be a part of what I'm going to do next. Because there is a next. There has to be. One final chapter before my freedom is curtailed.

It will complete my story, the one I'm going to finish and submit to a publisher. It's illegal to profit from a crime, so I will use a pseudonym, a name nobody could ever trace back to me. Things might be closing in but I still have some time. Already I have a title. All it needs is a closing chapter. Police investigations and autopsies and DNA results are notoriously slow. I have some breathing space to allow me to put the finishing touches to my manuscript, make it as polished as it can be.

My limbs feel lighter, my mood buoyant as I stand and head back to the high street. Excitement is a living breathing thing that thrums deep in my chest. The next part is the most exhilarating. The final denouement. The closing chapter of my life.

Buses thunder past as I wait at the stop, checking and rechecking the timetable. It is a thrilling sensation. I feel alive again, my movements no longer restricted by draconian rules and regulations. I am free to go wherever I please, and to see whomever I please.

And it pleases me to see Nigel.

Pain bites at me as my nails dig deep into my palms. I need that sensation as an anchor to steady me, stop me from falling from grace. What I am doing requires stealth and precision.

The bus journey drags, the place I am visiting farther than I remember. I sit at the back and stare out of the window, doing what I can to avert my gaze from other passengers. I don't want to appear furtive but neither do I want to be recognised. Not that it matters. I have burnt all my bridges. There is no going back now. No escape from my scandalous behaviour.

Familiar buildings come into view, the landscape around me sending my heart into a welcome flutter. I'm nearly there. I'm nearly at their house. I will get off at the next stop and that's where the next part of my story will really begin.

40

I'd forgotten how quiet it is, row after row of residential properties, each one a happy family home. I wonder if the people who live there realise how lucky they are? How fortunate they are to be born into a family that cares for them and wants them? I think of Lucy's daughter; the girl I tried to steal. I wanted her so badly, every fibre of my being screaming at me to do it, telling me over and over that I deserved her and that she belonged to me. I would have been a wonderful mother. That doesn't come from a place of selfishness; it's a feeling that stems from the pit of my stomach, from the marrow of my bones; a need I was born with. Something that still holds true to this day.

Where would I be now if Lucy and Nigel hadn't stopped me? Would I have managed to sneak the child out of the country and be living a life of luxury somewhere remote? A place where nobody would ever find us? Probably not, but I would be happy. I may not live as these people do with their neatly mowed lawns and expensive furniture, but money means nothing when you have the person you love by your side. And I desperately wanted that baby. I needed her to make me whole. I would have been delirious had I kept her. I don't want a large open plan kitchen or designer clothes. All I want is my child.

I hope Nigel has loved his daughter as much as I would have. Had she been mine, she may not have lived in a grand home or had access to all the latest hi-tech gadgets, but she would have felt loved and cherished and that is more important than having any expensive cars or attending some top-rated private school. That child would have been the centre of my world. I sincerely hope she is the centre of his.

The shrubbery where I used to hide is gone, a large gate and a sweeping driveway now free of foliage. All the flowers that once brought colour and calm to the area have also been ripped out. It's a sea of concrete and brick. Aesthetically ugly and drab enough to sour my soul.

I step back from Nigel's house, afraid of being spotted. My appearance has altered over the years. I've shed the extra weight I carried and now sport shorter hair. I also wear glasses, my cheap spectacles accentuating my dull small eyes. My face, however, is unchanged. Still bland. Still ordinary. Still the same dreary old me.

People come and go, climbing in and out of cars, striding through front doors, all except Nigel's house, which stands silently. Perhaps he's at work. Or maybe he has retired. I've lost touch with their lives, how they spend their days. I no longer know anything about them. That fact hits me hard. The pull of these people is something that has controlled my life for as long as I can remember. And now they are strangers. The disconnect momentarily winds me, sucking air out of my lungs.

I'm about give up and head home when I see something – the opening of their door and a young woman walking out onto the front step of the porch. She stops and lifts up her hands as if checking for rain, before pulling on a leather jacket and striding out onto the driveway.

Lucy!

Except it isn't Lucy. It can't be. But my God, she looks so much like her. Tall, slim, long blond hair. A face that could launch a thousand ships. Lucy's daughter. The child I longed for and wanted. The baby I tried to steal.

I stumble back and crouch near a wall, peering round at Lucy's daughter and the figure behind her. I drink in everything about them; the cut of their clothes, the confidence with which they hold themselves. A pocket of air is wedged in my chest. Because the figure behind the daughter is Nigel; older, broader, hair greying at the sides but definitely Nigel. And still as handsome as I remember. Time hasn't dimmed my memory of him nor my longing.

But no grandchild.

Of course there isn't a grandchild. That part of my story was a complete creation. But one day there will be. One day, this young woman will find a life partner and she will fall pregnant and then once again, Lucy, despite being completely incapacitated, will have exactly what I will never be able to have. Even in illness, her weakened body hooked up to an array of tubes that help keep her alive, Lucy will still be the victor. She will be surrounded by a loving supportive family and I will have nothing. *Be* nothing. An outcast. This chain, this vicious fucking circle, is never going to break.

Unless I decide to break it.

I take a rattling breath and stand up straight. It's time to jettison the old me, to discard the woman I used to be, like a snake shedding its skin, and become the confident person I have always longed to be. No longer the underdog, I crave satisfaction and contentment like a junkie after their next fix, and sometimes doing bad things to good people is the only way to get exactly what I want.

The breeze gathers pace. I shiver and rub at my arms, trying to erase my thoughts. Trying to dampen the demon that lives inside of me. It's a constant battle, the fight between good and bad, between right and wrong. They wrestle and squirm inside my veins, tics and twitches writhing beneath my flesh as I try to contain and temper each impulsive thought, each reckless action.

At the edge of my vision, I watch Nigel and his daughter as they head up the street, the sound of their laughter trailing towards me, their body language easy and effortless, as if they don't have a care in the world. As if their wife and mother isn't hooked up to a machine that helps keep her alive, an army of nurses continually turning her frail body to stop the bedsores from turning septic and killing her. A fusion of anger and envy collides inside me. My skin flashes hot and cold; a prickling sensation spreads across my scalp. So much injustice and unfairness in this world. So much left undone, the past a chilling reminder of how terrifying the future can be.

I pull up my hood and follow them, keeping a safe distance. Keeping myself salted away but always trailing in their shadow. I can do this. Following people is easy. I've had plenty of experience and, anyway, what's the worst that could happen?

* * *

The tremor in my legs is difficult to control. Ahead, Nigel and his daughter spin around, his hand cupped over his brow as he stares my way. I bend down, my head lowered, fingers numb and lacking in dexterity as I pretend to tie my shoelace, all the while watching them, my eyes narrowed against the sun. My hood remains lowered; a scarf is pulled tight around my neck. It's a coincidence is all. He cannot possibly recognise me, the distance between us too great, my thick garments a barrier to revealing my identity. It's been many years since we last met, both of us now middle-aged. Time can change people both physically and emotionally, our features a result of the lives we have lived. My face is not what I expect to see whenever I glance in the mirror, an image of a woman I neither know nor care for staring back at me. If I barely recognise myself, then the chances of Nigel remembering me must be almost zero.

Relief is a fluttering insect that bangs at my throat when he lowers his hand, shrugs and walks on, his beautiful leggy daughter at his side. They take the route over the bridge that spans the river while I attempt to keep my distance. I focus on Nigel's light tan-coloured jacket, his daughter's height, the sound of their chatter; anything I can to stay close and not lose sight of them.

I watch transfixed as the daughter enters a bookshop. She is followed by her father, their expressions serious, postures dipped. It's too risky for me to pursue them any further and yet voices in my head are screaming at me to keep them in my sights, to not lose them and find out more about their dynamics, and so I peer through the window, jaw clamped together in concentration. I lazily scan an array of strategically positioned books, my eyes travelling beyond them in the hope of seeing Nigel. Beside me, an older man stops, his gaze fixed on a hardback copy of a novel about sea life and the oceans.

'By heck those prices are a bit steep, aren't they?' The sound of his voice cuts through my thoughts.

I stand mutely, unable to drag my eyes away from the movements inside until I realise he is speaking to me and is waiting for a response.

'Yeah,' I murmur, wishing he would move on, leave me alone. Be anywhere but here. 'Everything is expensive lately.' I think of wreaths and the tiny spray of flowers I bought for my father's grave.

'Can't quite place your accent,' he says softly. I can feel the burn of his stare as he twists around to look into my face. 'You local or just visiting, then?'

The tic that pounds in my jaw is a conspicuous rhythmic movement. I can feel the flutter beneath my flesh, a vicious persistent demon fighting for freedom. I rub at my face, my smile forced.

'Just visiting,' I say, trying to keep my voice steady. It takes every ounce of energy I have to appear relaxed and unbothered by his presence. By his stupid, pointless bloody questions. 'Anyway, nice to chat but I need to get on. So much to do.' It comes out as a shriek, my tone testy, my body language defensive. I can feel the tendons in my neck as they stretch and creak, every sinew taut as cat gut. I run my tongue over my teeth to clear away spittle that has gathered there. A sour taste pools at the back of my throat.

I'm being pushed off course by this person, my objective thwarted by a stranger. It is like a form of torture to make it this far and have everything ruined by an elderly man who wants to engage in conversation about the cost of living and my bloody dialect.

'Aye, lovely to chat. Sorry to have kept you.'

Blood swills around my cranium when I nod, my movements brisk and mechanical. My feral grin is enough to send him scurrying away, his footsteps receding as he weaves his way past a gaggle of schoolchildren on their way to the local library. He stops for a moment to smile and say good morning, his friendliness returned with a sea of innocent grins. A wave of guilt pushes me up against the wall. I rest my head against brick, its rough, cold surface pressing into my scalp. I welcome the pain and close my eyes, willing myself to try harder. Is this what I wanted when I dreamt of being a free woman? Being rude to strangers, sending them scuttling away with my coarse manner and abrupt attitude? He was just an old man, a friendly guy making conversation. And I scared him off.

A noise close by prickles my flesh, pulling me out of my thoughts. I open my eyes and find myself standing face to face with Lucy's daughter. My feet are rooted to the spot, my limbs leaden. I try to spring free of the temporary paralysis but it's like staring into the face of the person I knew all those years ago, her eyes, her skin, the curve of her mouth; everything about her so familiar I almost reach out to make contact. Except I don't. I am stopped by the appearance of Nigel behind her, his eyes boring into mine with laser precision. Adrenaline courses through my veins, loosening my tightened muscles. Allowing me to escape. I try to sidestep him but feel his fingers as they clutch at my arm, pulling me closer, the heat of his breath misting my skin.

'You!' he says, a tremor evident in his voice as he calls out my name. 'Blake?'

It only takes a second for his daughter to identify me, for her beautiful glowing features to turn dark with hatred. She moves swiftly and faces her father, her mouth trembling. She reminds me of a young foal, helpless and fearful, and in that split second, I shake myself free from his grip, push them aside and run headlong into the crowd.

41

The shopping route has a maze of alleyways and narrow footpaths that branch off and lead down to the river. I lace my way through countless cut-throughs until I end up on a muddy track with the river meandering into the distance. Behind me all is silent. I stop to catch my breath, leaning forward with my hands resting on my knees. For my age, I think I'm reasonably healthy but if someone were to give chase, I would soon slow, my legs and lungs failing me when I need them the most.

I glance up at the line of trees that run the length of the water's edge and pray that I'm alone. It was a stupid move to allow myself to be caught off guard like that. Stupid and dangerous. My softness and feelings of guilt left me exposed and vulnerable. Should I have stayed and lied? Told Nigel he was mistaken? Insulted his intelligence by denying his accusations? None of those options seem feasible, but one thing I do know is that going back to my apartment is now out of the question. I have a small amount of cash on me and nothing else. Enough for my bus fare home with a little spare. Giving money to people like me isn't considered safe or sensible. I pull out my small purse and count the coins. Perhaps enough for a sandwich, maybe a small bottle of juice. And then what? I shiver and rub at my eyes. Sleep on a park bench? Conceal myself amongst the foliage like a wild animal hiding from predators?

Above me the sky feels heavy, as if it is about to fall to the ground, crushing me beneath the weight of its anger. I've done a terrible thing. A stupid thing. And now the clock is ticking, time, the weather, my limited finances all colluding against me.

In the distance a siren wails, its screech searing over my skin like white-hot lava. I stand and listen, my breathing laboured. The sound of the siren fades and is replaced by the chatter of birdsong as a flock of bluetits flit into a patch of shrubbery. My chest judders as I try to control my quaking limbs. The path is muddy, heavy rain making it slippery, its natural camber rendering it almost impossible to navigate without sliding down into the freezing water.

I stop and head back the way I came, mentally planning another route to a place where I can stay without being found. With no family or friends to call on, I find myself all out of ideas. And it is also freezing cold, the temperature dipping as the sun vanishes behind a long stretch of grey cloud. My coat and scarf provide little protection against the elements. In a few hours it will be dark. And then what? I shiver and crouch down, shuffling towards a snarl of branches hoping for shelter from the sharp unforgiving breeze. That's when I hear it – somebody calling my name.

Fire and ice collide in my head, a wave dizziness forcing me up to my feet. I stand and swivel in every direction, scanning the area for people. The rush of a passing train draws my eyes to the viaduct, the clatter as it hurtles past drowning out all other sounds. By the time it has passed, I am on red alert, my ears attuned to every tiny noise. Silence. No voices. Nobody calling for me. Nothing but the gentle chirrup of wildlife and the rush of the river. Did I imagine it? Is fear twisting my senses? And then it comes again.

'Blake!'

Driven by raw fear, I turn and run, my feet slipping on the mud, my legs scissoring wildly as I try to stop myself from falling. I'm gasping for breath, my leg muscles screaming at me to slow down, my teeth chattering, but I don't stop. I can't. I won't allow it to end like this. I had plans, dreams, things I need to do. I paid the price for my crime and have earned my liberty. I'm not perfect but who is? Show me a faultless individual, somebody who has never hurt anybody or broken a rule, and I'll show you a liar. We are all defective in one way or another, each of us flawed and damaged, our imperfections concealed deep inside of us.

I can hear voices getting closer, their shouts for me to stop obliterated by my need to remain a free woman. I'll fight for as long as I can. I'll fight until my body gives out. Sirens wail behind me, above me, the echo of their approach pounding in my ears.

I follow the curve of the river, hoping for a bridge or a dense patch of woodland and see nothing but a seemingly endless stretch of water. The power of the current grows stronger, the river widening as I follow its course. I stop and glance at its depth and darkness, wondering if I could make it to the other side. It would pull me under, the sheer strength of the water making it almost impossible for me to survive. My clothes are heavy and layered. I'm tired, my limbs dulled by exhaustion.

'Stop!'

I don't stop. I pick up my pace, trying to dip in and out of the shrubbery, thorns cutting at my face and ripping my clothes. The snarl of bushes slows me down as they snag at me. I pull myself free and pick up the path again, the quagmire of mud making it almost impossible to keep a firm footing. I end up falling, crawling on my hands and knees, taking whatever means possible to escape. Mud splashes in my mouth, my eyes, clumps of it landing in my hair. Using the trunk of a small tree, I pull myself back up onto my feet but the terrain is becoming more and more difficult to navigate, the slope of the path now almost vertical.

Behind me, the voices grow closer, the wail of the sirens louder. My whimpers are inaudible against the roar of their collective voices. Their pleas for me to stop. I can hear them shouting that escape is impossible, that my running from them is dangerous and that the river is high, the current fast, but none of it registers in my brain. All I can see is that building, those four walls. The thrum of the silence as lights are turned out and the night ahead looms like a dark spectre.

The wet slap of footsteps behind me frosts my skin. I try to run but once again fall, my body sliding down the riverbank towards the water. My arms and legs flail, my fingers clutching onto the branches of a clump of bushes. Spikes cut and tear at my flesh, a sudden line of hot pain forcing me to cry out.

'Hold on, we're coming!'

I try to roll to one side, to propel myself towards the gnarled roots of a tree, but miss my target, my body falling, legs curled beneath me. I land at the edge of the river, the rush of the water, the sheer power and speed of it enough to bring forth a flood of tears. Any movement results in me sliding closer to the edge. I stop, panting and sobbing. Doing what I can to stop myself from tumbling to certain death. Taking a deep rattling breath, I inch my body along the soil, my fingers digging for purchase. Ahead is a large tree, its canopy providing shelter and a small amount of cover from my pursuers. If I can reach it without falling, I might be in with a chance of staying alive. At this moment, not falling into the raging current is my priority.

The rustle of leaves and the crunch of snapping twigs freezes my blood. They're getting closer. In just a few minutes they will reach me, a team of police officers pulling at me, hissing in my ear as they read me my rights. I glance down at the river, trying to work out its depth, its speed. My chances of survival if I jumped.

'Blake Wallace!'

The sound of my name being called forces me into doing something unthinkable – anything – to escape and stay alive. I don't mean for it to happen. I try to stand but my feet slide about in the wet soil, the incline too steep for me to remain standing without falling. I find myself leaning awkwardly to one side, my body folding in on itself as I leave solid ground and clutch at thin air with freezing fingers.

I hit the water with a painful smack, my sodden clothes weighing me down. Above me, the voices continue to call out but quickly become distorted as I sink beneath the icy current and am pulled down, down, down before disappearing out of sight in the murk and silt of the raging river that swallows me whole.

42

TWO MONTHS LATER

I sit at my desk, a thousand random thoughts firing off inside my brain. It's been a busy few weeks. I don't mind. I like busy. Busy means less time for brooding and raking over the past. Less time for remembering what happened. And what I did. The old saying that truth is stranger than fiction has never been more pertinent. I hoped to have one last conversation with Nigel, a chance to tell him sorry I was, but after our encounter outside the shop, I knew my time was up. I never did get to speak with Lucy's daughter. I didn't get to hear the sound of her voice or look deep into her eyes. I didn't get to tell her how all those years ago I tried to take her with me to a place far from here and that I would have loved her more than life itself. In the end, it was all for nothing. All my plans and grand ideas crushed beyond recognition.

I was hauled out of the freezing river and resuscitated before being taken to hospital where I was treated for hypothermia and then questioned by police. The staff in my mother's care home had given a clear description of the last visitor to see poor old Isla which led the police straight to me. As for Harriet, she proved to be a tough old bird. Just a few stitches, some cuts and bruises and a night in hospital with concussion. The statement she gave to the police was also detailed enough to identify me. I knew it was coming; it just all happened sooner than I would have liked.

So now, here I am, back in my old room, surrounded by the same old people and doing the same old things day in and day out. Although, there is a new element to my narrative. It's taken me quite some time to finish writing my story, the past few weeks a blur of late evenings and early mornings spent hunched over my notebook, pen in hand. But eventually the many threads all came together to provide a fitting conclusion for my dark, joyless tale. I hope that I've provided an ending befitting of who I am, and what I've done. I hope readers try to unpick it all, to read between each line in a bid to unearth the truth. To understand what lies at the beating heart of me. The final chapter was the most challenging. It took me many sleepless nights and hours of toil to get the first draft of the ending down on paper, but I finally managed it. It wasn't easy; endings never are. The nightmares about Lucy have returned with a vengeance; that was the catalyst, the defining moment that implanted the idea in my brain for how to bring my story to its conclusion. What I do next is now clear to me and I don't know how I haven't considered it before now. Maybe I have. Maybe it all felt too terrifying, too surreal to see it through. Or maybe the change of environment has triggered something deep in my psyche, forcing me to peer closely into the shadows of my mind, to brush away those cobwebs, inspect what lies there and do something positive about it.

Lunch is a cheese sandwich that churns in my stomach and a cup of lukewarm tea that coats my tongue, leaving an oily foul-tasting residue in my mouth. The food in here is as bad as ever. Everything feels different and yet strangely the same. Yesterday I spoke with Maya and asked her to do something for me. We've become quite close in the past month or so. Her story is as almost as tragic as mine. Almost but not quite. Maya came to this country from India when she was a child, her mother bringing her here to escape an abusive father. She grew up moving from town to town, both of them terrified of being rooted out by the brutish man she had the misfortune to call her dad. Even in adulthood the fear was always there. She spent her life looking over her shoulder and then one day was convinced she saw him while out in the car with her mother. Gripped by fear, Maya sped up to get away from him and lost control of her vehicle, hitting a wall and killing her own mother. Turns out it wasn't her father after all, but having spent her entire life with the constant threat of him finding her, she became hysterical and one momentary lapse of concentration cost Maya's mother her life and Maya her freedom. Like me, she was sent here because we need guidance and help rather than punishments for our crimes. Some people take the wrong route through life because they choose to, and then there are the likes of me and Maya who stumble upon it because we can't find the right path. We end up heading in the wrong direction with no idea of how to get back to where we want to be.

Maya is leaving here tomorrow. She has served her time and is being picked up by her son who will take her to his large home in a village on the outskirts of County Durham. She is going to stay with him and his wife and will have her own small annexe where she can live independently. Maya has paid a hefty price for having an abusive parent and so must I. My stay here will probably be indefinite but that suits me. I'm not troubled by it. Not at all. My future is already sorted. I know what comes next.

I've given Maya my manuscript and a list of publishers and agents, and have asked her to submit it to them. Her son runs his own business and she has said that he will ask one of his office staff to put my work onto a memory stick. Apparently that's how it works now. Everything is digital, paper a thing of the past. Once Maya leaves here with my novel, I'll be free, everything I have planned for so many years now finally coming to fruition.

Outside, the weather beats against the window as if trying to claw its way in. There's something tremendously comforting about snuggling down under bedsheets while the rain and wind rage and howl in the distance. I think I prefer being alone. I've decided that the world is too frightening a place for me. Everything feels misshapen, my behaviour and conduct too bent and broken to fit in anywhere. Here is where I belong, and yet even here feels alien, as if it's a holding place for when I'm eventually moved on to somewhere else.

My eyes are sore, my body aching. Finishing my story has been a brutal experience both physically and mentally, leaving me exhausted and restless. I stare at the floor, then up at the ceiling. I dream of flying far away from here, soaring like a bird into an azure cloudless sky. Free. Weightless. Alone at last.

I should always have been alone. Pursuing Lucy was a futile exercise. She never wanted me, not the way I wanted her. Therapists in this place presume that because of my sexuality, I wanted her as a partner. It's not true. Yes, I adored her but not sexually. I simply wanted to be *like* her. I wanted to emulate her elegance and grace. I, too, wanted to be effortlessly beautiful; I craved that level of charisma and charm. Lucy was a flawless young woman whereas I was ugly and broken. The perfect antithesis to her exquisiteness.

I lie back on my bed, suddenly overcome with fatigue. Tomorrow is when I say goodbye to Maya. A part of me will leave with her while the rest of me will remain here with Sandra and others like her. I don't want to think about them. Maya is my future, making sure my story gets heard. She can take the reins and watch it soar.

Eyes heavy, I curl up on my side and feel myself being carried away into the darkness, contentment unfurling within me. About time, is all I can think as I edge my way into sleep. I'm rapidly approaching a level of happiness I've always longed to experience. After all these years, it's about bloody time.

EPILOGUE

SIX MONTHS LATER

It's been a difficult day. They're all difficult. Except today contained a small ray of sunshine. A tiny shaft of warmth amidst hellish weather that saw heavy rain and a howling wind battering the car as he drove into town. His visit to the care home to see Lucy was as traumatic as ever. Nothing changes. No improvements, no deterioration. She is aware enough to understand her predicament and cry silently for hours while he sits and holds her hand, but not physically able to do anything about it. Lucy longs to prop herself up in bed. She longs to walk and talk. To embrace her daughter and her husband and spend her days in her own home surrounded by her loved ones. But she can't and most likely never will. The road ahead of her is long, strewn with hurdles and debris. Doctors have offered no prognosis except to say the future is uncertain. Lucy's injuries were a combination of heavy bleeding and brain damage that renders her unable to move unaided. There are days when Nigel thinks death would have been easier. For all of them.

He pulls up his collar against the cold and rubs at his face. He's tired. Exhausted, actually. An early morning call dragged him from sleep. The manager of the unit where Blake was being detained said that he wanted to let Nigel know before he heard about it on the news or read about it in the papers. A man's voice explained that Blake Wallace had been found dead in her room the previous evening. No suspicious circumstances were suspected and the coroner's report is expected to state that she died by suicide. His first reaction was to cry. So many wasted, damaged lives. So much hurt and heartbreak. Then he gritted his teeth and smiled. Relief takes many forms.

He thinks now of Blake and her strange, unpredictable ways. Her behaviour and connection to Lucy made little sense to him. She and Lucy were polar opposites, their differences always greater, more noticeable, than their similarities. He never quite understood how somebody like Blake ended up so damaged, so full of envy and resentment, willing to do anything to wreak havoc and destroy those around her. It wasn't drugs and it wasn't alcohol. And although far from perfect, her home life wasn't dreadful. He had seen worse. Experienced worse, his own parents a couple of brutish people who preferred to dabble in crime and seek out other partners over caring for their own children. So whatever it was she endured, it is no excuse for what she did. He doesn't hate her even though many would. He pities her. In his darker moments, those long sleepless nights when he has lain alone in his bed watching shadows creep across the bedroom ceiling, he often wished that she and Lucy had never met. But hate? All that does is keep the chain intact. Fighting fire with fire is a preposterous idea. The world burns and turns to ash, and for what? So the winners can feel the heat of their victory and wallow in superiority while all around lies destruction and piles of rubble? No. Best to attempt forgiveness, to limit any further damage with mercy and tolerance.

The walk into town will hopefully clear his head. It's been a long morning. Visits to see Lucy are always exhausting. Their daughter Greta, the young woman who is the very image of her mother, is at college and today the house feels too big a place for him. He wonders at what point he will be able to introduce her to his new partner. Greta's future is slowly unfolding, the next step of her life at university growing roots and taking hold while he is stuck in a rut. Many wouldn't understand or approve; his wife is still alive, but what they all know but never speak of is the fact she will never come home. Such talk is thought of as callous and distasteful. But what about him and his future? Is Nigel really expected to spend his days alone while others move on with their lives? The nights are long, his days finite. He wants to spend the rest of his time on Earth with someone who makes him happy. And Rosa makes him so very happy. And if him being with somebody who makes his life brighter and easier is considered unseemly then those who disapprove can go to hell.

A small amount of anger unfurls in his chest. This morning's unexpected piece of news about Blake's death weighs heavily on him and he feels the need to be around people, to hear the sounds of idle chatter and be a part of the hustle and bustle as the world goes about its daily business. Thinking dark thoughts isn't healthy. It robs him of energy, makes his head pound. He shoves freezing fingers deep into his pocket and focuses all his energy on walking in a straight line.

It's almost lunchtime when he reaches the centre of town, notions of window shopping thwarted by hunger. A quick search of his pockets confirms he has forgotten his phone. This morning's call disrupted his routine, made him forgetful. He laid it down while collecting his keys and now feels cut adrift. He hoped to scan the news sites while eating, see if Blake's death has made the headlines. Possibly not. Probably not. His life is still on hold, his days stretching out like faded parchment, but others have forgotten; Blake's actions that day when everything changed beyond recognition for him and his family have been relegated to the archives. Forgotten and pushed to the backs of the minds of other people.

A queue snakes out the door of the bookshop as he makes his way over. If he can't browse the news on his phone, he will purchase a novel instead. People stand in line, clutching paperbacks, faces brimming with excitement as they wait for their books to be signed. Nigel slips through the throng and slides past, stopping to glance at the poster in the window. See what all the excitement is about. A debut author has written a psychological thriller about a series of letters exchanged between two old friends. Friends with dark secrets nobody knows about. Secrets that end in murder. The tagline is emblazoned in the window in bold font.

Best of friends or the worst of enemies?

He sidles past, the idea of reading a book about violence something he finds abhorrent. Does being entertained by acts of sadism and murder not appal other people? Is he the only one unable to stomach works that glorify gore and savagery?

Up ahead, a middle-aged female sits behind a desk, pen in hand, a simpering expression on her face as she dips her head and signs her name in a swooping cursive script – Maya Wallis. Nigel quietly moves past where she is seated, turning away, unwilling to act graciously towards a person who makes money by writing about death and violence. Maybe this lady has worked hard at creating her story; who knows, maybe she sat for hour after hour, day after day, pouring her heart and soul into creating characters, thinking up a grisly plot to hook in voracious readers, but he for one is sickened by the seemingly insatiable appetite for books that are mired in bloodshed and the dark, depraved ruminations of serial killers and murderers.

Nigel strides past, disappearing to the back of the shop where he stands alone, relieved to be leaving the queue of people far behind him.

* * *

MORE FROM J. A. BAKER

ACKNOWLEDGEMENTS

Writing this book has been exhausting so first and foremost I would like to thank my nice warm bed, the place I crept to after finishing each chapter and round of edits. On a more serious note, my thanks as always, goes to my brilliant editor, Emily Ruston and my copy editor, Jennifer Davies. Without their careful guidance this story would never have been fit for publication, so thank you, ladies! Thank you also to Rachel Sargeant for seeing things I had missed during the proofread.

Time is always an issue for me. With a huge family (four children and their partners, and five grandchildren), it is becoming increasingly difficult to set a routine for my writing, but with their help and understanding, I always manage to make those pesky deadlines. I owe an apology to my husband for being a hermit. When marrying me, I'm not sure he signed up for living with a reclusive individual who is half woman half laptop, but never complains, always offering support and guidance and a kick up the rear end when I need that extra bit of encouragement.

Thank you to the team at Boldwood who are unerringly patient and work hard at making sure my books get noticed. Thank you especially to Jenna and Nia for their constant support and for answering my endless questions that I should already know the answers to. More than twenty books released and I still haven't quite got the hang of this publishing malarkey!

A big thank you to the people who organise and participate

in the blog tours. You do a lot of work and ask so little in return. Your love of books is what keeps me and others like me writing.

I am on social media and aways available for a chat and can be found at:

Facebook.com/thewriterjude

Instagram.com/jabakerauthor

Best Wishes

J.A. Baker

ABOUT THE AUTHOR

J. A. Baker is a successful writer of numerous psychological thrillers. Born and brought up in Middlesbrough, she still lives in the North East, which inspires the settings for her books.

Download your exclusive bonus content from J. A. Baker here:

Follow J. A. Baker on social media:

facebook.com/thewriterjude
x.com/thewriterjude
instagram.com/jabakerauthor
tiktok.com/@jabaker41
bookbub.com/authors/JABaker

ALSO BY J. A. BAKER

Local Girl Missing

The Last Wife

The Woman at Number 19

The Other Mother

The Toxic Friend

The Retreat

The Woman in the Woods

The Stranger

The Intruder

The Girl In The Water

The Quiet One

The Passenger

Little Boy, Gone

When She Sleeps

The Widower's Lie

The Guilty Teacher

Hush Little Baby

The Good Daughter

Mother Knows Best

Such a Strange Little Girl

www.ingramcontent.com/pod-product-compliance
Ingram Content Group UK Ltd.
Pitfield, Milton Keynes, MK11 3LW, UK
UKHW041422250326
11488UKWH00039B/435

9 781835 612095